"Take off your coat," MacLeod ordered the rabbi.

"What? Why?"

"Just do it. There's no time to explain." MacLeod helped him off with his coat and guided him by his shoulders to the basement door.

They could hear the Germans fanning out through the neighborhood. *"Raus! Juden, Raus!"*

MacLeod lifted the hat from Rabbi Mendelsohn's head and placed it on his own. "You can't do this!" Rabbi Mendelsohn protested, beginning to realize what MacLeod had in mind. "I won't let you."

"Quiet!" MacLeod commanded, "I'll be back for you." He could hear soldiers banging on the front door.

"Jude Mendelsohn! Raus!"

"My life is not worth losing yours," the rabbi whispered urgently, begging. "Please!"

MacLeod gave the old man a gentle push onto the basement stairs and swiftly locked the door. "I will be back. I swear it."

The pounding grew louder, more insistent. "Mendelsohn!"

"MacLeod!" the rabbi cried. "Do not do this! No one comes back!"

ALSO IN THIS SERIES:

Available from
WARNER ASPECT

HIGHLANDER™
ZEALOT

A
NOVEL
BY
**DONNA
LETTOW**

ASPECT®

WARNER BOOKS

A Time Warner Company

WARNER BOOKS EDITION

"Highlander" is a protected trademark of Gaumont Television. © 1994 by Gaumont Television and © Davis Panzer Productions, Inc. 1985. Published by arrangement with Bohbot Entertainment and Media, Inc.

Aspect is a registered trademark of Warner Books, Inc.

Warner Books, Inc.
1271 Avenue of the Americas
New York, NY 10020

Visit our Web site at
http://warnerbooks.com

Ⓦ A Time Warner Company

Printed in the United States of America

First Printing: November, 1997

10 9 8 7 6 5 4 3 2 1

Acknowledgments

To Dennis DeYong,
who said if you've got yourself a dream,
go for it.

To Gillian Horvath and Amy Zoll,
who befriended a lonely computer geek
on a bus late one night and showed her a
whole new world.

To David Abramowitz,
who showed me how to use his toys
and let me share his wisdom.

To Bill Panzer and Betsy Mitchell,
who had faith in me.

Blessed is he who was not born,
Or he, who having been born, has died.
But as for us who live, woe unto us.
Because we see the afflictions of Zion,
And what has befallen Jerusalem . . .
—Baruch

Prologue

Allahu Akbar!

The tinny sound of the tape recording rang through the narrow streets of the ancient village of Hebron. The sound echoed from the uninspired facades of government housing built by the Israelis after the occupation. It echoed from the remains of massive granite walls built by invading Crusaders a millennium earlier. Wherever it went, it called the Muslim devout of Hebron to their Friday midday prayers.

Allahu Akbar! God is the Most Great!

The Akhirah Mosque just south of the Old Quarter wasn't the best mosque in Hebron. That honor fell to the majestic al-Haram al-Ibrahimi al-Khalil, a splendid edifice of gold and mosaics rising high above the cave where Abraham, Beloved of God, and his wife Sarah were buried, a site sacred to all of the People of the Book—Muslims, Jews, and Christians alike.

Allahu Akbar!

It wasn't even the second-best mosque in Hebron. Many in Hebron were larger, more elaborate, or simply more ancient than the Akhirah Mosque, which was a fairly new and nondescript block of utilitarian concrete at one end of the open market on the road to Jaffa. It was built near the site where a far grander mosque had stood for over five centuries before it was accidentally destroyed during the Six Day War. Only by its dome and minaret could the new mosque be distinguished from the shops and offices surrounding it.

Allahu Akbar! God is Most Great resounded from the loudspeakers in the minaret. The modest Akhirah Mosque couldn't even claim a live *muezzin* to climb the tower and issue the traditional call to prayer.

Ash-hadu an la ilaha illallah, the tape crackled. I bear witness that there is no God but Allah.

What the Akhirah Mosque had in its favor was its location. This Friday, like any Friday in Hebron, the Jaffa Road market teemed with Arab buyers and sellers, haggling over the price of a lamb, arguing over the quality of a crate of lemons fresh picked from a nearby orchard. Women hurried to finish their shopping before the market closed at midday, their heads and bodies covered despite the *hamsin* winds blowing hot off the desert, making a normally gentle spring feel like the blasting heat of summer. Old men, their dark faces wrinkled by the sun, filled the nearby coffeehouses, content to watch the constantly changing scene, while a few young men in crisp uniforms—members of the newly formed Palestinian police—patrolled the market as had their Israeli predecessors not too long before. At times the din of the market could nearly drown out the call to worship.

Ash-hadu ana Muhammadur rasululla. I bear witness that Muhammad is the Prophet of Allah.

Those Muslims who had the leisure streamed toward the magnificent al-Haram al-Ibrahimi al-Khalil for their Friday prayers alongside the many Muslim tourists on pilgrimage in Hebron. Those whose lives and work revolved around the Jaffa Road market preferred to stay close by and perform their ritual worship at the more humble Akhirah.

Hayya alas salah! Come to prayer!

By midway through the prerecorded *adhan* calling the faithful of Islam to gather, the inside of the tiny mosque was full of men ready for prayer. Most of the women of the market had hurried home to worship in the privacy of their houses. Those men arriving at the mosque too late to be accommodated inside simply spread their colorful woven prayer rugs on the ground, on the sidewalks, in the marketplace, wherever there was room, always facing holy Mecca to the southeast. For the Prophet said, "Wherever the hour of prayer overtakes you, you shall perform it."

Hayya alal falah! Come to salvation!

The din and clamor of the market, a place of chaos only minutes before, disappeared as if by magic, replaced by orderly rows of the faithful silently preparing their hearts and minds for communication with God.

La ilaha illallah! There is no God but Allah!

As the last echo of the call to prayer faded away in the *hamsin* winds, a serious young man joined the faithful in the marketplace outside the mosque. He hurriedly spread a prayer rug near the back of the throng before the communal prayers began. His skin was smoky dark, like that of the others, and he was dressed as any one of hundreds of Palestinian students from the nearby Islamic University, in his white dress shirt and dark slacks. His dark hair was cropped close to his head, covered by a knitted lace prayer cap, and he had a worn leather rucksack for his texts and research. He was a small man of slight build. With his boyish face, he looked nineteen, maybe twenty.

But as he stood at attention, his right hand over his left on his chest as prescribed by the Prophet, chanting "Glory and praise be to You, Oh God" in Arabic with the others, the eyes he raised toward Mecca were seemingly without bottom, round and dark. He might be seeing all the way to the spires of the holy city itself with those eyes.

"*Bismillahir rahmanir rahim,*" his prayers continued, followed by *ruku*, bowing to God in a show of love and respect. Three times the young man chanted "Glory be to my Great Lord and praise be to Him," and three times he bowed low in the presence of God with the other faithful.

Then the ultimate act of humility: proud men prostrate before God on the gravel of the marketplace, hands, faces, knees touching the ground. "God is greater than all else." As the worshipers returned to their knees for their personal prayers, no one noticed the young student in the back of the congregation reach into his leather bag.

The eerie quiet of a hundred men's silent petitions to Allah was suddenly shattered by the howl of an automatic weapon. Soundlessly, a row of pious men toppled from their knees to the ground, dead before their "Amen."

Then the screaming, the wailing, as the followers of Islam tried to struggle to their feet, to run in horror, to flee, but the young man, dark eyes burning with centuries of hate and vengeance, was merciless, cutting them down in the same orderly rows in which they'd prayed.

Before those inside the Akhirah Mosque even realized that their worship had been interrupted, forty-three Palestinian men lay dead or dying, their blood drenching their prayer rugs and seeping into the gravel of the Jaffa Road marketplace.

The avenger with his finger on the trigger of the automatic stopped firing only when he saw the squad of Palestinian police coming for him across the market, guns drawn. Whispering a sweet prayer to the God of his ancestors, the God of Moses and of David, he turned the muzzle of the weapon toward himself and pulled the trigger once again.

Chapter One

Paris: The Present

April in Paris. Despite all the threadworn clichés, there really *was* something magical about the City of Lights in spring. When the incessant winter rains and the graying slush finally went away, the city was reborn, dressed as if by way of apology in the finest Mother Nature had to offer. With the clouds gone, there was no doubt that whatever force had created the heavens, He or She had deliberately placed the sun so it would shine its brightest on the streets of Paris.

As he walked along the sunny Boulevard St. Germain crowded with shoppers and tourists, Duncan MacLeod wondered what it was that always seemed to draw him back to Paris in the springtime. After all, spring in Seacouver was perfectly nice, if a bit damp. In fact, he'd been in any number of cities and hamlets around the world with pleasant springs. He remembered lying beneath the cherry blossoms in old Edo with particular fondness—with Keiko, that was her name, he hadn't thought of her in ages—not to mention an occasional roll in the flowering heather in his native Highlands. But they just couldn't compare with Paris. Maybe it was something carried in the breeze that ruffled his hair as he walked. Maybe, he thought, looking around, just maybe it was the Parisian ladies, freed from the dour wool coats and boots of winter and allowed to bloom like the city. "*Bonjour,*" he said, and smiled his most charming smile as he caught the eye of a passing young mademoiselle in a daring skirt that went up to . . . there. He saw her blush just a bit and walk on with her girlfriend, giggling. When they thought he could no longer see them, they turned and watched him with great appreciation.

He remembered the first time he'd seen Paris. It had been spring then, too. It was a crowded, noisy place filled with more than its share of squalor and disease, but to an overgrown boy fresh out of Glenfinnan, it had seemed a place from a fairy story. Funny how some things don't change in four hundred years. He hadn't stayed long in Paris that first time. Eager to see it all and do it all, he was out and on his way to Italy before the first frost turned the leaves. It would be a long time before he learned that the real gift of Immortality was the chance to stop and savor the sights and smells of springtime.

Or that of a duck in—what was that? Rosemary? The smell greeted him on the sidewalk. MacLeod stopped outside a crowded café and checked the address against a card he pulled from his blazer pocket. Chez Nous. He was in the right place. A little pretentious for his tastes, but he'd heard the food was good. "Constantine, party of two," he told the maître d'. He knew he was a little late, but some days just seemed made for walking.

"One moment, Monsieur." MacLeod looked around the bistro, jammed with the well-to-do of Paris as well as a number of well-heeled tourists, all having a late lunch. Tessa had always said it was never hard to tell the two apart.

MacLeod had his own favorite restaurants in St. Germain. Café de Flore was one, where he and Sartre had argued 'til all hours, until finally the proprietor had bolted the door and gone home to bed, locking them inside until morning. And there was no counting the number of times Hemingway had stuck MacLeod with the check at Les Deux Magots. He still frequented them both, as much for the memories as the food. But the young upstart Chez Nous had recently received glowing reviews and a surprise two stars from the *Guide Michelin* and become The In Place to dine. It was just like Constantine to choose it—the Immortal curator could so rarely be pried out of his museum, the only restaurants he knew were ones he'd read about. "Is a table inside acceptable to Monsieur?"

"A table outside would be preferable to Monsieur."

"Right this way." He followed the maître d' to a small table on the patio near the entrance, which boasted a fine view of the busy boulevard. "Monsieur Constantine has not yet arrived," the maître d' informed him, handing him a menu and wine list before departing.

That was not like Marcus Constantine. MacLeod checked his watch—twenty minutes late. Not like Constantine at all. Although nearly a score of centuries had passed, Constantine still conducted his life the way he must have commanded the great legions of Rome, with discipline, punctuality, and a meticulous attention to detail. It had won an empire for Rome, but it sometimes made Constantine a pain to work with. Pity the poor museum archivist twenty minutes late for a staff meeting—at one point in Constantine's life, that offense would have merited flogging. Today, perhaps only a stern talking to. Still, MacLeod didn't envy Constantine's staff.

But now it was the General's turn to be late. MacLeod's first thought was of a chance encounter with another Immortal. Marcus Constantine may have taken himself out of the Immortal Game, but that didn't mean the Game wouldn't inevitably catch up with him. It was a part of being Immortal, like eating and breathing, that at any time another of your kind could challenge you for your head. But MacLeod didn't dwell on the possibility for long. It was more likely he'd been delayed by a traffic accident or a student demonstration, much more common in Metropolitan Paris than the occasional beheading.

The wine steward appeared by MacLeod's side, hovering in officious silence while he scanned the wine list. Arriving before Constantine meant that for once he got to choose the wine. Constantine's taste in wine tended to run to sweet, cloying vintages or wines aged practically to vinegar. While these may have been the height of fashion in Nero's day, MacLeod's tastes had been cultivated in far more civilized times. A quick glance at the menu told him Chez Nous specialized in the cooking of the south of France. Perfect. "L'Hermitage from Chavi. The 1990 if you have it." A proper wine for Provençal cooking.

While he waited for the wine, and for Constantine, to arrive, MacLeod watched the crowds go by along the boulevard, past the galleries and designer boutiques. He found himself, almost without thinking, naming where the obvious tourists had come from. The middle-aged couple in the matching brown coats and sensible shoes? German. The elderly man and woman? French, but not Parisian. Probably up from the South. It was a game he and Tessa would play for hours over coffee at a café or while strolling along the Seine. The only rule was you had to guess before hearing them speak. The two young lovers, no more than eighteen either of them, were too easy—English, his football jersey gave them away. Three blond women window-shopping at the jewelers across the way were more difficult. Obviously sisters, probably Scandinavian . . . Norwegian?

The woman walking past them caught his immediate attention. Her skin, the golden brown of sunset, bespoke a Middle Eastern heritage, but her walk, the way she carried herself, sure and confident, betrayed her time in the West. American, perhaps? But not by birth, he thought—she still carried the glow of the sands of Araby in her veins. She dressed simply, modestly. On most women her dark conservative suit would be severe, out of place on the fashion-conscious streets of Paris; on her, it created an aura of power and heightened, not hid, her natural beauty. MacLeod watched her with interest as she moved through the crowd until the wine steward offered him a taste of the wine he'd ordered for his approval.

MacLeod took a sip. "Delicious," he said, and the *sommellier* filled both his glass and the one at Constantine's empty place before departing. MacLeod scanned the passing crowds again for another glimpse of that woman. But she was gone.

The maître d' stepped into his line of sight. "Duncan MacLeod?" he asked, and MacLeod nodded. "There is a call for you." He handed MacLeod a portable phone and returned to his post.

"MacLeod."

"Ah, Duncan, thank goodness I caught you," said the voice on the other end.

"Marcus, where are you?"

"I am *so* sorry, Duncan, but there's been a slight emergency at the museum. I won't be able to meet you for lunch." Constantine's voice was apologetic.

"Come on, Marcus, what kind of 'emergency' can there be at an antiquities museum?"

"You'd be surprised. At the moment I'm tied up to my ears in red tape."

MacLeod laughed. "Now *there's* a pretty image."

"Funny," he heard Constantine say. "Can you meet me at the museum just after closing?"

"Sure, I suppose," MacLeod began, "but what about—"

"Perfect! Have to run, Duncan. See you at five." Constantine hung up before MacLeod could finish.

Great. He'd been stood up. It certainly wasn't the first time, but on the rare occasions it had happened in the past, the person standing him up had usually been a bit more . . . shapely than Marcus Constantine. He took a drink from his glass. At least the wine was good. He looked around for the maître d' to return the phone and found him at his podium near the entrance.

"I'm sorry, Madame," the maître d' said in a practiced monotone to another patron as MacLeod set down the phone, "but without a reservation, I cannot seat you. *C'est impossible,*" and MacLeod realized he was addressing the same remarkable Arab woman he'd seen on the street.

"You're sure there is *nothing* you can do?" she asked, her French a bit hesitant but her voice as smooth and rich as her skin. She slipped the maître d' a wad of francs.

He handed them back to her in a huff. "No, Madame," he said firmly, then walked away. MacLeod wondered if he'd been offended by the amount or by the thought of being bribed by a woman. Obviously disappointed, the woman put the money into a jacket pocket and turned to leave.

"I think I can help," MacLeod found himself saying almost before he realized it.

She stopped and turned to him, her dark eyes taking in his finely chiseled features, his well-kempt ponytail, his body so obviously fit and muscular beneath the tailored blazer. Her eyes crinkled as she smiled, clearly liking what she saw. "Yes?"

"I . . ." Under the full power of her smile, he nearly found himself tongue-tied. Four hundred years of experience stripped away and for a solitary instant he was once again

Duncan MacLeod the Chieftain's son, pretty good with a sword but shy and awkward around the lassies. But only for an instant, then Duncan MacLeod the charmer kicked into action. "My lunch appointment just canceled and I've got a fantastic Hermitage that'd be a shame to waste. Care to join me?"

"What if I told you I didn't drink?" He could tell she was interested, testing him.

"What if I confessed that was only a ruse so I might have the pleasure of your company?" He turned on his own thousand-watt smile and watched her reserve start to melt.

"Well . . ."

"I'll be the perfect gentleman. Scout's honor."

"I'm sure you will," she relented, unable to resist those eyes. With a quick glance back toward the street, she offered MacLeod her hand, and he escorted her to his table. As they passed the maître d', she smiled her most demure smile and gave him a little wave, startling the maître d'. "Arrogant little bigot," MacLeod heard her mutter under her breath in Arabic as he ushered her to Constantine's place.

MacLeod looked back at the maître d'. "Don't mind him. He's French," he said in Arabic. Then he switched to English, playing a hunch. "I'm sure he's like that with everyone."

The woman sighed as she settled into her chair. "Maybe some days I'm just more paranoid than others." Then she looked up at MacLeod with new appreciation, realizing he'd tricked her into answering him in English as well. "So, you know a little Arabic, Mr. . . . ?"

"MacLeod. Duncan MacLeod. A little. And your English is impeccable, Miss," he noticed a gold band on her finger, "Mrs. . . . ?"

"*Doctor* Amina," she stressed. "I'm . . . no longer married. And you may call me Maral." The "r" rumbled in the back of her throat like a contented cat's.

"Maral," he echoed. He liked the way that felt.

The waiter approached their table and rattled off the day's specials. Maral ordered "just a salade nicoise." The waiter waited patiently for MacLeod to order, but MacLeod was admiring Maral's hair. It was thick and long, caught in simple but elegant combs up onto her head, where it shone black as burnished jet in the Parisian sunlight. He had a sudden urge to reach out and gently remove the combs, to watch the hair cascade around her shoulders . . . "Duncan?" He loved the way she pronounced his name. "Doon-can?" Maral reached up and touched her hair self-consciously. "Were you planning on having any *food* with your wine?"

"Right. Food." MacLeod covered quickly. "I'll have the dorade grillée and some pommes frites." Then he dismissed the waiter and turned to Maral. "So you're a doctor?"

"PhD," she replied. "Chairman of the Western Studies department at Bir Zeit University."

"In Israel?"

She shrugged. "That depends on whom you ask. It's in Ramallah, a little town on the West Bank. It's where I was born."

"You're Palestinian," MacLeod said. "That explains it."

"Explains what?" MacLead wasn't prepared for the intensity of her defensiveness.

"Your accent. I couldn't quite place it." He thought for a moment. "But you've spent some time in the States, haven't you?"

Maral bristled. "Would you like to see my identity papers? How about my travel permits?" As she busied herself with her water glass, MacLeod could feel a wall click into place between them. He'd obviously rubbed a sore wound.

"Maral, I'm sorry," he said earnestly. He turned his charm up a notch. "If you let me take my foot out of my mouth, I'll make it up to you. Promise." He smiled a wee smile, hoping she'd follow suit.

After a long moment she finally did, her smile a little wry, her dark eyes a little sad. "I'm sorry, too, Duncan. I'm usually not like this. It's the end of a very difficult, very disappointing week." She looked beyond MacLeod toward the gothic spires of Saint-Germain-des-Prés, towering over the next block. "I just thought maybe Paris would be different somehow. I always thought that Paris would be magical."

"Maybe you just need to give Paris a chance. Magic can happen when you least expect it."

He liked the way her eyes brightened with flecks of copper when she smiled. "When I was eleven, my father took a position teaching political science at Rutgers University in New Brunswick, New Jersey." The way she pronounced the name made it sound like a kingdom in a fairy tale. "He wanted to keep us safe from the trouble at home."

As Maral spoke, MacLeod came to the sudden realization that he was being watched from the sidewalk.

"So I guess you could say I spent my formative years as a 'Joisy Goil.' " Her attempt at a New Jersey accent made him laugh. As he did, he subtly turned his chair to get a better view of his observer. Olive-skinned, dark glasses, bushy mustache, surveillance earpiece. "I went to college at Rutgers, got my PhD from Columbia." His first guess was that the man was a Watcher, one of the secret society of mortals dedicated to observing and chronicling the Immortals, but he'd never seen a Watcher as badly trained at surveillance as this guy was.

"What made you go back to Ramallah?" he prompted. He needed to keep her talking, didn't want her to get alarmed.

"I needed to discover who I really was. I couldn't turn my back on my people like my father had."

"You mean you weren't cut out to be a Bruce Springsteen song?" he added, glibly, his mind only half on their conversation. It was obvious that whoever the guy was, he'd learned his surveillance technique from old Cold War spy movies. MacLeod was waiting for him to start talking into his sleeve.

When Maral laughed, it reminded him of wind chimes. "I went home to teach. And then I met someone . . ." MacLeod's mysterious observer turned to the side to light a cigarette and MacLeod spotted the telltale bulge under his left arm that confirmed this was no Watcher. Maybe the guy was inept, but he was deadly serious.

"Maral," he interrupted her quickly, "hold that thought. I have to . . ." He gestured vaguely at the interior of the café. "I'll be right back."

"Of course," she said, and watched him sprint into the restaurant.

MacLeod made a beeline for the kitchen. The maître d', seating a young couple at a table inside, called out to him with concern—"Monsieur?"—but MacLeod kept moving, pushing past a waiter in the narrow aisle between tables, nearly upsetting a tray of drinks. He startled the kitchen help as he slammed through the swinging doors and stalked into the kitchen.

"Are you lost, Monsieur?" a surprised busboy asked. The *sous*-chef made a move to stop him, but MacLeod was out the back door and into the alley beyond before anyone could reach him.

Slowly, cautiously, MacLeod crept along the side of the restaurant. He spotted his man leaning against a letterbox, smoking with studied casualness. The gunman watched with great interest as the Chez Nous waiter brought their lunch to their table on the patio. MacLeod slipped into the crowd of pedestrians on the sidewalk and, pulling from his pocket the notecard on which he'd jotted the restaurant's address, strode toward the letterbox as if he was going to mail it.

In front of the letterbox, he made a great show of dropping the card. Recognition dawned on the face of the gunman as MacLeod bent down to pick it up. Before the gunman could react, MacLeod elbowed him sharply in the groin.

The man bent double in pain, howling. MacLeod delivered a roundhouse kick squarely in the man's gut, driving him hard back against the letterbox.

A well-placed hit to the back of the man's neck dropped him neatly to the pavement before the passersby on the sidewalk were even aware anything had happened.

MacLeod had the man's gun almost before the gunman hit the ground. A passing tourist screamed at the sight of the automatic, alerting everyone on the street and in the café as well, but MacLeod had eyes only for the battered gunman at his feet.

"Who are you?" MacLeod growled, pressing the automatic nearer the man's face. "Why were you spying on me?" He tried again, in Arabic this time. *"Shú ismak? Min wáyn inta?"* but still there was no response. The man simply closed his eyes, as if expecting MacLeod to pull the trigger.

Suddenly, MacLeod felt a hard ring of steel jammed in his own side, insistent. "Doon-can," Maral's purr pleaded in his ear, "put the gun down. Please, put the gun down." He could feel her hands shaking, felt her gun vibrate against his ribs. For the safety of all of them, he decided to do as she said. He set the automatic on the pavement by the letterbox.

The man on the ground made a quick move toward it, intent on using it. Maral barked a sharp *"la!"*, no, and reached out her hand to help him gingerly to his feet. "Assad, Duncan MacLeod," she said to him by way of perfunctory introduction as she helped him up. Assad, in pain, held his ribs and glowered at MacLeod. To MacLeod she said, "Duncan, this is Assad. My bodyguard."

"Your WHAT?" MacLeod was livid.

Maral, hearing the distinctive whine of Parisian police cars in the distance and seeing the size of the crowd their little drama had attracted, begged him, "Please, there's been a horrible mistake. Let's just go someplace quiet we can talk."

"I think we've gone way beyond 'mistake.' " MacLeod took her by the arm and led her off through the crowd, Assad lagging a short distance behind. "This had better be good."

"So it was all a lie? Bir Zeit? New Brunswick? All of it?" MacLeod paced angrily across the sumptuous lobby of the Hôtel Lutétia, feeling used. Across the lobby Assad and an Arab gentleman in a traditional headdress were speaking with a *gendarme*, straightening out the little "misunderstanding" at Chez Nous. Maral, looking tired and worn, sat in an armchair near MacLeod, trying to get him to understand.

"It *is* true. Every word of it."

"So tell me again the part about how the schoolteacher conveniently forgot to mention she was a negotiator for the Palestinians, with a gun in her handbag and an armed bodyguard." He pulled her to her feet. He was in her face. He didn't care.

Maral gave it right back to him. "What am I supposed to do? Announce to every Don Juan who comes on to me in a restaurant 'I'm with the PLO! Come kill me and all my friends?' It's my job, Duncan, it's not who I *am*." He started to walk away from her. She grabbed his arm and pulled him back, looking him dead in the eyes. "Tell me *your* life's an open book. You swoop in like James Bond, you take down Assad without even breathing heavy. Maybe there's something you'd like to tell me about Duncan MacLeod?"

He stared at her and realized she had him. She hadn't told him she was a Palestinian diplomat in Paris to negotiate the future of East Jerusalem with the Israelis, and he'd neglected to mention he was born in the Highlands of Scotland in 1592 and couldn't die unless someone took his head. In retrospect, he had to admit his was probably the more egregious omission. He led her to a couch, the wind out of his sails, and they both sat. "Okay," he said simply, "tell me about the gun."

Maral wasn't quite as ready to stop fighting. "I'm planning on hijacking a busload of schoolchildren, what did you think?" MacLeod just gave her a long, long look, one that seemed to see right through the shield of her anger and into her soul. "I just want to survive, Duncan," she said. "Is that so much to ask for?" Her anger seemed to evaporate into his look and with it her bravado, leaving her tired and looking just a little . . . lost. "The man who had this job before me was blown up in his own car at a traffic light while taking his son to school, did you know that?" MacLeod had to shake his head, no. "I just want to be around long enough to know I've started something that might someday stop the killing. More than anything, I want peace—but I'm not stupid, and I'm not suicidal. There are a lot of crazies out there, on both sides. And I refuse to go down like a sacrificial lamb. I'm no martyr, Duncan—does that make me evil?"

"No," he said quietly, "no, it doesn't." He of all people could understand her plight, trying to do what she knew was right while all around, it seemed, the whole world conspired to stop her. It was a battle he'd faced for four hundred years. He looked into her coffee-colored eyes and felt a moment of intense connection between them. He started to put his free arm around her shoulders to bring her close to him, wanting to kiss her, to seal their link. Instead, she pulled away and stood up, breaking the bond. He looked at her, surprised—he knew from the look in her eyes she felt the spark, too.

"Not here. Not now," she whispered. "Islam forbids it." MacLeod thought back on his travels in the Arab world, and remembered that public signs of affection between unmarried men and women were taboo. Some societies, he remembered, even refused to let them speak to each other—and punished with death. He was amused to think that he, at his age and experience, would be subject to those rules, but he nodded that he understood. Maral continued in a low voice. "We have several what you might call 'fundamentalists' in our party. While I may not share all their beliefs, I must respect them. I have no wish to offend them publicly."

MacLeod nodded his understanding. "I should go." He stood and started for the great revolving door that was the lobby's entrance.

"Duncan, wait," she called out to him as he walked away. He turned. "Will I see you again?"

"Dinner tomorrow?" Despite their rocky start, he found himself looking forward to spending some time alone with this woman.

Maral beamed, flattered he would consider seeing her again after such a debacle. "I'd like that very much."

"Great. What about your friend?" He gestured toward Assad.

"I think I can arrange to give Assad the night off." She laughed as she walked MacLeod to the door. "After your little display today, I don't think I'll be in much danger with the mighty Duncan MacLeod protecting me."

"But who will protect you from Duncan MacLeod?" he teased, with a raised eyebrow and a wicked grin.

Maral gifted him with an alluring smile as he headed out the door. "Who says I want to be protected?"

Chapter Two

Paris: The Present

The Musée National des Antiquités had risen up from the remains of a thousand-year-old abbey gutted and looted by the same misguided crowds who had stormed the Bastille. The corridor, whose granite paving stones eerily amplified the sound of MacLeod's footsteps, was once the cloister-walk surrounding a garden where generations of monks had tilled the earth. Now the walk was enclosed in glass and the garden planted not with medicinal herbs but with sculpture that would have scandalized the poor monks—Grecian youths at play, a nymph and a shepherd boy celebrating the beauty of the human form, some of those lusty busty women Rubens and his crowd had been so partial to nearly two thousand years later. Centuries of human history frozen in time under the chisel of human genius.

MacLeod always felt that museums after hours took on the air of a crypt, a pregnant silence as if waiting for the dead to arise. As his steps rang down the hall, MacLeod half expected the shepherd boy to come to life, or the monks to return to claim what once was theirs. Irrational, he knew; but, then, not everything in life was rational. He approached the entrance at the end of the corridor, two massive wooden doors hand-carved and blackened with age that once separated the garden from the monks' quarters. Wary as he was in the eerie atmosphere of the deserted museum, he was not prepared for the ancient doors to spring open on their own as he reached out to touch them.

MacLeod stepped back quickly, waiting until the doors had opened fully. As he did, he sensed the presence of another Immortal. He stepped through with caution. Most likely Constantine, he thought, but it never paid to drop your guard until you were sure.

"Marcus?" he called out, looking around. There was no response.

The old monks' quarters had been completely destroyed in the violence following the Revolution and in its place the Musée National des Antiquités had created an immense hall of marble in the Classical style, part of nineteenth-century architecture's sad attempt to recreate the splendor of the ancient world. MacLeod had trouble envisioning a display of Monet's works installed in this room, or the paintings of Georgia O'Keeffe—although, come to think of it, there were a few of Henry Moore's more amorphous sculptures he thought might feel at home here.

For Constantine's new exhibition, however, the room was perfect. Two Corinthian columns secured a large banner bearing the name of the exhibit in precise Latin lettering: *Hostes Romae—Hostiae Romae*. Rome's Enemies—Rome's Victims.

Passing under the banner, MacLeod approached a freestanding stone archway built in the style of the Roman triumphal arches he remembered from his days in Italy with Hugh Fitzcairn. He smiled, remembering the morning after the duke's wedding, waking up barely clothed on the top of one such arch near the ruins of the Forum, Fitz nowhere to be found and him with one hell of a headache, wondering how the devil he'd managed to get up there. Or how the devil he'd get down. Then along came Fitz with a hay wagon. Good old Fitz.

This particular arch wasn't actually stone, he realized as he got closer, just a clever simulation. And the opening in the archway was barely taller than he was, probably only a fifth of its original scale—no hay wagon necessary to break the fall. He admired the workmanship in the gilt statue on top of the arch—some triumphant Roman emperor in a chariot pulled by four fiery steeds, their muscles rippling. He brushed off his Latin to read the inscription. Titus. This particular triumphant Roman was Titus.

He tried to remember which one Titus was. "Caesar, Augustus, Tiberius," he chanted under his breath. In the back of his mind, he could hear Brother Paul chanting it along with him, night after night, all those years ago in the Monastery of St. Christopher. "Caligula, Claudius, Nero . . ." Paul had tried hard to teach MacLeod about the history of the world he'd begun to explore, but MacLeod had been so young then. So very young. He could name the kings of Scotland and those were the only kings worth knowing.

"Galba, Vitellius . . ." No, wait. "Otho, Vitellius . . ."

"Ach, it's no' fair—four in one year!" he could hear his frustrated younger self say, and Brother Paul had just laughed.

"Otho, Galba . . ." It was no use. He couldn't keep them straight then, he couldn't do it now. He gave up and walked on.

The floor plan had been deliberately designed in such a way that any visitor coming into the great hall was compelled to pass through the Arch of Titus to enter the exhibition. As MacLeod walked beneath the arch, he noticed the light-beam sensor just before he was about to trip it. Cautiously he reached out and broke the beam of light with his hand. Drums and horns blared around him. He looked around for the source, on alert. Then, over the martial music, came chanting and cheering:

"Ave, Caesar!" "Hail the conquering hero!"

He stepped cautiously through the archway and found himself surrounded by the frenzied citizens of Rome. Life-size mannequins garbed in Roman finery, caught in uncanny tableau as they seemed to cheer, applaud, strew his way with flowers. Each face individual, expressive, filled with the emotion of their leader's triumphal march into the city, of his glorious victory over the barbarians. Lights and sound flickered, highlighting this group, that person, flash, flash, giving the Romans the illusion of movement, almost giving them life. MacLeod turned quickly one way, then the other, taking in the crowd, receiving their adulation, and for one brief instant perhaps, he felt it, *knew* what it was like to be a king. To be the Emperor.

Then, in mid-rapture, the crowd abruptly silenced. Marcus Constantine stepped from beside the Arch of Titus, a key in his hand, and walked toward MacLeod.

"So? What do you think?" he asked, more than a little proud of his creation.

MacLeod caught his breath. "Impressive." He looked at the curator, so comfortable in a suit and tie, at home in his museum with his books and artifacts, so much the academic, and tried to see the legendary Roman general beneath it all. "Is that what it was like?"

Constantine's eyes shone bright, remembering, and he smiled. "On a good day." Then he laughed. "On a bad day you were up to your waist in swamp water trying to keep your provisions dry and the Emperor was trying to bribe your aide to poison you."

"Office politics?" MacLeod remarked.

"Precisely." Constantine pointed to the Arch. "He came after Vespasian, by the way. Julius Caesar, Augustus, Tiberius, Caligula, Claudius, Nero, the Year of Four Emperors that ended with Vespasian, then Titus, Vespasian's son." In response to MacLeod's look, he said, "Don't let it bother you, I can't remember them either." Then he winked at MacLeod and whispered conspiratorially, "And I was there."

MacLeod followed Constantine past displays arranged to give the museum visitor a quick foundation in the rise and power of the Roman Empire. These exhibits, too, were full of light and color, with computer animation and games and plenty of buttons to push to keep the kids amused. "A little sad, don't you think?" MacLeod commented. "Those men were once the most powerful men in the entire world, and now no one even remembers them."

"We of all people know that power doesn't guarantee Immortality, Duncan." MacLeod nodded in agreement. "Which is, in fact, part of the point of my new exhibition."

"I thought you must have an agenda, Marcus. It's not like you to glorify Rome like this."

"Ah, no, no, my friend, just the opposite. Consider this exhibition as a tribute to the assimilated. A memorial to the societies that were lost to history when the Romans came through like a giant steamroller, flattened their native cultures, carried off their best and brightest, and turned everyone into second-class Romans." Constantine stopped at one display in the center of the next section of walkway. As far as MacLeod could tell, it was a waist-high circular railing about six feet in diameter that enclosed nothing but floor. Constantine fit his key into a control box under the railing and turned it. "Watch," he said.

Suddenly, a round column of light appeared in the center of the enclosure, filling the space from floor to ceiling. MacLeod watched, waiting for something more to happen. After a moment, he prompted, "And . . . ?"

"Patience," Constantine counseled, looking more than a little like a wizard conjuring a spirit as he gestured at the light. "It takes a moment for it to warm up."

MacLeod saw a word begin to spiral down the column of light. Etruscan. "Hologram?" he asked, and Constantine nodded. Then there were more words. Samnite, Umbrian, Carthaginian, Sardinian. Faster. MacLeod realized he was watching a roll call of the assimilated. The technology fascinated him. Corsican, Corinthian, Syrian, Numidian, Celtiberian, Cimbri, Teuton, Egyptian. Like in a whirlwind, the names of vanquished peoples spun down from the ceiling, sucked into the floor. Samaritan, Dacian, Thracian, Illyrian, Macedonian, Epirote, Parthian, Helvetii. Faster and faster the vortex spun, the names descending fast and furious—CaledonianMaeataeArverniSenonesNerviiGalatian— so fast MacLeod could no longer read every one, could only pick out random cultures before they disappeared without a trace. Insubrian. Gaesatae. Boii. Iberian. Belgae. Suebi. Iceni. Parisii.

Finally the last name was consumed by the floor and all that remained was the column of light. Constantine turned off his new toy. MacLeod shook his head in wonder, and asked, "Whatever happened to the days when museums were places with dusty relics in big oak cases?"

"Just keeping up with the times, Duncan—we have to compete with EuroDisney now." He gestured for MacLeod to follow him into the next room of the carefully orchestrated exhibition. "We still keep a couple of cases around, for purists like yourself." A Plexiglas case taller than MacLeod filled the center of the cubicle, accessible from all sides. On a nearly transparent pedestal, parallel to the floor, rested an Egyptian sarcophagus. Above it, apparently hovering as if by magic, several smaller artifacts were suspended by fishing line. The arrangement seemed a little off, a large space left empty on the right side of the display, but MacLeod's attention was drawn to the sarcophagus.

"Marcus, that's Nefertiri's." MacLeod remembered the day he'd freed the handmaiden of Cleopatra from her two-thousand-year imprisonment in that sarcophagus. He also remembered the day he'd been forced to kill her.

"I guess you might call it a little selfish, wanting to get a curator's exclusive, but I called in a few favors from some of our kind. I wanted to bring a few pieces to the public that had never been on exhibit before. Pieces like this drinking horn from my old friend Bato the Illyrian"—he pointed out a translucent vessel carved from alabaster—"some rare pieces that could exemplify the beauty and sophistication of one of the cultures we destroyed or that in some way would symbolize the brutality we were capable of."

MacLeod had raised an eyebrow at Constantine's "we." Since his arrival he'd suspected that this exhibition was Constantine's way of trying to make amends, to atone in some small way for what he felt were the sins of his past. It certainly explained the exhibition's scale—it must have taken years to design. He wouldn't be surprised to learn that Constantine's own money was funding it—he knew the modest Musée could never afford an installation so state-of-the-art. But MacLeod said nothing about it, noting with wry sadness instead, "I don't think Nefertiri will need it back. And I think she'd be pleased that her people were being remembered."

Constantine seemed a bit relieved that MacLeod approved. "Recognize this one?" he asked, pointing to one of the artifacts "floating" in the case on hidden wires.

A Celtic torque gleamed in the case's spotlight, the golden terminals at the ends of the elaborate neckpiece clasped together to form a delicate ring, finely wrought and crafted by artisans whose skills had rarely been equaled. "Ceirdwyn's?"

"How'd you guess? She rarely lets it out. I nearly had to pry it off of her. You should have seen the look she gave me when I asked if I might borrow her sword, as well."

"She brought it out when her husband Steven was killed."

Constantine looked grim. "Sad business, that." He was

silent for a moment, then went on. "The Celts were such an amazing people, Duncan. You should have seen them—they were passionate, they were spontaneous. They loved life with a gusto I'd never thought was possible. And then the Romans came through and we made them . . ." Constantine seemed at a loss for the right words.

"English?" MacLeod ventured with a wicked grin, and they both laughed. He looked at the next item in the case. The foot-long piece of iron was flat black next to the gleaming torque, maybe an inch in diameter, and marked only with a ring of rusty oxidation about halfway up the shaft. "What's that?"

"Slave boy from the northern provinces was crucified by his Roman master because the master's wife tried to seduce him."

MacLeod looked more closely at the nail and shuddered. "Nasty way to die, even for one of us."

"You should have seen the master's wife." Now it was Constantine's turn to shudder. "Personally, I think crucifixion was the better part of the deal. The slave kept one of the nails as a souvenir. Sick sense of humor, if you ask me."

MacLeod pointed out the empty section of the case. "So what goes here? A piece of the One True Cross?"

"Actually, that's why I asked you to come by."

Ah, here it comes, MacLeod thought. "Somehow I knew you wouldn't make a lunch date just because you enjoyed the company, Marcus."

Constantine, a little embarrassed, asked, "That transparent, am I?"

MacLeod smiled. "Whatever I have is yours. You know that." He looked around the room. "But I don't know what I have that would fit in with all of this."

"Paul Karros's sword?"

"Karros?" MacLeod was intrigued.

"I tried to locate him and found out you had . . . taken care of him, as it were. I thought you might have kept the sword. It was a *gladius*, an iron short sword, beautiful piece of work. He used it during the Spartacan revolt, you know. He was Thracian, like Spartacus, trained as a—"

"I know, trained as a gladiator to fight in the Roman games. He must have told me a thousand times," MacLeod explained.

"Really? I didn't realize you were that close."

"We were once," MacLeod said quietly, and Constantine needed no further explanation. They'd all been there.

"So you *do* have the sword?" Constantine asked eagerly.

MacLeod nodded. "I know where I can get my hands on it. Tuesday soon enough?"

"Perfect. The exhibition opens on Wednesday." Constantine looked pleased. "Well, that was simple enough—and I didn't even have to spring for lunch," he added with a devilish look at MacLeod, who thought he could almost detect a small gleam of victory in his eyes.

"Uh-uh, not so fast," MacLeod said, shaking his head. "You still owe me, Marcus. And this time I pick the restaurant. I don't think we'll be welcome at Chez Nous again."

"What did you do, Duncan?" Constantine scolded with fatherly concern.

"It's a long story. But no lame excuses about curation emergencies next time."

Constantine acted shocked at the very notion. "Lame? Not lame at all, I assure you. Look at this." He led MacLeod toward another case, this one made of a tinted plastic. "I spent the entire day wrestling French Customs for this piece—you thought facing Karros was tough. But if I hadn't, it would have ended up in some bureaucratic warehouse next to the Ark of the Covenant." MacLeod stopped and looked closely at Constantine for a moment, then decided it must just be museum humor. With Constantine, you couldn't always tell when he was kidding. "It will come as no surprise to you, I'm sure, that the Israelis don't look kindly on removing antiquities from the country. You'd better have your paperwork in order. In triplicate."

Constantine flipped a switch at the back of the case and a dim light illuminated the contents. An old, worn fragment of papyrus, apparently blank in the half-light. MacLeod looked at it for a moment. "Am I waiting for it to warm up?" he asked.

"No holograms here, my friend. This is the real thing. But I believe we can help it out a bit with the magic of technology." He flipped another switch, bathing the scrap in infrared light, and suddenly MacLeod could make out a tiny, delicate script covering the papyrus. Hebrew, he realized, very old. He looked up at Constantine, questioning.

"A fragment of the Torah, Duncan." Both Constantine's voice and face conveyed a reverence MacLeod had not expected from a man who could be considered an ancient relic himself. "Recovered from Masada. It just arrived today from my student, Avram Mordecai."

To get a better look at the delicate writing, MacLeod moved closer to the Torah.

Chapter Three

MacLeod moved closer to the Torah, taking the precious scroll carefully from the shaking hands of the man who clutched it to his chest for protection. "*Rebbe*, please, we must hurry."

"My son, he is *gut?*" Rabbi Mendelsohn asked for perhaps the third time in the ten minutes since MacLeod had roused him from his sleep in the predawn gloom. The old man was smaller than MacLeod had expected, stooped and bowed with the effects of age and three years of deprivation, confined behind the formidable walls of the Jewish Ghetto. Only the rabbi's clothes, carefully patched and mended and hanging from his gaunt frame, bespoke the strong, robust man his son Shimon had described to MacLeod in such loving detail back in Paris.

"Shimon is fine, *zai'er gut*," MacLeod reassured him. MacLeod knew only a little Yiddish, although Shimon Mendelsohn had tried to teach him all he could before MacLeod left. The rabbi's Polish was rusty, Yiddish having been the language of daily life and commerce in Warsaw's Jewish community for centuries, but quickly they'd discovered they could communicate in a rough pastiche of the two languages, mixed with a little German, a little Russian. It was enough. "He's living with monks outside of Paris. He is safe there."

"Safe." The old man savored the word and his eyes grew bright with unshed tears. "*Danken Gott*, Shimon is *safe*," he repeated to himself while MacLeod set the Torah down carefully by the rabbi's hat on a low table near the door. The table and an old wing chair were the only furnishings left in the room. "Then his story has been told?" Rabbi Mendelsohn asked him, tugging eagerly on MacLeod's sleeve for emphasis. "The West knows? Shimon has told them?"

How to tell the old man the messenger had gotten out safely, but not the message? How to tell him his only son fought his way to the West to proclaim the word, eager to expose for all the world the atrocities of the Warsaw Ghetto, and the world had turned its back on him? How to tell him Shimon Mendelsohn had escaped the death camps, broken the news that the Germans were systematically destroying his people, and instead of finding aid, found only apathy and disbelief?

He didn't have to tell him. The rabbi, no stranger to the human heart, read it in his face, saw the despair and the shame in his eyes.

"They didn't have ears to hear him, did they?" A deep sigh of resignation seemed to stoop the old man's shoulders even more. "Everyone's got their own problems. Their own war." He sat heavily in the wing chair, tugging nervously on his graying beard. "Nobody's got time for the *tsores* of a bunch of 'worthless Jews' in Poland." He spit out the words with surprising venom.

"*Rebbe*, it's not like that," MacLeod protested.

"No, Mr. MacLeod? Then you tell me what it *is* like."

The silence between them was long and heavy. MacLeod couldn't tell him, not in Yiddish, not in Polish, not in any language on earth, because there *was* no rational explanation he could find for the Allies' disregard of Shimon's plea for help. He tried a different approach. "Shimon feels that if you and your wife can join him and get to England, or even America, to bear witness with him—"

"My wife is gone," the rabbi said quietly, not looking at MacLeod.

"I'm sorry," MacLeod said after a moment. "I . . . I didn't know."

"Irena was taking medicines to her sister on Franciszkanska Street. That was at the end of August, two weeks before the *Aktsia*, the expulsions, stopped. I never saw her again . . . A neighbor said he saw her and Irka at the *Um-*

schlagplatz—those Nazi demons were putting them on the train to Treblinka." The rabbi stood and turned to MacLeod. "In two months, they took a half a million people—my wife, my neighbors, my congregation. All gone. And now those of us they've left behind wait in fear of the day the demons decide to come and finish the job." His voice was quavery but his eyes were hard, boring into MacLeod. "So you tell me again how no one cares, Mr. MacLeod. You tell me again how they can say *this isn't happening!*"

MacLeod could say nothing. Instead, he reached out and placed a hand on the rabbi's shoulder, for strength, for comfort. Rabbi Mendelsohn grasped his arm like a lifeline and buried his face in MacLeod's chest, his own shoulders shaking with mute anger and grief.

MacLeod gave him a moment, then gently reminded him, "*Rebbe*, we have to go. There is transport waiting to take you to Shimon, but we have to hurry."

The old man released MacLeod's arm and stepped away, nodding his understanding. He wiped his eyes. "Yes, yes, but first, I must get the rest of my things." He hurried to a basement door.

"No, wait—" MacLeod tried to stop him, but he disappeared down the dark stairs.

MacLeod checked his pocket watch, concerned. This was taking longer than he'd expected. It was nearly six in the morning. Soon the sun would be up. He hurried to the window and cautiously pulled back a corner of the drape.

She was still there, across the street on the corner, still vigilant, keeping watch for the soldiers just as she'd promised she would. It was a good sign.

Her name, she'd told him, was Rivka. MacLeod knew she couldn't be any older than thirteen. He first saw her soon after he arrived in Warsaw. He'd traveled from Paris as a German businessman—his German and his papers were both impeccable and "Herr Münte" had had little trouble passing border guards and checkpoints throughout the New German Reich. But "Herr Münte" couldn't help him in occupied Warsaw, where most of the Poles would sooner spit on a German than give him the time of day. It certainly wouldn't get him past the formidable iron gates and machine-gun emplacements barring the entrances to the Jewish Ghetto.

He'd spent a day carefully studying the Wall surrounding the Ghetto, analyzing it surreptitiously from the apartment buildings and shops across the narrow streets. It was almost beyond his comprehension—wherever he stood outside the Wall, Polish children played in the streets while their mothers went about their daily chores, shopping, chatting with their neighbors, trying to maintain some semblance of normalcy in the face of the Nazi occupation. Meanwhile, less than twenty yards away, if the sketchy reports reaching Paris were at all accurate, hundreds of thousands of their fellow human beings were being systematically murdered. It just didn't seem possible.

When he thought no one was looking, he'd stood by the Wall, touched it. In some places it was as tall as he was, in others it must have been as much as six feet taller, all of it of sturdy red brick and mortar. At the top, barbed wire spiraled its length, supplemented in places by shards of broken glass embedded in the mortar. A serious wall, designed to let no one in, and no one out. He could take the Wall, he knew—especially under the cover of night—and make it into the Ghetto. But back out, with an elderly rabbi and his wife . . . He had to keep looking for a weakness in the Germans' design.

It had been midafternoon when he noticed Rivka near a bakery on Zelanza Street, close to the western face of the Wall. He had remembered seeing her in another market earlier in the day, the dark-eyed waif remarkable among the other pigtailed Polish girls because of the tattered and frayed overcoat that seemed way too large for her but not nearly warm enough for the January cold. But now the coat seemed to fit her, in an odd sort of way.

From across the street, he had watched her go into the bakery and, quick as a flash, stuff two loaves of bread into the coat while the baker was distracted. She scurried from the shop before the baker had even looked up from his customer, then she strolled casually down the street as if nothing had happened.

Smuggling. Stealing food to smuggle back into the Ghetto, MacLeod was willing to bet. And she was good at it, too, by the look of things. If she could get in and out of the Ghetto, there must be a way for him, as well. He had followed her from a distance.

Soon they had reached a section of the Wall that faced onto several blocks of apartments blown to hell by the Germans in the battle for Warsaw. Corners of brick buildings jutted up out of rubble a yard deep, bleak monuments to those who had lived and died there. There were no other pedestrians around, no shops, no residents. Only devastation, and a young girl on a mission. MacLeod was careful to stay hidden in the shadows.

She looked around carefully, then started toward the Wall. Then, in that paranoia that is only bred of desperation, she must have heard something, or caught a glimpse of something, because she turned around abruptly and spotted MacLeod.

Her eyes grew wide with fear, but the fear quickly mixed with something that could have been defiance when she realized he wasn't a soldier and he was alone. MacLeod spoke fast, before he lost her. "Little girl," he said quietly, "I need your help. *Proszę.*" But his strangely accented Polish had only proven to her he was an outsider, and she turned and ran through the rubble, away from the Wall as fast as she could, as if the devil himself was chasing her.

MacLeod had tried to follow—she left a clear trail of food dropped from her overcoat that would have pleased Hansel and Gretel—but when he'd made it through the shifting rubble and back to a busy street nearby, he had lost her.

All the next afternoon he had hidden in the rubble, hoping against hope that she'd make her rounds again and have to return his way. Just before sundown he finally saw her, coat bulging with stolen food, looking around her constantly as she walked, wary, waiting. He took a big chance—*"Shimon Mendelsohn shikt mir,"* he called out in halting Yiddish.

She stopped, looking around for him, frightened but not running. At least, not yet. "Shimon sent you?" She was wary, waiting for a trap.

"I've come to see the *rebbe.*" He threw a large bag over the ruined wall behind which he was hiding, and it hit the ground with a thunk. She moved away from it quickly, then cautiously approached it again when it was clear it would not explode. "Please, can you help me?" MacLeod asked. After looking around quickly, furtively, like a squirrel with a nut, she opened the bag, rifling through bread and potatoes and cheeses. She touched them reverently, like manna from heaven, then reached farther in the bag and pulled out the sausages. Stunned, she looked around for her benefactor, still wary, but with tears pooling on her cheeks. Looking at her gaunt bare legs, red with cold, and her dark sunken eyes, MacLeod wondered how long it had been since she'd had any meat.

Slowly, arms spread to show he had no weapon, that he was no threat to her, MacLeod came around the wall. She hurriedly stuffed the food back into the bag, as if afraid he'd take it away from her. "Will you help me find *Rebbe* Mendelsohn?" MacLeod asked again and held his last treasure out to her—a sturdy woolen coat, lined with fleece. He'd purposely gotten one too large for her, so she could still ply her craft in it. But at least she'd be warm.

She snatched it from his hand and stepped away from him. She considered him solemnly for a long moment, child's eyes, shadowed with hunger and fatigue, searching him. MacLeod met her eyes with sincerity, and realized hers were a child's eyes no longer. He'd seen those eyes before, in many lands, in many wars—eyes that had seen too little happiness and far too much death.

"Two hours before sunrise," she finally said in Polish. "Meet me here. I will take you." Before she had even finished speaking, she scooped up the bag of food and, with bag in one hand and new coat in the other, hurried away from him.

"Wait!" he called after her. "*Vi haist ir?*"

"Rivka," she called back from the shadows, and disappeared.

She'd kept her promise, returning in the dead of night to lead him silently to a breach in the Wall, hidden away behind a tailor's shop on Krochmalna Street. Though Rivka could pass easily through the small opening, it was a tight fit for an adult, but with effort MacLeod managed to make it through to the Jewish sector.

More relaxed in the relative safety of the Ghetto, Rivka took his hand and led him through the dark, abandoned streets to the rabbi's home. There she promised to wait outside and lead them back to the Aryan side again.

"Best lookout in the Ghetto," she told him proudly.

MacLeod had smiled at her warmly. "I have no doubt," he said, playfully tugging at one of her plaited pigtails. He was rewarded with the first smile he'd seen from her.

Now, as he watched her on the corner, there was no trace of that smile. He watched her hunker down in her ragged cloth coat as the wind blew against her. A light snow was just beginning to fall. He wondered why she hadn't worn her new coat, then realized with sadness she had probably sold it for more food.

MacLeod heard Rabbi Mendelsohn coming up the basement stairs and turned from the window. The rabbi was carrying a large metal strongbox. "No, no, *Rebbe*, you don't understand," MacLeod explained patiently. "We have to travel light. You'll have to leave that here."

"No, Mr. MacLeod, it is *you* who does not understand." He pushed the box toward MacLeod, who took it reluctantly. "These are my writings, my journals. I keep a history for *Oneg Shabbat*. It is all there—the expulsions, the camps, the hunger, the disease—everything that has happened since the Germans." The old man was adamant. "What happens to me does not matter. But *these* must survive. These must go to Shimon. These *must* bear witness to the world when we no longer can." He pleaded, "That is the only voice we have left. You cannot allow it to be destroyed, Mr. MacLeod, or everything we are, everything we were will vanish into nothing, like the smoke from Treblinka. And then the Germans will have won." He grabbed MacLeod's arm with surprising strength. "Promise me."

MacLeod could feel his voice catch in his throat. "I promise."

"*Gut*," said the rabbi, suddenly all business. "Now my coat, and we'll be on our way to Shimon." He fetched his coat and shrugged it on, the dingy white armband with its blue Star of David prominent on one sleeve. Settling his hat on his head and picking up the scroll of the Torah, he said "After you, Mr. MacLeod," gesturing toward the door.

Suddenly, two sharp whistles pierced the predawn quiet. MacLeod quickly pushed the rabbi behind him and looked out the small window embedded in the door. Rivka was gone.

And coming around the corner where she once stood was a small convoy of German vehicles.

Damn.

"Vos?" the rabbi asked. The squealing of wheels and the shouts of the soldiers answered his question before MacLeod could even try. *"Tei'er Gott!"* The rabbi grew pale. Dear God. It was a sound he'd not heard in nearly four months, a sound he'd prayed every night he'd never hear again. "The *Aktsia*—it has started again."

MacLeod thought fast as he watched the Germans pile out of their trucks. Too many to try and fight. Too many to try and hide. He turned from the window, setting the strongbox on the table and removing his jacket. "Take off your coat," he ordered the rabbi.

"What? Why?"

"Just do it. There's no time to explain." MacLeod took the Torah from the rabbi, placing it on the table, then helped him off with his coat. Pressing the Torah and the strongbox into the old man's arms, he guided him by the shoulders to the basement door.

They could hear the Germans fanning out through the neighborhood, calling the Jews from their homes. *"Raus! Juden, Raus!"*

MacLeod lifted the hat from Rabbi Mendelsohn's head and placed it on his own. "You can't do this!" Rabbi Mendelsohn protested, beginning to realize what MacLeod had in mind. "I won't let you."

"Shvieg!" Quiet! MacLeod commanded, "Stay here. I'll be back for you." He could hear soldiers banging on the door.

"Jude Mendelsohn! Raus!"

"My life is not worth losing yours," the rabbi whispered urgently, begging. "Take the box and run! Please!"

MacLeod gave the old man a gentle push onto the basement stairs and swiftly locked the door behind him. "Wait for me. I *will* be back. I swear it."

The pounding grew louder, more insistent. "Mendelsohn!" They were trying to break the door down.

"MacLeod!" he could hear the rabbi cry out as he began to put on the old man's coat. "Do not do this! No one comes back!"

Quickly, he tugged on the coat. Even at his prime, the rabbi had been a smaller man than MacLeod, and the seams of the old coat strained but held.

The same could not be said of the door, which finally broke under the force of the battering, and suddenly the room seemed full of uniforms. Two of the soldiers grabbed him by the arms and forced him painfully to his knees.

"Mendelsohn, Zalman?" their leader barked in his face, and MacLeod nodded in mute acknowledgment. The soldier looked at him suspiciously for a long moment—MacLeod held his breath—then signaled to his men to take him away. As they dragged him roughly from the house to a truck waiting in the street, he overheard the leader tell another soldier he probably wasn't Mendelsohn, but they had a quota to fill and "one dead Jew's as good as any other" as far as the final tally was concerned. MacLeod had been counting on that.

The canvas-covered truck stank of stale urine and fear. Three guards, armed, rode the tailgate, completely ignoring their defenseless cargo. There were about two dozen Jews packed tightly in the truck, mostly women, a few children, a few old men, all terrified. As the truck pulled away, MacLeod maneuvered his way toward the tailgate, trying to calculate the best way to escape and take the others with him. Or at least not get them all killed in his attempt. He had a pistol in his boot and knew he could take out the guards before they could get off an answering round. Surprise was in his favor—they obviously weren't expecting any resistance.

His dilemma was the vehicle he could see out the back of the truck, an open car with six more Germans. Yes, he could take out the guards, but at the first shot the chase car would be alerted, and then there would be nothing to prevent them from opening fire on the truck.

He heard the other passengers whisper nervously among themselves. They were nearly to the *Umschlagplatz*, the railway station that led to Treblinka. Pressed against one canvas wall of the truck, a toddler in his mother's arms began to wail, as if hearing the name of the bogeyman. His mother hurried to shush him, clutching his face tightly to her bosom, but the wailing grew louder.

"Stille!" a soldier on the tailgate commanded, annoyed by

the sound. The young mother did what she could to quiet the little boy, putting her hand over his mouth, cooing words of comfort in his ear, but the boy was inconsolable. The others in the truck looked at each other with helpless dread. The wail became a scream as the toddler fought to get away from his mother's suffocating grasp.

"STILLE!"

A single shot rang out. The scream was silenced. The young Jewish mother slumped where she stood, killed by the same bullet that had passed through her child, but her body could not fall, held in place by the crush of the other prisoners. Behind her, the splatter of her blood leached into the fabric of the wall.

One of the old men near her, his hair, his clothes, his face all gray, rocked back and forth, eyes closed, lips moving in silent prayer.

MacLeod reached down and cautiously pulled the pistol from his boot. At the train station would be more soldiers, and more innocent victims. He knew he didn't dare make his stand there. He felt trapped. He had made a solemn promise to Shimon, and then to Shimon's father, but how many lives was he willing to sacrifice to keep that promise? He watched the gray man praying. They both would need a miracle.

Then, before MacLeod's eyes, someone's prayers were answered. The chase car erupted in flames!

Not stopping to thank God for this unexpected blessing, MacLeod acted on it. As the three guards registered what had just happened behind them, he fired three shots in rapid succession. Just as rapidly, three stains of blood blossomed on three brown shirts. One guard fell from the tailgate to the rapidly moving pavement below. MacLeod pushed the other two from the truck as the other prisoners looked on in astonishment.

The sound of gunfire was all around now, and another explosion rocked the truck. "Get down!" MacLeod ordered the stunned passengers. *"Vart doh!"* He pushed the gray man to his knees for emphasis and the other passengers followed.

As the truck lurched to a halt, MacLeod vaulted over the tailgate, landing on the street in a crouch, then rolled under the truck. From there he surveyed the situation. He could see they were about a block from the train station. All around, hundreds of people wearing the white armband were fleeing, taking cover, or dropping to the ground where they stood, covering their heads. In the midst of them, a fire fight—a handful of Jews, maybe twenty in all, young men and women, practically children, were taking on the Germans with nothing more than some pistols and a few grenades. And, incredibly, the Germans were retreating to cover under the barrage!

Another grenade impacted nearby and rocked the truck. MacLeod could hear the occupants still above him in the truck scream. He crawled along the underbelly of the truck until he reached the cab. Reaching up from below, he threw the driver's side door open. When the driver leaned out, MacLeod grabbed him by the shoulders and pulled him from the cab to the ground.

"Guten Morgen!" MacLeod said cheerfully to the surprised German, then punched him hard in the face, knocking him out against the pavement.

Climbing into the cab, he saw that the copilot had already bailed out. He threw the truck into gear and started to drive.

As he did, he sensed the presence of another Immortal nearby.

Shit, he thought, *not now*. He drove on for several blocks, taking the truck far from the line of fire, but still he couldn't shake the sensation. Once sure that his passengers were safe for the moment, he stopped the truck and knocked against the back of the cab, yelling "Go! Hurry! *Gai a'vek!*" The rocking of the truck assured him his charges were taking his advice and getting the hell out.

Just as MacLeod turned to get out of the truck and face the other Immortal, the other Immortal came to him. The passenger door opened and a young man of slight build jumped in. His skin was smoky dark, very different from that of either the Poles or the Jews who inhabited the area. He had black, almost bottomless eyes and a boyish face that could have been considered friendly under other circumstances—circumstances where he wasn't holding a pistol to MacLeod's head. MacLeod slowly raised his hands.

"I'm Duncan MacLeod of the Clan MacLeod," he said, "and we don't need guns."

"I am Avram ben Mordecai of . . ." he thought for a moment, trying to match MacLeod, "the House of Judah. And I don't have time for this Immortal bullshit right now. Get out of the truck."

MacLeod got down from the truck and Avram slid across the seat to exit behind him, gun still trained on the back of MacLeod's head.

"Why are you here?" Avram demanded.

"I came to help."

"Funny, you don't look Jewish." A threat.

MacLeod turned to face him. "I didn't realize that was a prerequisite for compassion."

"These days, it is." Avram studied him closely, taking in the too-small coat, the Star of David. "You know, *goy*, I could shoot you right now and take your head."

"You could," MacLeod acknowledged. "But I think you have more important things to do. And I have a promise to keep to Zalman Mendelsohn."

"The *Rebbe*?" Then he realized, "You wear his coat!" He pressed the gun closer to MacLeod's face. "What have you done to the *Rebbe*, you bastard?"

"Tzaddik, don't!" a young voice cried out. Keeping his pistol to MacLeod's face, Avram turned his head to see Rivka racing down the block toward them.

MacLeod called to her in alarm, "Rivka, stay back!" but she kept running.

"Tzaddik, don't hurt him. Shimon sent him—all the way from Paris!" Reaching them, Rivka threw her arms around MacLeod protectively. "We're going to get the *Rebbe* out of the Ghetto!"

"Shimon? You've seen Shimon?"

MacLeod nodded. "He made it to Paris. He's with the Resistance." Avram stepped back from him, regarding him intently but not dropping his gun. The two men sized each other up. MacLeod thought he could sense that Avram was much like himself, a man of honor. From blocks away, they could still hear the sound of sporadic gunfire. "Listen to your heart, Avram," MacLeod appealed to him urgently. "Believe me. Trust me. I'm not here to hurt anyone. I just want to help Shimon's father. And your people need you back there." Avram's expression didn't change. "If you don't believe me, then send the child away and we'll settle this honorably."

"Tzaddik, please . . ." Rivka begged.

In the distance, another explosion sounded. Avram was torn. This was the moment he and the surviving youth of the Ghetto had worked and drilled endlessly for—when the Germans would return in force to eradicate the last remaining Jews in Warsaw and the Jews would finally rise up with weapons and face their murderers in battle. His people needed him. But, this Immortal, this Gentile, this *goy* MacLeod . . . he could prove a danger to his people as well . . . He looked from Rivka's eager eyes to MacLeod. "Well," he said after a long moment, praying he was making the right decision, "if Shimon and Rivka vouch for you . . ." Sometimes he could only go with his gut feeling. He reached into a pouch at his waist and pulled out a grenade, handing it to MacLeod. "Here, you'll probably need this. Now go, you and Rivka keep your promise. Give Shimon my regards. Tell him he still owes me two tickets to the pictures." He turned and climbed into the cargo truck.

"Avram!" MacLeod called after him, and Avram hung out the window. "I'll be back to help when the rabbi's safe."

"Sure you will, *goy*," Avram called back, unconvinced. He threw the truck into gear and drove off.

Chapter Four

Paris: The Present

MacLeod pulled his Citroën close in behind the truck stopped in front of the Hôtel Lutétia, tossing his keys to a uniformed doorman as he got out. As he adjusted his gray turtleneck sweater and buttoned the single button of his blue sports coat over it, he thought he could almost detect the vaguest shiver of nervousness in his stomach.

Some things never changed, not even after four hundred years. Certainly first dates hadn't changed—all the possibilities, all the uncertainties. At least he wouldn't have to meet Maral's parents. The thought brought a rueful smile to his lips. Fighting the most despicable Kern or Kalas on the planet had always been easier than facing a girl's parents for the first time. With a deep relaxation breath he entered the great revolving doors and passed into the grand lobby of the hotel.

Four Arab men in suits and surly looks were waiting for him inside. They surrounded him as soon as he entered. "*Masá al-kháyr*," MacLeod bade them good evening in his friendliest voice, flashing his most sincere smile. It never paid to piss off guys carrying automatic weapons under their coats before finding out what their problem was.

"Duncan MacLeod?" asked one of them, an older man in a traditional Arab headdress, the *kaffiyeh*, and MacLeod nodded.

"Dr. Amina is expecting me," he said and immediately two of the other suits each grabbed him by an arm. This wasn't exactly what he expected on a first date. He looked at the two men holding him, then at the older man in the *kaffiyeh*, who was regarding him sternly. "You wouldn't happen to be her father, would you? Look, I promise, I'll have her home by midnight," he joked, but the Palestinian was not amused.

"Search him," he commanded, his face implacable. The suit holding MacLeod's right arm pulled MacLeod's wallet and a small box in colorful gift wrap from his jacket and tossed them to the older man. The fourth suit proceeded to pat down MacLeod's chest and under his arms.

"Hey, watch it, that tickles," MacLeod protested. The Palestinian, ignoring him, frisked him around the waist, then up and down each leg. MacLeod pulled away. "Sorry, buddy, you're not my type." The friendly edge was beginning to wear off his voice.

"He's clean," the one frisking him reported to his boss. The two suits restraining MacLeod released him.

"Sorry to disappoint you, gentlemen." MacLeod casually tugged the sleeves of his jacket back into position. "What do we do next? Retinal scans? IQ tests? Or do I get to see Dr. Amina now?" At the older man's nod, one of his men began to speak quietly into a small walkie-talkie.

Kaffiyeh tore the paper from the box and opened it, scrutinizing the contents. Apparently convinced the palm-sized box didn't contain an incendiary device, he closed the box and made a halfhearted attempt to stuff it back into its wrapping. Then he opened MacLeod's wallet and gave it a cursory look before handing them both back. "Our apologies, Mr. MacLeod," he said, anything but apologetic. "She will be down directly. Please wait here." He indicated a chair in full view of all corners of the room.

"And you're not going to tell me what this is about, are you?" MacLeod asked as he put away his wallet and tattered gift. The Palestinian merely turned and walked away. "Somehow, I knew that was a rhetorical question." MacLeod sat down in the specified chair, drumming his fingers on his thighs as he waited for Maral. There were others in the lobby seemingly going about their business, all of them careful not to be caught watching him, but he could feel a dozen eyes burning into him in secret. It was a relief when he saw Maral coming across the lobby toward him a few minutes later.

He moved toward her, took her hand in his and kissed it gently. *"Káyf hálik?"* he greeted her in her native language, asking her how she was.

Maral smiled at him. *"Mabsúta,* Duncan," she assured him she was well, and the words were warm and throaty. Her hair was still worn up in combs, but she had exchanged her conservative suit for a moss-colored dress that swirled around her calves and brought out the burnished gold in her skin. It was Paris *haute couture* and yet somehow still the epitome of Arab modesty. MacLeod couldn't decide whether it was the dress that enhanced Maral's natural beauty, or Maral who enhanced the dress's.

"You look magnificent," he said, meaning every word of it.

She laughed. "How often does a girl get to Paris?" She did a quick little turn in front of him. "I don't think I've worn anything quite this fancy since my wedding."

Over one arm Maral carried a silk shawl in whirls of greens and golds adorned by intricate beadwork. "May I?" MacLeod took the shawl from her and draped it around her shoulders. "Spring nights here can still be chilly, but we don't have too far to go." With a light touch, he stroked the silk as it lay across her shoulders. It was soft and cool. "This is lovely," he said, but he meant so much more than the shawl, keenly aware of the curve of her shoulder, the gracefulness of her arm as he caressed them beneath the silk.

Maral tied the ends of the shawl in front of her, then playfully guided his hand along the edge of the silk as it passed gently over her breast before holding his hand tight against the knot of the shawl where it lay just beneath her bosom. Her dark eyes met his own and a moment sparked between them. It wasn't a promise. It was a possibility.

"This was my grandmother's," she finally said, but MacLeod could tell that wasn't what she really wanted to say. "It was part of her dowry from my great-grandfather." She abruptly released his hand and his gaze as her bodyguard Assad and yet another man who had obviously been shopping off the rack at Spy City approached them.

"We're ready, Doctor," Assad announced.

"Then I guess so are we." Maral offered her arm to MacLeod. "Duncan?"

He looked at the two men, who were obviously armed to the teeth and who clearly intended to accompany them. "I didn't realize this was a double date." He turned to Maral. "I thought you were going to arrange to leave Toto at home."

Maral's face reflected her deep concern. "Farid didn't tell you?" She looked across the lobby toward the man in the *kaffiyeh*.

"I'm afraid they were too busy measuring my inseam. Not a very chatty bunch. Tell me what?"

She reached out and touched his hand. "There's been more trouble at home." Her eyes grew darker, her voice took on a note of pain. "Forty-three people were murdered outside a mosque in Hebron yesterday by an extremist Jewish student with an automatic weapon."

That would explain the smell of paranoia in the lobby, the heightened security. He understood immediately. "And you're afraid of retaliation."

Maral nodded. "All of the peoples of Palestine are children of thousands of years of blood feuds and retribution. A Jewish attack like this will only lead to an Arab counterattack. Then an Israeli response, then a Palestinian uprising. And then the military will crack down, and the next thing you know, five years of compromise and negotiation and movement—however so slowly—toward peace could be gone. All because of one fanatic. Everything we fought for. Everything we've gained. We will be prisoners again in our own country." MacLeod caught a glimpse of the combination of eloquence and a hard edge of steel that bred a strong negotiator. "We cannot let that happen."

"Then you *are* in danger?"

"No more here than in Ramallah, I think. But you see, don't you, why Farid and his security people would not allow me to go to dinner with such a charming, mysterious stranger without proper"—she looked at stern-faced Assad and his brooding associate and said wryly—"chaperones?"

"Well, the more the merrier, I always say." MacLeod took Maral's arm and started toward the door. He glanced back at Assad. "You coming, Toto?"

"I will drive," Assad announced.

"I thought we'd walk," MacLeod said. "The restaurant's

only a few blocks away, and it's a nice night. C'mon, the exercise'll do you good."

"I will drive," Assad reiterated.

"I'm afraid Farid has picked a different restaurant for us," Maral told MacLeod apologetically, "one he knows is secure. I hope you don't mind. It was either this, or I would be having room service alone in my hotel room again."

MacLeod smiled at her. "It's fine. I don't care where we eat or what we eat, as long as it's with you."

Maral laughed. "I'm beginning to think you have the patience of a saint, Duncan MacLeod."

"If it keeps you from becoming a martyr, I can be anything you like." He ushered her through the revolving doors to a dark Town Car waiting outside.

The ride to the restaurant was an uncomfortable one, Maral sandwiched in the backseat between MacLeod and the sullen Arab whose name MacLeod still didn't know. With the two bodyguards listening to their every word, it wasn't the best place for conversation beyond remarks about the weather and the sorry state of Parisian traffic. It was to everyone's relief when they finally arrived at the restaurant.

MacLeod escorted Maral inside to find the place completely empty. "I hope this isn't a commentary on the food," he remarked, surveying the empty tables.

"We have it all to ourselves this evening," Maral explained.

"Just the four of us? How romantic."

The owner of the establishment, a rotund Frenchman with a handlebar mustache, hurried over to greet them and ushered them to a table. MacLeod helped seat Maral and then sat himself down opposite her. The two bodyguards took up their positions, standing like twin towers of doom and gloom at the corners of the table.

Maral removed her shawl and draped it on the back of the empty chair to her right, but the silk was slippery and slid from the chair to the floor. Immediately, both guards swooped in to rescue it as if throwing themselves on a live grenade. Maral had to laugh at how ridiculous they looked, and once she'd started, found she couldn't stop. "I can't do this," she said through her laughter. "This is all too surreal. I'll never get used to it." Tears came to her eyes, though whether they were tears of laughter or frustration at their situation, MacLeod couldn't tell.

He got up and pulled two nearby tables a little closer to the table where he and Maral were seated. He pulled a chair out from under one table, grabbed Assad by the shoulders and directed him to the chair. "You, Beavis, sit." He pulled a chair out from under the second table and indicated it to Assad's partner. "And you, Butthead, over here." The partner was about to protest, but one glance at the look on MacLeod's face and he sat where ordered. MacLeod sat back down in his own seat. "Better?"

"Much better," Maral agreed. "Thank you."

MacLeod reached for the wine list, then stopped. "Would you be offended if I had a drink?"

"Offended? Why would I be offended?"

"Islam. You said at lunch yesterday you didn't drink, and I thought . . ."

Maral shook her head. "I'm afraid the last devout Muslim in my family was my grandfather. I don't drink, but it's not a religious obligation. You should help yourself." MacLeod called the owner over and ordered a glass of wine.

"Would Monsieur like to see a dinner menu?" the owner asked.

"No . . ." MacLeod looked over at Maral with a twinkle in his eye. "Surprise us." The owner hurried off to confer with the chef. "Now," he said to Maral, "tell me more about your family."

"My father was raised in Islam, but he was always full of doubt, even as a child. He grew up in a Palestinian refugee camp in Jordan, and he always had trouble understanding why my grandfather believed it was written that peasants from Russia should take away the farm that had been in our family for nearly three hundred years. My mother was a Christian, from Bethlehem. My uncles, who still raise sheep there, like to claim that it was our ancestors who saw the great star over Bethlehem and found the baby Jesus. That's how long they say my mother's family have herded sheep in that area."

MacLeod could remember many sunny afternoons as a boy spent off adventuring with his cousin Robert, even though they'd both been warned to mind the sheep. And many's the cold, lonely night spent helping a ewe bring new life into the world. "I come from a long line of shepherds, myself."

The owner brought MacLeod's wine to the table, but MacLeod, fascinated by this glimpse into the complex layers that made up his dinner companion, didn't touch it. "So, your mother was an Arab Christian, your father an apostate Muslim. How about you?"

She shrugged. "I guess you could say my brothers and I are interested spectators. Respectful of both traditions and practicing none. That's why my father wanted to move to America, where race and religion wouldn't matter so much anymore."

MacLeod knew better than that and could tell she did, too. "And did it?" he prompted.

"Of course it still mattered. 'Dirty Arab' hurts a child as much in English as it does in Hebrew. And we could never truly get away from everything that was happening back home." She stopped talking for a moment, as if unwilling to peel back a deeper layer on such short acquaintance, then continued on with her story. "My father managed to drink himself to death by the time I was nineteen. So much for that American dream, huh?" Her little laugh was mirth-free. "I've seen alcohol. I saw it promise my father the peace he was looking for, then strip it all away from him. And, since I'm told I'm very much like the stubborn old fool in other ways, I've decided it's best I stay away from it."

MacLeod touched her hand across the table. "I suspect you are neither old nor a fool."

"Ah, but don't forget stubborn." She turned her hand over so that his palm rested in hers, then held his hand. "So, now I have bared my soul to you, it's your turn." Her purring voice, her chocolate eyes flecked with gold, the way she stroked the back of his hand, she was certainly persuasive, and even the sudden arrival of the first course would not deter her from her request. As the owner left the table, she pinned MacLeod's hand beneath hers when he tried to reach for his fork. "Tell me about Duncan MacLeod." Stubborn she was, indeed.

"Not much to tell, really. I own a small barge on the Quai de la Tournelle. Cold in the winter, but you can't beat the view. I run a dojo back in the States. I like to read. I like to run." He gave her a little self-deprecating grin. "I'm really rather boring, when you get right down to it."

"Yes, I know these things. You have a martial-arts studio that barely breaks even, you have no other visible means of support apart from dabbling a bit in antiques. And despite that, you always pay your taxes on time, and you give extremely generously to charities, especially those involving orphaned children. Your last traffic ticket was two years ago. You have no criminal record, yet your name seems to come up quite frequently as a witness in police records, which tells me you are a 'do-gooder' with an overgrown curiosity."

MacLeod rolled his eyes. "Your Farid does good work."

"I asked him to. And while all that interests me, it still tells me nothing about Duncan MacLeod. Tell me how he feels, tell me how he thinks."

"He thinks your food is getting cold and you should eat it before the main course arrives," MacLeod said, picking up his fork. He tore into his choucroute with great relish. "Otherwise, we may offend our host," he continued between bites.

Maral seemed to give in, taking a few dainty bites. Then she said, with studied casualness, " 'MacLeod'—your family is English, then?"

"Scottish," he corrected her through a mouthful.

She took another careful bite. "Scottish, English, there's not really a difference anymore, is there? I mean, after all, it all belongs to England now."

"There is too a difference," he explained. "The Scots didn't give up their identity just because the English took the land. There's a lot of dead Scots who wouldn't take kindly to being called English. A lot of live ones, too." Then he realized he'd walked right into her web.

Placing her elbows firmly on the table, Maral leaned across toward him and gave him a blistering smile. The light in her eyes was positively wicked. "Gotcha."

Humph. "If I'd known there would be a test, I would have studied," he groused good-naturedly.

"Call it a pop quiz," she said. "You seem to know your genealogy, so tell me: How long had there been MacLeods tending their sheep in Scotland before the English came? Before some English lord suddenly owned all the sheep pastures just because some foreign king said so and made your ancestors tenants on their own land? How long, Duncan?" She could tell by the shadow that had come over his face that her words had somehow struck a chord deep within him. "And how long was it before your people sickened of being treated like animals and rose up against the English and demanded their rights?" She pressed her point. "And how many Scottish lives were lost over the centuries in their fight to keep their identity?"

Her words *had* cut him to the bone. He who had buried generation after generation of young martyrs to the cause of Scotland. He who'd witnessed the trail of the dying, the mutilated, the violated left in the English wake. Even now, he could almost hear their voices begging him to help them. "Too many," he said quietly, haunted.

She did not relent. "Then think about this: Was Scotland's William Wallace really that different than Yasser Arafat?"

"It's not that simple anymore."

"Isn't it? One man's terrorist is another man's hero. Whether they fight for the freedom to raise sheep in the Highlands or the Golan Heights." She reached across the table to grab him by the arm, almost blinding him with her intensity. "Hasn't there ever been anything in your life so precious you were willing to fight for it?"

How could she know? How could she understand? She dredged the word up from his soul. "Yes."

Maral released his arm and her urgent energy seemed to dissipate into the empty restaurant. "Good," she said, settling back into her chair, relaxed. "So Duncan MacLeod is a man of great passion and principles. I like that." She picked up her fork and resumed eating, a look of satisfaction clear on her face.

"So, Professor, does that mean I pass?" He was a man of many secrets who'd been interrogated by some of the best inquisitors of their generations, but had never talked, never broken. Yet this woman had found all his buttons and had played them like music. With a few deft cuts, she had laid bare his soul. She continued to amaze him. "Or do I have to try for extra credit?"

"Maybe just a little homework." That wicked look was back.

MacLeod looked at her and felt something strong stir within him. The promise. The possibilities. "I'll do whatever it takes, Professor."

"I'm sure you will."

The chirping sound of a ringing cellular phone filled the restaurant. Assad, seated at the next table pretending not to eavesdrop, pulled the phone out of his jacket and flipped it open. "Assad," he announced, then listened intently. "*Halan*"—immediately—he responded. Standing up, he handed the phone to Maral and moved quickly toward the kitchen. As he left he barked "*Árabaya!*" to his partner, who immediately left to fetch the car.

"Amina," Maral said into the phone. MacLeod couldn't hear the voice on the other end, but he could follow the language of her body, the emotion in her face as it changed from interest to concern, briefly to fear, and then finally to sorrow. "*Iwa*," she said heavily into the phone, but agreeing to what, MacLeod didn't know. When she toggled off the phone, she looked ten years older.

"What's wrong?" he asked.

"We have to go back." She pushed back from the table and stood, reaching for her shawl. It was clear she didn't intend to tell him anything more. MacLeod took her by the hand and held it.

"Maral, tell me what's happened. Let me help."

"You want to help? Build me a world where husbands and fathers and sons aren't gunned down in the street because of the way they choose to worship God." Her words were brittle as she tried to pull away from him. He wouldn't let her go, giving her a calm, steady look that plainly let her know he would patiently wait until she was ready to share her pain with him. She tried halfheartedly to pull away again, then acquiesced with a sigh. "The shooter yesterday. His body's gone—someone's stolen it."

Missing bodies always caught MacLeod's attention. "You're sure no one has it?"

"The Hebron police thought the military had it. The military thought the civilian coroner's office had it. You know how it goes. And by the time they realized it was gone, someone had called today claiming responsibility for the attack. An organization we've never heard of before, called *Oneg Shabbat*."

"Sabbath surprise?" MacLeod translated the Hebrew, releasing Maral's hand, trying to place why he knew the name.

Assad, returning from the kitchen, overheard him. "You know them?" he asked, reaching for his gun.

"No," MacLeod said, exasperated, "and put that thing away before you hurt yourself. *Oneg Shabbat* is a party for children after worship." He stopped a moment, thinking. "But it was also the name of a group of scholars in Poland who documented the Holocaust and kept the records hidden from the Germans."

"So you have heard of them," Assad pressed.

MacLeod shook his head. "They died fifty years ago. And they were scholars, not fighters. It's got to be some other group using the same name."

"Put away the gun, Assad," Maral said, and he complied. MacLeod retrieved the shawl and draped it over Maral's shoulders. She pulled it eagerly around her, as if a shield, but drew no warmth from it. "Whoever they are," she said, "this changes everything. It wasn't just some lone fanatic listening to voices in his head. This is different. This is organized, deliberate. We don't know anything about them—they could be anywhere, planning anything." A shiver ran through her, and instinctively she pulled the ancient shawl, the emblem of her family and her people, more tightly to her. "Forty-three men praying is only a start for them, Duncan—my God, just think what could be next."

Despite a murderous look from Assad, MacLeod put an arm around her trembling shoulders and drew her to him in a comforting embrace, willing the heat and strength of his body into hers. They'd known each other such a brief time, but there was something about her—her beauty, her inner strength, her vulnerability, maybe all of the above and more— that called forth the Protector in him. "We should go back now," he whispered. "You'll be safe there."

"It's not *my* safety, Duncan. It's my people." At Assad's signal to depart, she pulled away from the embrace, but allowed MacLeod's arm to stay protectively across her shoulders as he escorted her to the door. "It's the children on their way to school, women in the marketplaces. I'm not afraid for me, I'm afraid for them. And for the future. We're so close to peace, Duncan, *so* close. Something like this could ruin everything."

As he helped her into the car, MacLeod looked at her and a hint of sadness touched his heart. A beautiful but poignant mix of East and West, of the runways of Paris and the caravans of the Arabian desert. The legendary Palestine of her past and the very real Israel of her present. Maral Amina might claim she was no martyr, but he'd seen devotion like hers end in tragedy too many times. It took a very special kind of person to put the onus of three thousand years of history ahead of her own life.

As he settled next to her and Assad closed the door behind him, he pulled the gift box from his pocket. He'd hoped to give it to her at a more auspicious time, but now it appeared that such a time might never exist for them. "I'd like you to have this." He did his best to make the tattered paper more presentable.

Maral had to laugh at his earnest attempt at the impossible. "Don't tell me—you have a puppy?" she said, looking at the sorry wrapping. Her face brightened with anticipation as he handed it to her and although she reached for the box with studied casualness, he thought he could see peeking out the excited little girl held barely in check. He suspected Maral was a woman who could use more unexpected gifts in her life.

"A puppy named Farid. I don't think he's housebroken yet, either." As they touched and he transferred the gift to her, the last traces of paper fluttered away, leaving Maral with a plain white box the size of her hand. "You can't say he's not thorough, though," MacLeod said wryly.

Maral quickly pulled the top from the box and withdrew her prizes—two gazelles, intricately hand-wrought of iron, their elongated faces wise but sad. Their graceful legs had been carefully formed into combs for a lady's hair. With a quick intake of breath, she was beaming like a ten-year-old with a new bike. "Duncan"—she held them out in front of her to admire them—"they're breathtaking."

"Then they're in good company." With Assad and his trusty sidekick in such close proximity, MacLeod resisted the temptation to reach up and remove the wooden combs binding her luscious hair. Some other time. "There once was a small tribe in a region of the grasslands of East Africa where metals are very, very scarce," he said in his best storytelling voice. "The people of the tribe believed that Father Iron was the most sacred of all the metals, and those in the tribe who could work with iron were considered blessed." In the back of his mind, he could hear the singsong voice of the ancient *griot* who once told him the tale. He hoped he was doing her memory honor in his retelling. "Now, to these people, the greatest of the animals that roamed the grasslands was not Lion, with his cruel and vicious hunger." The *griot* had growled at that point, but MacLeod wasn't sure that would be appropriate in his current setting. Assad might take it personally. "It wasn't Elephant, all-mighty and powerful. The greatest of the animals was Gazelle."

"The gazelle," she repeated and the tone of her voice said she wasn't buying this for a minute but would happily play along.

"Are you always this tough an audience? This one always wows 'em at the preschool." He took one of the gazelle combs from her hand and continued as if uninterrupted. "Gazelle. Now Gazelle didn't have the power of the lion or the strength of the elephant. But Gazelle had a special magic all her own. She could fly with the winds. She could run until she caught the horizon. Gazelle had heart. She had courage. She had grace and passion. And with this special magic, she could escape Lion's cruel hunger and she could direct Elephant's all-mighty strength." He cocked his head toward Maral. "You getting all of this?"

"The greatest of all the animals," she said, stroking the slender coil of horn that rose above the dark wise eyes.

"Now, metals being scarce and all, this was a tribe that wouldn't just cast any warthog into sacred iron—that they reserved for Gazelle. Because, so they said, when a truly skilled craftsman created Gazelle in Father Iron, he could imbue the piece with her special magic, and those same qualities that made Gazelle the greatest of all the animals would bless the bearer." He pressed the second comb back into Maral's hands. "Fly with the winds, Maral. Run until you catch the horizon."

She stared at him, openmouthed, and the streetlight glinted from a tear in the corner of her eye. She started to speak, then stopped, at a loss for words, then as she tried to speak again, Assad interrupted.

"We are here," he announced, and the car stopped abruptly in front of the hotel once again. Immediately the car door was opened and MacLeod was pulled out by security guards intent on Maral's safety.

As she exited the car, Farid moved quickly to spirit her away into the fortress of the grand hotel, but Maral stopped him with a hand. She turned back to MacLeod. She didn't dare touch him, couldn't in front of this crowd of men so concerned for her protection, but he could see it smolder in her eyes, feel it flow between the two of them like a thing alive. The possibilities. The need.

MacLeod moved toward her and, despite a fierce look of warning from Farid, kissed her chastely on one cheek. "So how much of that was bullshit?" she whispered to him.

"Does it matter?" was his reply, as she was pulled away from him.

"*Ana muser,*" Farid said harshly. I insist.

MacLeod called after her. "You need anything, anything at all, you call me."

I promise—she mouthed the words as Farid and his men swept her into the great revolving doors and away from MacLeod's sight.

Chapter Five

Israel: 14 Nisan, The Present

The sun shone bright over the Dead Sea, its rays reflecting off the shimmering blue surface. On the road that skirted along the edge of the sea, Avram Mordecai reached into the glove box for his sunglasses. With one hand he flipped them open and put them on, relieved to be able to see the road again.

There wasn't much traffic on the narrow road that wove its way through the craggy desert surrounding the sea of salt. It wasn't yet high season for the seaside resorts, despite the unseasonably warm spring, so the hordes of tourists who flocked to the area to encase themselves in mud baths or just float in the briny waters had not yet begun to clog up the roads. He could never see the attraction, himself.

He was only a couple of miles out of the oasis town of Ein Gedi, the last speck of green for miles in this wilderness, when he spotted it, up ahead in the distance—Masada. Its sheer rock facings towered more than a quarter mile above the sea far below and then stopped abruptly to form a vast plateau, as if God had begun to make a mountain, and then been called away halfway through. Avram was still some miles away, but the promontory on which King Herod had built his fortress dominated the landscape.

Avram glanced at the dashboard clock. It had taken him less than two hours to make the drive from Jerusalem. The first time he had made the journey, it had taken over a week. He and his father had nearly died in the wilderness, and their first glimpse—like now, shimmering through the heat in the distance—of the impenetrable stronghold high atop the mesa had seemed like a beacon of hope sent by God.

The rock loomed ever larger as Avram sped toward it. A trick of the light, a small cloud shadowing the sun—he was certain he saw, just for a moment, the magnificence of Herod's palace perched precariously on the steep north face, resplendent in white and gold. But he knew it was illusion, nothing more. He'd been with the party that unearthed the secrets of Masada in the years after the liberation of Israel, slung a trowel and hauled rock with the other students and soldiers and housewives eager to find the truth. Avram had seen for himself that nothing remained now but patterns of rocks and the sands of time.

He pulled his car into the parking lot by the youth hostel at the foot of Masada and got out. In a pair of faded jeans, hiking boots, and a T-shirt proclaiming a popular Tel Aviv coffeehouse, he could easily pass as one of the many Israeli teenagers who made the pilgrimage to Masada each day, looking for their cultural heritage, looking for their own identity. And in many ways, he was.

A cable car whisked tourists from the base to the summit in a matter of minutes. Avram rolled his eyes disdainfully at the idea of such laziness and walked on. To truly know Masada, one should suffer, at least a bit. There were two other paths up the face of the rock for those who preferred to climb under their own power. Most chose the huge earthen ramp that sloped from the foot to the top, an easy ten-minute walk. Avram refused. The enormous ramp was all that remained of the giant siege engine the Romans had constructed to take Masada. He'd watched it built, day by day, bit by bit, on the blood and death of ten thousand Jewish slaves forced to toil in the desert heat. Each day it had crept closer to the summit, each day closer to the last remaining bastion of Jewish freedom. He'd sooner die than justify its existence now.

He chose instead the torturous serpentine path that wove its way in and among the rocks on the craggy eastern face of the rock. It was by this path he had originally come to Masada, it was by this path that Herod had created his fortress a hundred years before that. During his work with the archaeologists excavating Masada in the 1960s, Avram had needed some fancy excuses to explain why he always preferred the fifty-minute hike up the serpentine to the easy walk up the Roman ramp— Professor Yadin thought he was an exercise nut—but he'd sworn he'd never take his ease on the broken backs of ten thousand of his Jewish brothers.

Once he finally reached the top, Avram wasted no time. Bypassing the bathhouse, the synagogue, the swimming pool, and the other remains where the excited tourists all gathered, he moved away from them to the far southern end of the site, to the thick stone wall that had surrounded the plateau, creating Herod's fortress. Avram passed through an opening in the rocks. Just beyond him, another wall of stones. Together, the two walls formed concentric rings around Masada. And within the space between the walls, the remains of walls more narrow, partitioning the space into smaller rooms. He moved quickly, confidently through a maze of ruined stone partitions standing no taller than his waist, sure of his destination.

Avram stopped in an opening between the rocks where a door once stood. In front of him the stones marked out a tiny cubicle, hardly bigger than a closet. He entered with reverence. In one corner, set into the walls, a small clay oven, worn and eroded by time. Still, he thought he could smell bread baking . . .

Masada, Idumaea: 14 Nisan 3833 (A.D. 73)

"More bread?" The flat rounds of dough were still warm from the oven and filled their tiny stone room with a fresh, homey scent. Deborah reached across the tattered cloth that functioned as their table and served her husband, placing more bread next to his bowl of pottage. Avram took both her slender hands into his own and brought them to his lips, kissing them gently. His face was filled with love and the certain knowledge that he was the luckiest man in the world. He turned one of her hands in his and covered her palm with kisses. Her hands still smelled of yeast and flour, and he drank in the perfume. Then his lips moved down her hand to her delicate wrist, stopping only at the embroidered sleeve of her gown.

Deborah laughed, a silvery sound like the jangle of coins. "Does that mean 'thank you' by any chance?" In the sputtering lamplight that bathed their chamber in a golden glow, her eyes were burnished chestnut, and they sparkled at his touch. Her thick, black hair, free and loose only in the seclusion of their room for the delight of her husband, adorned her face as no jeweled bauble ever could.

Deborah's whole world was the barren plateau on the heights of Masada. She'd come here when she was ten, her parents dead of fever, her brother Judah one of the fighters who helped Menahem the Galilean recapture Masada from the Romans early in the Great Revolt. In the seven years since, Jerusalem had fallen, the Great Temple destroyed, but Masada had held and Deborah had grown into a beautiful young woman within its protective walls. "Whatever you don't eat, we'll just have to burn before *Pesach* begins tomorrow."

Avram pushed aside the bread and pottage. "Funny, I don't feel hungry anymore." He rose to his feet from his seat on the floor and offered Deborah a hand to stand. "Not for food, anyway," he said with a smile, as his young wife stood before him, willing, wanting. He touched her cheek, her hair. Even now, after three months of life as man and wife, the simple act of touching her sent sparks through his body. He knelt at her feet, carefully removed her sandals, kissing the dusty tops of her feet.

Avram had been nineteen when he arrived at Masada three years before. He was a scholar and a Pharisee like his father before him, and his father before him. His whole life had revolved around the study and interpretation of the Law and the Prophets and strict adherence to the ancient traditions of the Jews. He and his parents had been trapped in Jerusalem when the Roman forces of Titus laid siege during the festival of *Pesach*. Every day, like the rest of the besieged city, they had scrabbled to find a little food, enough water to stay alive. In the fourth month of the siege, Avram's mother Tamar finally succumbed to the hunger and disease that was claiming thousands each day, and died. But somehow Avram and Mordecai, his father, managed to hold on. At the end of summer, the Romans finally breached Jerusalem's defenses and took the city.

In front of thousands of starving Jews, they burned the Great Temple to the ground, trapping hundreds inside. His father was in shock at the destruction of the Holy of Holies, but Avram managed to get him out of the city in the midst of the chaos.

They escaped to the wilderness. Mordecai, all spirit gone, had begged to be left there to die, but Avram, the scholar who had never held a bow or a sling, was determined to fight for his birthright. He herded, cajoled, and sometimes even carried his father across the wasteland until they came to Masada. There, Avram had found purpose in his life, united with his fellow Jews to reclaim their homeland. And there, Avram had found Deborah.

Avram's hands slid up the sides of Deborah's legs, gathering and raising her woven tunic as he stood, hands tracing the gentle curve of her hips, her waist. Deborah dropped to one knee, arms raised high, and he pulled the linen garment off, revealing her splendid body in the light. Slowly, almost ritually, she untied the lacings that twined up his calves, and removed his sandals. He shrugged off his mantle and pulled his tunic off over his head.

The body lit and shadowed by the oil lamps was no longer that of a boyish scholar. Three years of hard work on the rock had tempered it. Sinews defined his calves and forearms; muscles rippled down his firm belly; the dark tendrils of his hair curled to touch powerful shoulders. A boy had come to Masada wanting to play war with the Romans. Now, despite the Romans, a man hoped to start a family there. He bent low and gathered his wife in his arms. As she reached out to kiss him, he carried her to his bed.

Avram and Deborah had been betrothed for a year before their marriage, a year of waiting, of dreaming what might be. Neither Deborah's brother nor Avram's father had consented to the engagement at first, both men firm in their belief that the times were too unsettled, their situation too precarious for marriage. The young couple and the love they shared grudgingly won them over. But soon after the betrothal, the Romans came with their siege walls and their engines of war, trapping the fighters and their families on the mesa top. They all watched in horror as their enslaved Jewish brothers, once their friends and neighbors back in poor Jerusalem, built the earthwork ramp that slowly crept up the mountainside toward them. Preparations for the wedding had helped keep their minds, especially those of the women of Masada, from dwelling on the encroaching danger.

They wed in borrowed finery, Deborah wearing a simple gown and veil she'd covered with intricate needlework in the year of their betrothal. There was no dowry, no bride-price, no elaborate procession on horseback. But all of the nearly one thousand residents of the rock were gathered when Avram met his bride beneath the canopy in the courtyard of Herod's palace. The feast afterward lasted until dawn, the musicians playing and the revelers singing as loud as they could, to make sure the Romans far below them had no doubt there was celebration, not fear, on Masada.

During the dancing and merriment, a group of men including Deborah's brother Judah and Eleazar, the commander of Masada, had escorted Avram to the tiny stone chamber built into the double wall surrounding the fortress that would be his and Deborah's new home. No longer would he live in the bachelor's barracks with his father. Amid last-minute advice and lewd jokes, his drunken friends departed, leaving him alone in front of the wooden door. Suddenly, he felt very nervous. With sweating palms, he pushed it open.

On a pile of mats and skins that nearly filled the room, Deborah waited for him. She was arrayed in nothing but gold and gems, collected from a dozen women. They had anointed her body with oils so that her dusky skin glowed with a marble-like luster and had painted her face with rouges and powders. It was said that the wise King Solomon had had a thousand wives—Avram knew not one in that thousand could compare with his Deborah.

He stood in the doorway for some time, speechless, simply staring at the vision of beauty that was his new wife. Deborah looked to her new husband, waiting for a sign, a word, something to indicate that he was pleased. Neither of them moved.

Finally, when she knew if the silence went on much longer she was going to scream, Deborah spoke. "Avram, my love," she began, "would you mind closing the door? I'd rather the neighbors weren't watching."

His trance broken, Avram looked out at the open corridor, then at Deborah, and they both started to laugh. Avram shut the door, still laughing, so great was his relief. He sat on the bed of skins and embraced his closest friend, this woman who was now his wife.

Their marriage bed had been tentative, full of false starts and friendly laughter, both partners fumbling and inexperienced. Now, three months later, as they'd grown to know each other's needs, their lovemaking was confident and lasting. It was sensual, yet spiritual, as they sought to express their love for each other and for God in the creation of a child from the joy of their bodies.

After Avram had filled her with the promise of children yet to be, the couple lay back on the mat that was their bed, Deborah's head on Avram's shoulder. She drew idle patterns on his chest with a gentle finger as he played with a lock of her ebony hair. "What do you think of Mattathias?" he asked.

"It's . . ." Deborah crinkled up her nose, "quite a mouthful for a child, don't you think? I always think simple names are the best. How about Simon?"

Avram shook his head. "I have an Uncle Simon. Can't stand him." He thought for a moment, wrapping her hair around his finger. "We could name him after my father."

"Mordecai? But then he'd be frowning and grumpy all the time, just like your father. I wouldn't wish that on a child."

"He hasn't always been like that." Mordecai had never really recovered from the death of his wife and the destruction of the Temple. "I just wish you could have known him before."

"I know. I wish I could have, too." Deborah had never gotten along well with Avram's father. He'd made it abundantly clear he felt his only son had married far beneath his station. It was Deborah's hope that once they had children, Mordecai would accept her as the mother of his grandchildren. "If it makes you happy, we'll name our firstborn Mordecai."

"Now, what makes you so certain our firstborn will be a boy?" Avram wondered.

Deborah laughed. "Because you're a man, and that's all men ever want."

"Haven't you realized by now, I'm not like other men?" Avram tugged playfully on one of her ears. "A beautiful little Deborah or two will always be welcome. Or three. Or five. As many as you want."

She ran a hand across his taut belly. "Easy for you to say, you don't have to bear them all." She rolled over slightly so she could look him in the face. "And we name the first girl-child Tamar."

"Tamar." His voice caught a bit as he said the name. "I think my mother would be very pleased."

Deborah lay her head on Avram's chest. "Then it's decided. Tamar and Mordecai."

"And Zebediah and Benjamin and Dan and Tabitha and Esther and—"

She reached up and put a hand across Avram's lips. "Stop!" she laughed. "I'm exhausted just thinking about it."

There was a knock on the wooden door to their chamber. Deborah and Avram sat up. "Yes?" Avram called out as he stood, reaching for his tunic.

"It's your father, Avram, I need to speak with you."

"It's late, *Aba*, give us a moment." Avram handed Deborah her gown with a weak smile and a shrug, then pulled on his own tunic. When he was sure his wife was decorously clothed, he untied the latch and opened the door to his father. "Welcome, *Aba*."

Avram's father stepped into the room. The years of the Revolt had not been kind to Mordecai ben Enoch. He was a bearded man of middle age, grown gray and stooped beyond his span of years. Lately he'd taken to walking with aid of a cane. He inclined his head briefly toward his daughter-in-law. "Deborah."

"Welcome, *Aba*. Would you like some wine?"

If he had heard her, Mordecai did not show it, moving straight to his son. "Avram, we must talk."

Avram waited a moment, and, when further conversation was not forthcoming, he prompted: "So, talk."

"Not here." He indicated Deborah with his eyes. "Alone."

Avram looked at him, unable to read his expression, then reached for his girdle and began to tie it around his middle. "Fine," he said, "alone." Without prompting, Deborah found his sandals and knelt at his feet to lace the thongs.

The silence in the tiny room was palpable. Helping her husband dress, Deborah thought to lessen it. "Guess what we've decided to name our first girl, *Aba*. Tamar, after Avram's mother, God rest her soul." There was no response from Mordecai. "I hope that pleases you."

A dark shadow passed across Mordecai's face, then he said, as gently as his gruff demeanor would allow, "That would please me." He stepped out into the corridor, "Come, Avram."

Avram picked up his mantle and followed his father out of the room. Deborah closed the door behind them.

As soon as they had passed out of earshot of Avram's room, his father took him to task. "Why do you fill her head with such things?"

"What things?"

"You know. This nonsense about children . . . and the future. She should know the truth."

"Why? So we can all share this pit of despair you've been living in? What's the harm in living with a little hope?" Avram stopped walking and turned to face his father, angrily. "What should I tell her, *Aba*? That in a week's time she'll be forced to pleasure some oily Senator and his pagan friends in a house of decadence in Rome? Or that by sundown tomorrow I'll be dead on a cross along the road to Ein Gedi? Or that maybe I'll be lucky, and face the wild beasts in the arena at Caesarea instead? Is *that* what I should tell her?" He could feel his eyes beginning to well with tears, tears he could never allow his father to see. He turned away from the old man and started walking quickly down the corridor that ran between the two walls ringing the fortress.

Mordecai hurried to catch up. "Son, I—"

"She's not stupid, *Aba*. She knows. Everyone knows. But when we give up hope, we've lost." He tried to look his father in the eyes, but the tears came again. He turned away and leaned his head against the stone wall, his shoulders shaking with sobs.

"Avram . . ." Mordecai reached out and touched his son on the shoulder.

Avram shook him off roughly and turned on him with an icy glare. "Why did you come here? You said you wanted to talk about something. For once, let it not be about my wife."

"The wind has shifted. The last barricade is on fire," Mordecai said quietly. "Now even God has forsaken us."

Avram's heart sank. When the giant Roman battering ram built at the top of the earthen ramp had broken through first one, then the second stone wall just days before, the defenders of Masada had quickly built wooden walls in the breach with loosely packed dirt between to cushion the blows of the battering ram and render it useless. But what the Romans couldn't batter down they attempted to burn, hurling flaming torches at the wooden wall. When the fires were first lit, the winds suddenly shifted to the south, blowing the Romans' fire back upon them and their siege engines, clearly a sign of God's intervention in the eyes of many of the besieged.

Now the winds had shifted to the north, driving the fire quickly through the barricades. There was no use in denying that the Romans would try to take the fortress at first light. "So now we fight," Avram said, resigned. "After three years, maybe it's finally time."

"I don't know what we do, Avram," his father said. "There are ten thousand men down there, and we are less than a thousand, even if you count the women and children. I don't know what we do."

Through the stone walls, they could hear the sounding of the shofar, calling the men of Masada to gather. "It sounds as if we're about to find out," Avram said, putting on his mantle as he led the way to the door leading to the interior of the fortress.

Chapter Six
===

Masada, Idumaea: 14 Nissan 3833 (A.D. 73)

The men gathered at the crossroads near the northern end of the mesa, where the paths between the palace, the villas, the barracks and the storehouses all converged. It was a long walk, nearly a third of a mile from the tiny stone room in the southern wall Avram shared with Deborah, a walk made longer by his father's halting gait. Far below them in the camps of the Romans, they could see the lights of a thousand campfires, hear the shouts and obscene songs of the soldiers passing the night as clearly as if they occupied the rock with them. Tonight Avram thought he could detect more activity and a tension-filled energy from the camps than on other nights, as if the Romans could sense as well that the coming dawn would spell the end of the siege of Masada.

Despite Avram's urging his father to hurry, the meeting had begun by the time they arrived. Eleazar, Masada's commander, stood at the top of the stairs to the administration building, addressing his people. Eleazar was a tall, muscular man with flowing hair and beard who carried himself like a soldier, and in Avram's eyes he could do no wrong. As he came within earshot, Avram was astounded to hear Judah, Deborah's brother and one of Eleazar's most trusted captains, openly confronting his commander.

"You are a coward! In your fear, you have lost your manhood, and I will follow you no longer." The crowd of men shouted in response, many trying to shout him down, others sounding their allegiance with Judah.

In the crowd, Avram found Simeon, another of his unit, and tapped him on the shoulder. "What's happened?"

Simeon turned to him, his face a mix of fear and confusion. "Eleazar says that we've no hope against them. That we should burn the complex and kill ourselves before daybreak."

"No." Avram was astounded. He was ready to fight, eager to take as many Roman devils with him as he could before he died. "This can't be."

On the stairs, Eleazar bore the shouts and jeers from the crowd with great patience for some time. Then he spoke again. "We cannot win a battle of weapons against the force arrayed against us. The Empire has us outnumbered twenty to one. To believe otherwise would be madness. On this, we are in agreement. Correct?"

Begrudgingly, the crowd acknowledged their agreement. After watching the massive military force of the Roman Empire marshal beneath them, only a foolish few harbored belief any longer that the meager forces of Masada could somehow defeat Rome and liberate their homeland.

Eleazar continued, "Then if we cannot save our lives, I say we save our honor. And the honor of our people."

Judah climbed the stairs, challenging. "There is no *honor* in suicide. You want honor for the people of Israel? I say we fight like men and we die like men. Let our deeds be remembered."

"That's fine for you, Judah. You fight like a man and preserve your honor. But what about our wives? Our daughters? Look on them." Although it was forbidden, more than a few of the women of Masada had gathered in the shadows of the buildings surrounding the meeting place to hear the decision of their men. It was toward them Eleazar addressed his words. "What of their honor? Look them in their sweet and trusting eyes and tell them you wish to see them captive on a Roman's couch. Made whore to the Romans' lust, slaves to their perverted appetites." Some of the women present began to cry. Some fled away into the shadows back to their homes, a few braving the wrath of the assembly to run to their husbands, clutching them for comfort. Eleazar took little note of them. "And what about your sons, Judah. Dragged in chains to heathen lands, raised as heathens to service heathens. Is that how the People of God are to be remembered?"

Judah was obviously affected by his leader's words. Head low, eyes downcast, he started back down the stairs to join the throng at Eleazar's feet. But Eleazar stopped him, holding out his hands. "Put away your pride, Judah, and join me in one final victory over the Romans." Judah hesitated, the pain of his decision on his agonized face, then grabbed Eleazar's hands like a lifeline. The commander pulled Judah to him in a close embrace, then, with his captain by his side, turned to his people. "We will save the honor of our fathers and their fathers before them. Our deeds here today *will* be remembered!"

The meeting ran late into the night, and by the time it had ended, the men of Masada were united in their resolve to snatch the prize of victory from the hands of the Romans. Even Avram, who once dreamed of confronting the Romans face-to-face, conceded theirs would be a victory in the eyes of God and of history. Each man would be responsible for easing his own family's passing. The ten unit captains would then help the men join their families. As the meeting ended, Eleazar, Judah, and the other captains cast lots on shards of pottery to determine which of them would dispatch the others and put Masada to the torch.

The corridor running between the fortress walls was empty as Avram returned to their chamber, but behind the doors that lined it, Avram could hear the wailing and howls of grief as the men told their families what must be. He didn't know how he was going to break the news to Deborah. How to tell her that everything they'd hoped for, everything they'd dreamed of was gone. That their brief taste of life was over. He knew the look in her eyes would kill him more surely than any blade.

He opened the door to their chamber with trembling hands. Deborah sat on the edge of their sleeping mat, dressed in the embroidered robe she'd made for their wedding, her hair and face obscured by the wedding veil.

"You know," he said softly. He moved quickly to sit by her side, pushing back the veil to reveal her face.

"Hard to keep a secret in Masada," she said, her eyes ringed red from crying, her face dark with the shadows of grief. Avram reached out to her and pulled her close to him, embracing her as if he'd never let her go. He wished he had words with which to comfort her, words that would make it all go away, that could restore their happiness. But the only words he had were "I'm sorry" and the only thing he could tell her was how much he loved her. And he did, over and over again.

"Will it hurt?" she asked in a small voice.

Avram pulled back from their embrace so he could look into her chestnut eyes. "I don't know," he said honestly. "Deborah, if I could take this away from you, you know I would." His anguished words were choked.

"Avram, it's all right," she comforted him. "I can be brave, because I know we'll be together. We'll live as man and wife for all eternity in the world to come."

"And here I always thought I was boring you with my studies," Avram smiled wistfully. It was the foundation of Pharisaic belief, he had once devoted his life to its study, and yet in his dark hour of need it had taken an uneducated woman to remind him that death was not the end, it was only the beginning. "On the day of Resurrection, we *will* be together again."

"And for all the days to come," Deborah added. "I'm not afraid of death, my love. I'll be with you."

Off in the distance, the shofar sounded. Avram drew Deborah near to him once again, kissing her lips, stroking her face, pretending he hadn't heard it, willing it to go away. Then his father appeared in the doorway.

"It's time, Avram."

Avram looked up at his father and nodded, the face of agony. "May we do this privately, *Aba*?"

"In a moment," Mordecai said, entering the room. He moved to Deborah and slowly, painfully, knelt beside the mat where she sat. He took one of her hands and held it close to his heart. "Thank you for making my Avram happy, daughter," he said. He kissed her awkwardly on the forehead. "God bless you."

"Good-bye, *Aba*," she managed to say, stunned at his show

of affection, and then the tears started and she could speak no more. Avram helped his father back to his feet.

"I'll be outside," Mordecai said, gripping his son by the arm, willing them both strength to face what must be done.

As his father left the room, Avram went to the small wooden chest in which they kept their few belongings. He removed an iron knife, testing its edge as if he was about to carve a shank of lamb. He moved back toward the bed, where Deborah waited in her wedding finery. She turned her head away, unable to bear the sight of the knife. He sat beside her.

"Kiss me, Deborah. Let's remember each other as lovers." They kissed—a deep, longing kiss made more passionate by the taint of death. "I love you, Deborah," he murmured.

"For all eternity," she whispered back into the kiss, then a small, surprised sound cut off as the cold iron of Avram's knife sliced into her throat.

He pulled her to him even more tightly. He could feel her blood surge over them both, washing them in her life's essence as it ebbed away. He could feel her tighten in panic, then slowly relax as life left her, draining her, leaving her empty.

When he knew she was gone, he released her and carefully arranged her body on the sleeping mat. Her bridal garments were stained in her blood like their marriage bed had once been. He lovingly placed her wedding veil over her beautiful face, so she would not be disgraced by the gaze of some lecherous Roman pig.

Avram heard movement in the doorway. "It's done, *Aba*," he said, not taking his gaze off Deborah.

Mordecai entered the room. With sorrowful eyes he took in his son kneeling by the body of his dead bride, covered in her blood. "Avram, I'm so sorry."

Avram stood and faced him. "No, *Aba*, I'm the one to be sorry, sorry I ever brought you here. We should have gone to Galilee, or Bethlehem, somewhere we could have had a normal life."

Mordecai shook his head. "Any life under Roman rule is not normal. You did the right thing. I lived to see my son grow into a man, to see him take a bride. What more could a father ask for?"

Avram looked at his father in amazement. "Then . . . you're

not angry with me?" Mordecai hugged his son close to his bosom as he'd not done since Avram was a child.

"My little Avram, I have never been more proud of you than I am right now. Yes, we die, but we die free. See, you've even taught your old *Aba* something." He reached up to kiss Avram on the forehead—Avram had never before noticed that he was taller than his father. Then he picked up the bloody knife and handed it to his son. "Let's get on with it. The sooner we get this over with, the sooner I see your mother again."

Mordecai painfully lowered himself to the floor near the sleeping mat and lay down, carefully adjusting his tunic, making sure the fringes on the corners of his mantle weren't tangled. He folded his hands on his chest and closed his eyes in prayer. "Blessed art Thou, O Lord our God, King of the universe, Whose judgments are true." Then, with a sigh, he tilted back his head, exposing his throat. "Strike well, son. Trust in God."

Avram knelt beside his father. "Good-bye, *Aba*," he whispered, then pulled the knife swiftly across his father's throat.

Avram didn't know how long he knelt there, watching the blood rush, then run, then trickle from his father's throat. He was numb. Completely numb. Beyond pain. Beyond grief. Numb. He stared at the knife in his hand, watching the patterns the red fluid made against the iron blade, his Deborah's blood mingling with the blood of his father.

Finally, he managed to rouse himself, his task still unfinished. He opened the wooden box that housed their possessions and removed the few pieces of pottery and glass inside. With all his strength, all his anger, all his grief, he hurled the bowls, the cups, and Deborah's cooking pots at the wall, shattering them, until nothing remained that the Romans could use. The rest of their meager possessions—their clothing, a few wooden implements, some cloth—he placed in the wooden box and moved it near the oven. He emptied the last of the lamp oil on the box and set it alight with the wick of a lamp.

He was still staring wide-eyed into the flames when Eleazar came for him. His commander was covered with blood, like a demon butcher, and his face was haunted with the horror of his deeds.

"Avram."

Avram turned to look at his commander, haunted by his own demons. "I killed them." The anguish in his soul manifested in his voice. "God forgive me, I killed them," he wailed.

"He will, Avram. You know He will."

Avram nodded numbly. He moved to the sleeping mat, lay down beside the body of his wife. He put one arm around her lovingly, protectively, then looked to Eleazar. "Now," he said. Avram closed his eyes and prayed as Eleazar's sword drove into his heart.

Masada: 14 Nisan, The Present

Avram opened his eyes and wiped away an escaping tear with a shrug of his shoulder. Nearly two thousand years had passed, yet the memory stayed with him, as sharp as if it had happened only yesterday. He could still feel the pain, not of Eleazar's sword, but of his heart as it broke when he awoke to discover that he had failed, that he could not die. That he could never be with Deborah.

Today was the anniversary of her death, of all their deaths. He had faithfully kept the anniversary ever since, in the decadent villas of Rome, the tiny Russian *shtetls*, the teeming cities of Eastern Europe, wherever his life had taken him. With the liberation of Israel, he'd finally been able to return to the rock, to this tiny room where they had loved, to the room where he had killed her.

Avram knelt by the clay oven, bowed his head, and began to recite softly, so softly only he and God could hear. "Extolled and hallowed be the name of God in that world which He is to create anew, and to revive the dead and to raise them to an everlasting life. Then will the city of Jerusalem be rebuilt, the Temple be erected there, the worship of idols be erased from the land, and the Holy One, Blessed be He, will reign in His Kingdom in majestic glory. May this happen in your lifetime and in your days, and in the lifetime of the whole house of Israel, speedily and near in time, and let us say, Amen."

The words were in Aramaic, the language of his childhood, a language nearly forgotten, but which gave him great comfort. It made him think of his father, who had drilled him in his prayers from the day little Avram started to speak, confident that his son was smarter and quicker than all the other boys. One of the hardest parts of being Immortal for Avram had been learning that Mordecai ben Enoch and his wife were not his natural parents, that Mordecai had adopted a foundling child to be his only son. At first he was devastated, but as time passed Avram came to realize that no father could ever have loved a son of his loins more than his father had loved him. He remembered the beaming look of pride on his father's face the first time he'd read aloud from the Torah in front of the other men of the synagogue. After all these centuries, he hoped his father would still be proud.

"Let His great name be blessed forever and to all eternity. Blessed, praised and glorified, exalted, adored and honored, extolled and lauded be the name of the Holy One, blessed be He; though He be high above all the blessings and hymns, praises and works of solace which are uttered in the world; and say ye, Amen."

Avram stopped on the "Amen," hearing footsteps nearby. He turned his head to see a man, gray-haired, yet tanned and very fit, coming toward him.

"Son, are you all right?" One of the guides who helped patrol the complex and conducted tours for the visitors stopped in the ruined doorway.

Avram smiled at the old man. "I'm fine. Just resting a bit." He shrugged, embarrassed. "I had to be Rambo and come up the long way." They shared a chuckle at Avram's expense.

"The next tour's starting up in about fifteen minutes." The guide was full of enthusiasm. "Bet you I can show you some things you never imagined were up here." He gave Avram a wink. "I promise I won't go too fast for you."

"Fifteen minutes? Sure," Avram said amiably, "meet you there." With a wave, the guide continued on his way.

Avram turned back to the corner by the oven, reached out to touch a faint mark of scorched rock on the wall nearby—

still marking the spot where he had burned the last of their possessions. He bowed his head and continued.

"May abundant peace and life descend from heaven upon us and upon all Israel; and say ye, Amen. May He who makes peace in His heights bring peace upon us and upon all Israel; and say ye, Amen."

Then he stood up and removed a handful of pebbles from his pocket. He had collected them during his hike up the serpentine path. Pebbles that predated the concession stands, the sound and laser show, the cable cars. Pebbles that predated even the Romans. He rolled them around in his hand for a moment and then set them down in a little pile on top of the clay oven, marking his visit. His *kaddish* complete, Avram took one last long look around the ruined fortress and started the journey back down the mountain. He'd be back in Jerusalem before *Pesach* began with the setting of the sun.

Chapter Seven

Paris: The Present

According to Monday morning's paper, which MacLeod read over a leisurely pot of coffee and a fresh baguette smothered in grapefruit marmalade on the deck of his barge, the previous day's negotiating session had been relatively undramatic. No fistfights had broken out over minor points of protocol. No one had walked out in a fit of pique over some slight, imagined or otherwise. No one on either side had threatened to pick up their toys and go home. But, once again, for the seventh day of the Israeli/Palestinian talks, only an impasse had been reached. No agreement. No understanding. No movement toward a peaceful resolution of the fate of East Jerusalem, which the Palestinians envisioned someday as the capital of their new autonomous nation, and which the Israelis viewed as an inviolate part of the Holy City.

MacLeod spent most of the day on the barge, washing her glass, touching up her paint, polishing her chrome, and getting her ready to embrace the spring after a long, hard winter. Puttering, really, though he probably wouldn't admit that to himself. It was the first day of Passover for the Israeli delegation, there would be no negotiations that day, and he worked with half an ear toward the phone—but Maral's call never came.

Later that night, as he settled on the couch in front of a cheerful fire with a snifter of brandy and a copy of Joyce's *Ulysses*, he tried to see her in the back of his mind. Alone in the sumptuous appointments of the Lutétia, picking over a first-rate dinner delivered on a room-service tray. A beautiful bird in a gilded cage.

It had been a long time since he'd been this infatuated with a woman, a long time since his waking thoughts were preoccupied with the image, the touch, the smell of a woman. Probably not since that day he'd leapt onto Tessa's tour boat not far from the spot where his barge was now moored on the Seine. But with Tessa, even from their first meeting, he knew it was more than simple infatuation, more than pure physical attraction that brought them together like two halves of a broken locket. Beautiful and intelligent as she was, Maral wasn't Tessa, could never be Tessa. There would probably never be another Tessa for him, even if he lived a thousand years.

Still, there was something to be said for physical attraction. If she didn't call tomorrow, he would find a way to contact her.

Tuesday morning dawned with the threat of showers, but by midmorning, the clouds had fled and the sun shone bright off the waters of the Seine. A promising knock on the barge door after lunch had proven only to be the international courier service, bearing the box containing Karros's sword from the States. Wearing a pair of jeans with a T-shirt under his brown leather jacket, MacLeod started off for the museum with the sword case under one arm.

As MacLeod passed through the massive wooden doors into the marble hall where the *Hostes Romae* exhibit was installed, he realized the gallery was awash in rugrats. Three young boys played an impromptu game of tag in and out of the columns of the Arch of Titus, their voices shrieking above the martial music their antics in the Arch kept triggering, over and over again.

There were children everywhere. He moved into the exhibit rooms and found them punching all the buttons, climbing on the equipment. He stopped for a moment as he sensed Constantine at the far end of the marble hall. Two little girls careened into MacLeod at great speed, jolting him from his reverie, both armed to the teeth with Nerf swords and cardboard bucklers, whaling away at each other—and MacLeod— with great abandon, like extras in a gladiator film. He managed to disentangle himself and move away quickly, leaving them to their own private Circus Maximus.

"Marcus!" he called out over the din of young voices and chattering displays as he neared the end of the exhibit, and Constantine poked his head out of a side cubicle.

"In here, MacLeod."

MacLeod followed him into a room with a large glass case on a dais, its top removed while Constantine fiddled with the contents. "What in heaven's name is going on here? I thought you didn't open until tomorrow."

"Beta testing. If we can survive St. Catherine's fifth grade, we can survive anything. We've had a minor disaster in here, but nothing that a rigorous application of glue couldn't fix." Constantine reached into the open case and pulled out a small figurine. He turned toward MacLeod, holding the figurine up against his own face. "Not a very good likeness, don't you think?"

"That's you?"

"Unfortunately. Not that I told that to the model makers, of course." He gestured expansively over the architectural model in front of him. "Behold Jerusalem's Second Temple, King Herod's greatest masterpiece." The Temple Mount was encircled by a wall of massive stones—an engineering marvel, the wall in some places twenty times higher than the figurines representing people—and paved in stone. The Temple itself was of gleaming marble highlighted in gold. Against the splendid backdrop of the Temple, the figurines of the Roman conquerors were painted a ghostly gray. "And behold Rome's finest," he continued, placing the figure he called his own discreetly behind and to the left of the commanders. "Fools, every last one of them."

Constantine tapped a finger against a wall labeled Court of the Gentiles and seemed pleased when nothing moved. "That should hold it." He picked up one end of the glass lid, and MacLeod helped him lower it into place on top of the case. "It's amazing what havoc the average ten-year-old can wreak."

"This," MacLeod indicated the Temple model, "isn't from memory, is it?"

Constantine laughed. "Oh, no, no, no. Based on the most sound archaeological evidence available. Archaeologists have very set ideas about what these sites looked like and where everything was. Far be it from me to rock their boat with the unprovable truth. If the great minds of archaeology want to insist that some hole in the ground is a swimming pool, then it's a swimming pool. Let them have their fun."

After the Temple was safely back behind glass, MacLeod handed Constantine his box. "Paul Karros's sword, per request."

Setting the box on the top of the Temple's display case, Constantine opened it and withdrew the short sword, admiring the way it caught the light as he sliced it through the air in a short combination pass. "Oh, that *is* nice." His face lit with the pleasure of a fine blade in his hands and he felt a sense of power tingle through his body. God, how he missed it sometimes, locked away among his books and papers. He lunged and slashed, and the sword danced in the light.

"Marcus, the children," MacLeod warned quietly as a couple of St. Catherine's finest dashed past the doorway.

Constantine put the sword back in the box with obvious regret. "I'll indulge some other time. Come, we'll put it in its case, so I won't be tempted."

MacLeod looked at the delicate Temple model once again, remembering his visits to Jerusalem. The first had been nearly 250 years before, in those dark, tortured years after the Scottish failure at Culloden. He'd fled Scotland like a banshee, trying to escape the ghosts of his people and the demons in his own mind. For a time he'd thought perhaps the answers would lie in the Holy Land. Instead he'd found a land in many ways like his beloved Scotland, occupied by invader after invader, downtrodden, her holy places in neglect and decay. Even then, only a fragment of the Western wall remained of what was once Herod's magnificent temple. It was hard for him to envision this splendid edifice atop Jerusalem's Temple Mount, where the Dome of the Rock—the center of the world, to Islam—had already stood for a thousand years when MacLeod saw it for the first time. "Marcus, you've been around . . ."

"That, my dear man, is an understatement."

"You know what I mean. What's your take on Israel?"

Constantine laughed. "Much more favorable since the invention of air-conditioning, I'll tell you." He saw MacLeod's earnest look and took the question a little more seriously. "Two hard lessons learned from four of the worst years of my life. First, always remember that, no matter what, incompetence will always rise to the highest level possible. And second, never, ever get involved in the politics of Palestine. It will only bring you grief." He paused, remembering. "I swear, the only decent thing to come out of my service there was Avram Mordecai."

Masada, Province of Judaea: 10 Avrilis in the fourth year of the reign of Imperator Caesar Vespasianus Augustus (A.D. 73)

"The men are ready, sir," Gaius Marius, the First Centurion, announced to Governor Silva's aide, Constantine. Constantine and Marius, the *Primus Pilus* of the legion *X Fretensis*, stood to the side on the staging platform in the dim light inside the massive siege tower. With the battering ram removed, the wooden platform accommodated nearly the entire First Cohort, nearly 360 men, all ready and eager to put an end to the year they'd spent camped in the miserable desert, waiting for the traitorous Jews of Masada to surrender.

Constantine was more than ready for it to end, as well. More than ready to brush the dust of Judaea from his heels and regain the brilliant military career he'd once given up. Thirteen years prior, while a general quelling a different rebellion, that one in Britannia, he had chanced upon one of his own, newly Immortal, amid the bodies of the recalcitrant Britons on the blood-soaked field of battle. He'd always disliked taking students. Like wives or children, they were a drain on his resources, both in terms of money and time. But above all things, Marcus Constantine was an honorable man, and honor dictated he initiate the Briton female into the Game. He had known it would be a challenge to civilize the blue-painted hellion called Ceirdwyn, but almost more than life itself, Constantine relished a good challenge.

He had resigned his military commission and retired to Rome, where he became both teacher and lover to Ceirdwyn, but never master—she made that abundantly clear. She was, indeed, a challenge. They were happy together, or so he thought, but slowly he realized that Rome was killing them both. Ceirdwyn pined for the untamed freedom of her native land as much as he longed to return to the order and discipline of the military life. With many regrets, they finally parted.

Constantine began to rebuild his military career. He had had to remake himself, a Marcus Constantine from a new generation, and work his way back up, if not from the bottom— a few forged records of meritorious service in Germania took care of that—then at least from the middle. It would be years before he could be General Marcus Constantine once again.

Or maybe longer, if this posting was any indication: aide-de-camp to Provincial Governor Flavius Silva, a mediocre general with a few family connections, in the absolute armpit of the Empire, Judaea. One might as well be exiled to a deserted island, for all the good service in Judaea did for a military record. The gala celebration of Vespasian and Titus's heroic triumph over the Jews was three years past, the citizenry of Rome totally unaware of this last holdout of cursed Jewish stubbornness on a barren spit of rock in the middle of nowhere. When Masada finally fell, there would be no triumphant procession through the streets of Rome for the legion of Flavius Silva. In the camps, the men of the *X Fretensis* joked about the bitter irony of receiving their pay in coins proclaiming *"Judaea Capta,"* when far above them the allegedly conquered Jews sang and feasted and openly mocked them. They, like Constantine, were more than ready to take the hilltop and be done with Masada.

Constantine raised his arm, signaling the engineers to break through the final fire-damaged barricade to the summit. Flanking each engineer were two legionnaires, with shield and *pilum* at the ready, prepared to use the thrusting spears to protect the engineers if necessary from the onslaught of the armed rebels waiting within the fortress. The charred wood was brittle and gave way easily. Constantine raised his other arm, and, with a huge cry, the First Cohort thundered through the debris and into Masada. The great siege tower shook with the force of their charge and the rush of the Second Cohort up the tower to the staging platform to move into position behind them.

This day would never have arrived without Constantine. Silva had seemed content to wait the Jews out, counting on time and hunger to bring Masada to its knees. The survivors of the Roman garrison who had occupied the rock prior to their defeat by the insurgents seven years previous told of tremendous storehouses of supplies and weapons and huge cisterns of water, but Silva had discounted their reports. Constantine knew a small army could hole up on Masada for a decade. It was Constantine who had calculated the precise spot for the earthen ramp to scale the heights, Constantine who designed the siege engine to batter down the walls, and most importantly, Constantine who convinced the Provincial Governor of Judaea it was all his own idea. Silva would more than likely receive a commendation from the Emperor for his brilliant tactics once the fortress fell, perhaps even the governorship of a much more desirable province. All Constantine wanted was a ticket out of Judaea.

The Second Cohort held at the ready on the staging platform like runners at the starting line eager for the race. All they lacked was a signal from the *Primus Pilus* of the First Cohort to join the fray.

Suddenly Constantine realized he could hear no fray. Where were the sounds of battle? The clashing of sword against shield? The battle cries? The screams of dying men and the shrieks of their women? He started toward the opening in the wall as Marius returned, signaling to him.

"Sir, I think you need to see this." Constantine pulled his *gladius* from its sheath and weighed it in his hand for a moment before following.

The troops parted in waves as Marcus Constantine passed through the rubble of the breach in the Jewish defenses and strode onto the top of the mesa. It was no secret to the men of the *X Fretensis* who was really in command of the legion. In the brilliant sunlight of the summit, Constantine's helmet and *lorica* shone bright, his cloak rippling behind him in the mild breeze, and he carried himself with strength and pride. No matter his rank, he bore himself like a general, a talent the weaselly Silva had yet to learn.

Constantine looked around warily. Masada was silent and still, the only movement that of his own troops as they moved cautiously from building to building. "What's happened here, Marius?" he asked the First Centurion. "Where have they all gone?"

"They're dead, sir, all dead," the Centurion answered, making a sign with his hands to ward off evil. Like the majority of the legion, he was from the provinces and still clung to his primitive superstitions. Constantine had little patience for such nonsense.

Constantine turned a hard look on the Centurion. "You can't mean *all*—where are the women? The children?"

"All, sir," he confirmed, a bit spooked, "the old men, the women, the babies . . ." He made the symbol again.

"Show me," Constantine commanded.

The First Centurion indicated three men to accompany them, then led the way to a Roman-style villa just south of the breach. He motioned for two of the legionnaires to enter first, alert for ambush, but none came. Then Constantine and the Centurion entered. The third soldier stationed himself in the doorway to protect their backs.

As they passed through the foyer toward the center courtyard, Constantine could smell death. He gripped his sword tighter and pushed past the soldiers leading the way, impatient. In the villa courtyard he saw for himself that the Centurion was right. Infants and small children silenced by a knife to their throats, cradled protectively by their parents, just as dead. Old men, young women barely past their girlhood, no one was spared. At least forty people in this one yard, dead in the arms of those they'd held dear. And one man, alone, who'd obviously fallen on his sword after he'd helped dispatch the others. From the blood lying in pools around him, Constantine knew it had taken him a long time to die.

"Damn them!" Constantine raged. "Damn them all!" He stormed across the courtyard to the rooms beyond. He broke open one door with a kick of a hobnailed sandal, then another door. And another. Every room, the same story. The same death.

He sheathed his sword angrily. "Cowards!" he roared, frustrated beyond belief. "Cowards!" But in his heart he knew that wasn't true. It wasn't their cowardice that angered him, but their nobility. In his four hundred years in the service of

Rome, never before had he seen such determination, and it ate away at him. Damn them for flaunting their dignity in his face.

Constantine moved farther into the living quarters of the villa. Here the paint could barely be seen on the soot-blackened walls and the tiled floor was covered in ash. "It's the same throughout the complex, sir," the Centurion reported from the doorway behind him.

Constantine crouched down and picked up a handful of broken, charred pottery shards. "They couldn't take it with them, but they made sure we couldn't have it. What kind of people are these, Marius?"

Before the Centurion could answer, Constantine suddenly knew there was another Immortal on Masada. The sensation surprised him with its unexpectedness, and the Centurion could note the sudden change in Constantine's face as he looked up. "Are you unwell, sir?"

Constantine quickly schooled his expression and stood up. "Bring in the Second Cohort," he ordered. "Initiate a room-by-room search of the fortress. Every storehouse, every cistern, inch by inch. I want a complete accounting. Start at the northern palace." He started to leave the room through a door to the south. The Centurion called to him.

"You should take a guard."

"Why, Marius? In case the dead rise up and come for their revenge?" Constantine laughed a bitter laugh. "Let them come." He dismissed the Centurion and strode purposefully out of the villa through the southern porch.

He pulled his *gladius* again and proceeded cautiously, tracking the sensation south along the outer wall of the fortress. Within earshot of an entire Roman legion was not the optimum place for a Quickening, but he wanted answers, and this was the only indication of life on the entire cursed rock. He hoped it wouldn't have to come to taking a head.

At 150 paces from the villa, he found an entrance into the wall surrounding the complex. Sword first, he entered the dimly lit stone corridor. Oil lamps stood in niches along the wall, but most had long run out of oil, and only a few still sputtered. The Immortal was closer now, he could tell, possibly within only a few feet. Constantine set himself and drove his hobnailed sandal into a wooden door, forcing it from its hinges. He planted himself in the doorway and announced, *"Mihi nomen est Marcus Constantinius."*

Two bloodied bodies lay on the floor. One, a Jewish graybeard. The other, veiled, unmistakably a woman. And near her, cringing against the wall, wild eyes wide, a Jewish youth trying in vain to shake away the lightning flashing in his brain. He looked up and with effort focused his eyes on Constantine, suddenly aware that the Roman was the source of his pain.

"I am Marcus Constantine," Constantine announced again, waiting for the answering challenge. Avram dived for the bloodstained iron knife lying on the floor and Constantine raised his sword, on the defensive. "I don't want to fight you." The youth's information would be more valuable to Constantine than his head.

Avram screamed something incomprehensible to Constantine and, before Constantine could stop him, plunged the knife into his own chest. The Jew fell to the ground, dead once more, and Constantine realized that the young man had no idea of his own Immortality. Like it or not, Constantine had just inherited another student.

It was only a few seconds after Avram revived, chest still burning with fire, that he realized his hands were bound behind him. He thrashed about on the floor, then on his knees, desperate to free himself.

"It's for your own good, boy," Constantine explained gently. He had removed his helmet and his shining breastplate in order to appear less intimidating when the terrified young man awoke, but his flame red tunic and noble bearing still proclaimed him as Roman. *"Quod nomen tibi est?"* he asked.

Avram, breathing hard, glared at the Roman with hate in his eyes, but did not speak.

"What is your name?" Constantine asked again, less gently. Damn these Jews! They all knew Latin well enough, the dogs, but they would not dignify it with a response. "Tell me your name!" he demanded.

Avram's only response was to spit in the Roman's face.

Constantine grabbed the Jew viciously by the length of his hair. Marcus Constantine tolerated such insubordination from no man! He drew a fist back to strike—then hesitated. Angrily, he pushed the youth away from him and took a step back. This was a student, he reminded himself, not an interrogation. He would need a different tactic.

He knew no Aramaic, rarely bothered to learn the native languages of the subjugated peoples because they were so quickly supplanted by Latin. But the young Jew refused to respond to Latin. A compromise: *"Athanatos,"* he said in Greek. "You are Immortal, you cannot die." The Jewish scholars all seemed to know some Greek, and the robes of the dead old man on the floor proclaimed him a scholar. With luck, his boy was one as well. "We are alike, you and I. We are Immortal. I am Marcus Constantine, and I've come to help you."

Avram sat back on his heels, stunned, no longer struggling against his bonds. "I cannot die?" he repeated, wary. "Never?"

There were terms and conditions they would get into later, but for the moment that would suffice. "Never," Constantine confirmed. "You've seen so yourself." He cut Avram's bonds with the iron knife, and Avram scrambled away from him, moving to the woman's body.

Avram pulled the veil from Deborah's head and gazed longingly at her lifeless face. "Never?" he asked again, his voice filled with anguish.

"Accept the gift, Jew. We are blessed by the gods. We will live forever—Immortal."

"Blessed? I'm *cursed*, don't you see? Cursed by God." He clutched Deborah's body tightly to his own. "God in Heaven, what have I done to you to deserve this?" He rocked her cold body back and forth, back and forth, tears welling in his eyes. "Deborah!" he bellowed in a voice he hoped would crack Heaven. "Deborah!"

Paris: The Present

"I don't think Avram ever got over Deborah. How he'd lost her. How he'd betrayed her. And how he'd betrayed his God. Over and over, I heard about how he'd betrayed God by not dying. I remember thinking at the time what a demanding God that young man had. But now I know it's Avram who's the demanding one." Constantine paused a moment, then continued. "I took Avram and we left Judaea not long after. I've never been back. And I've never been able to get the images of Masada out of my head."

"I don't know how anyone could," MacLeod concurred.

Constantine picked up the sword box and led the way out of the Temple room. "But that's not actually what you were asking about, was it? You wanted to know about Israel now, not Israel then."

MacLeod followed him back through the exhibit. "Don't you have to understand one to understand the other?"

"If more people realized that, Duncan, maybe we wouldn't still be debating the future of Palestine two thousand years later."

A flock of wayward children came running down the aisle, screaming and laughing. MacLeod dodged out of their way and they swirled around Constantine like an ocean wave engulfing a rock. Behind them, a harried teacher's aide called out, "Stop! It's time to leave." But the children paid her no mind as they pushed past Constantine toward the next exhibit.

"FREEZE!"

And the voice that had commanded a hundred generations of fighting men to his will reverberated through the marble hall like the voice of God. The children froze in their tracks, silenced by the general's order.

With a grateful look, the teacher's aide gathered her charges. "Come, the bus is waiting," she told them, and they followed her toward the exit in a quiet and orderly fashion.

Constantine shrugged and gestured for MacLeod to follow him into the next cubicle of the exhibition, the room with the case containing Nefertiri's sarcophagus. "Hold this." He handed the sword box to MacLeod, then opened the locked cabinet. Carefully, he removed the gleaming short sword from the box and attached two lengths of nylon monofilament to the terminals of the hilt, suspending the sword in the space reserved for it.

"You were pretty certain I'd come through on this, Marcus," MacLeod noted, and Constantine just smiled, knowingly.

The jangle of MacLeod's cell phone added to the general clamor in the gallery. He flipped it open. "MacLeod."

"Doon-can?" her voice purred velvet in his ear.

"Maral," he said, and watched Constantine raise an indulgent eyebrow at the softening of his voice. "Are you all right?"

He could hear her sigh through the phone. "Arafat left the negotiation in a huff and the Israeli foreign minister broke off the session. I need . . . I don't know what I need . . ."

"How about a hug? For a start." Constantine's face broke into an almost patronizing smile, and MacLeod waved him away.

"That would be lovely," she agreed. "But they won't let me out. I'm suffocating here. Can you rescue me?"

"One knight in shining armor, coming right up."

"Really? You'll help me?" The joy in her voice was clear even over the ragged cellular connection.

"Daring rescues, my specialty. I'm on my way. Wear comfortable shoes." MacLeod toggled off the phone and turned to Constantine, who was grinning with fatherly pride. "I think I'll be going now."

"I won't wait up."

"You don't have to be so smug," MacLeod said, starting from the room.

"You don't have to look so happy," Constantine countered, as MacLeod left.

Chapter Eight

Tel Aviv, Israel: The Present

The four o'clock train from Haifa was late. The four o'clock train from Haifa was always late. Inside the crowded Arlozorov Railway Station, it was stifling hot. The antiquated air-conditioning system was out of commission again, as it so often was, and Avram, seated on a bench near the gate where the train from Haifa would someday arrive, berated himself for his choice of garb.

Heavy black suit, black overcoat, black-rimmed spectacles, black felt hat pulled low and tight around his ears to conceal his close-cropped hair and anchor the false prayer curls he wore, he was traveling as one of the ultra-orthodox *haredim*, one of the "black hats" as they were known colloquially throughout Israel. Packed tightly on the bench between an enormous Jewish matron and an unwashed European backpacker, he was certain he was dying. If it was the purpose of the "black hats" to suffer before God, they succeeded admirably. He admired their discipline, but wanted nothing more than to strip off the oppressive black wool and plunge into the Mediterranean, so blue and inviting just a little over a mile away.

The arrival of the train brought some relief as his seatmates hurried off to meet it. Avram stayed where he was, his briefcase on his lap, watching from beneath the brim of his hat as the passengers just off the train from Haifa passed through the gate and into the railway station. Businessmen mostly, returning from a day of transacting business in the northern city. A number of tourists rushed through the station, afraid to miss their connection to Jerusalem. More backpackers, French and Italian, off in search of the youth hostel. As the surge of people off the train began to thin, he spotted a small group of Israeli soldiers in uniform, three men and a woman, coming through the gate with duffel bags slung over their backs. Avram watched them pass his position, laughing and joking with each other in that easy camaraderie that's forged in the trenches. As they started to exit the railway station, he picked up his briefcase and followed them out.

The four walked to a nearby bus stop, Avram not far behind them. After a brief wait in the blazing sun, the bus arrived and the soldiers boarded along with a handful of civilians. Avram followed, choosing a seat near the front of the bus behind the driver, away from the soldiers who sat at the back. The bus was nearly full, but at least the air-conditioning was working. There was no room for his briefcase on the crowded seat beside him, so he slid it under his seat. Several of Avram's fellow passengers looked at him curiously. It wasn't every day that they saw one of the black hats on the streets of very secular Tel Aviv—many of the *haredim* considered the city a modern Sodom or Gomorrah. Good. Avram had counted on being noticed.

The bus ran west, away from central Tel Aviv and into the western suburbs. The line terminated near the Ben Gurion National Defense Base, where the soldiers were returning from their Passover leave. There had been no Tel Aviv when Avram was young, just a few fishing villages near the already ancient port of Jaffa. When he'd returned to liberate his homeland after World War II, the tiny hamlet founded by struggling Zionists only fifty years earlier was already a city. Now nearly a third of Israel lived in the sprawling metropolis. As the bus continued on into the suburbs, picking up and discharging passengers along its way, Avram noted that throughout the world, one modern cement suburb looked pretty much like any other.

Several stops from the military base, the last civilian got off the bus. Now only Avram and the soldiers remained. He chanced a look at them from beneath his hat. They were so young, all of them. Soldiers always were. One of the men looked even younger than Avram did. He probably didn't need to shave yet, either. Why was it always the young, so vibrant and full of potential, who were sacrificed so the old could survive?

He caught the eye of the woman, who smiled at him, teeth white against her tawny skin. Avram noticed how attractive she looked in her olive uniform, dark hair pulled back beneath her cap, but he resisted the temptation to return her smile. While Avram had supported a young woman's right to fight for her country since the liberation and had fought side by side with many he'd been proud to serve with, to the black hats she was anathema. He turned away from her pointedly.

It was always regrettable when soldiers had to die in war. But these Israeli soldiers, like those who had gone before them, like Avram himself, had stood among the ghosts of Masada as new Israeli recruits, had sworn the oath of allegiance to their homeland—"Never again"—and vowed to fight and to die in her defense. As long as Israel was threatened, such sacrifice would be necessary.

Avram reached up and pulled the cord, signaling his intention to leave the bus at the next stop. When the bus began to slow, Avram stood and moved toward the door as the stop neared. He looked through the glass door and stopped cold. Two young girls stood at the stop in front of a corner market carrying a cat in a small cage.

Avram took a deep, calming breath, then reached into his pants pocket and pulled out a large handful of coins. The bus pulled up to the curb and the driver opened the doors. Avram started down the top step, then tripped over his own feet, sprawling onto the pavement below. Coins clattered away in all directions.

"Please, children, can you help me?" he begged piteously, crawling on the ground to retrieve his shekels. To his vast relief, the older girl, almost a teenager, set down the cat carrier to chase after the coins, and soon her younger sister helped as well. Avram waved the bus driver on with a smile.

After the girls handed him the coins they had gathered, Avram thanked them. "And I'm so very sorry I made you miss your bus, girls," he said, handing them each a ten-shekel piece. "Here, you should take a taxi." He reached through the bars of the cage with one hand and began to scratch their cat under the chin. It purred against his hand. With his other hand, he reached into the pocket of his long black coat and pressed the "record" button on a small tape recorder there. "I'm told taxis are much safer than public buses." The resulting explosion as his briefcase detonated blocks away shattered the windows of the market behind them.

Chapter Nine

Paris: The Present

The room was large, larger than her entire apartment back in Ramallah, and it commanded a lovely view of the Square Boucicaut just outside the Lutétia. Maral knew every inch of the view by heart, the way the light of the setting sun traveled across the marble fountain and played in the spurting waters, the patterns of the pair of pigeons nesting between the ears of a bronze horse bearing the effigy of some dead French king. She'd eaten most of her meals by these windows—but not too near, thank you, Farid—taking in as much of Paris as she could from the confines of the narrow panes of glass.

Art nouveau monopolized the decor of the room, a style she'd never been partial to. There was nothing homey about this place she was forced to call home. She knew she was supposed to consider herself fortunate. Paris hotel rooms were notoriously small—she heard the usually stalwart Assad complaining he was barely able to open his suitcase in the tiny room he'd been given. Part of her envied him his cozy accommodations. Her room was dominated by a huge bed hung with heavy draperies, a bed so tall a mahogany stairstep was provided. She found any bed lonely since Ali's death, and this monster doubly so. When she was alone and awake in the middle of the night, she felt very much like the princess and the pea, a nagging thought in the back of her mind that someday they'd discover she wasn't a real princess and send her back to her classroom.

Maral had no delusions about why she'd been selected for the negotiating team. She was raw and untried, the junior member of the team, but she was secular and she was female, an important symbol to the Western world, which believed that all Palestinians were intractable religious fanatics with rags on their heads and automatic weapons in their hands. Token symbol or not, she was determined to make her presence felt. If true peace were ever to be created in her homeland, it would come not from the religious bickerings of the fanatics of either faith, but from those who could step back and see those seated on the other side of the table as people, not ideologies. And it would hold not because of posturing warriors showing off the size of their manhood, but because of women, Israeli women, Palestinian women, women sick of burying their husbands and their brothers and their sons, women who became mothers who would instill the message of peace in their children and their children's children.

More than one of the old-school Palestinian diplomats she worked with called her naive, treated her like an impetuous daughter. They could patronize her all they wanted—she knew she was having an impact. Hers was the voice of reason that had kept them at the table when more extremist minds threatened to shatter the fragile understanding they'd managed to cobble together. Hers, the hand that had slipped what they dismissed as "womanly" concerns like education for the children and health care for the poor and displaced into a platform more concerned with the placement of guns and the movement of troops. As long as she knew Arafat supported her, she had no qualms against butting heads with the stodgiest of the traditionalists.

But it was lonely work. And lately, its only reward had been coming back to this lifeless room, after a long, hard day at the table, to watch the pigeons play in the square. The few times she'd been able to venture out into Paris shone like bright jewels in the bleak memory of the past two weeks of negotiations, and that mysterious Duncan MacLeod seemed to be at the heart of them.

She didn't know what she was expecting when she called him. Just to hear his voice, really. Just to talk to someone who didn't give a damn which side of Suleiman Street was the border or who would guard the Garden Tomb. When he said he would come to see her, her heart was lighter than it had been since she'd left Ramallah. She'd changed clothes twice since, and finally settled on a pair of tailored slacks and a silk tunic in shades of rust and cinnamon that she knew highlighted her skin and brought out her eyes. She hoped a pair of suede loafers would satisfy his request for comfortable shoes.

As the sun went down, there was a knock on her hotel room door. She got up quickly from her perch near the window and moved toward the door. A voice called out, "Room service!"

Oh. "I didn't call for room service," she answered, disappointed.

"No, no, madame," the voice outside protested in Pakistani-flavored French. "You put in your order about three hours ago. The kitchen has been backed up."

Three hours ago? She threw the door open. In a crisp waiter's uniform and fake mustache, Duncan MacLeod stood behind a room-service cart covered in white linen. "Room service!" he announced with a bright smile and a wave of his hand over the contents of the cart, inclining his head to one side a bit to indicate the security men posted down the hall by the elevators.

Maral gestured for him to enter, managing to keep from laughing until she'd closed and locked the door behind him. "What are you doing?"

"You ordered a rescue, madame," he said in his outrageous fake accent. "Here at the Hôtel Lutétia, we aim to please. Would you like that rescue for here or to go?"

"To go? You mean, out of the hotel?" She knew that's what she had asked for, but she hadn't actually dreamed it possible.

"Well, technically, it wouldn't be much of a rescue if we just stayed here," he said, resuming his normal, charming voice.

"But how?"

He lifted the linen skirt around the room service cart and indicated the empty platform below with an expansive gesture. "One getaway vehicle, at your service."

"You think of everything, don't you?"

"I try," he said with a modest shrug. "What do you say, game for a little adventure?"

She was torn. A good little girl would stay in her room alone, safe, secure, content to watch the pigeons. But she was so tired of being everyone's good little girl. A little adventure . . . One look at his face—caring, inviting—and her decision was made. "I should leave Assad a note, tell him not to worry." She pulled hotel stationery and a pen from the desk, scribbling as she talked. "I get a wake-up call at six-thirty in the morning. Usually no one tries to contact me until then, but just in case, I'll let him know I'm with you." She propped the note up on the pillows of her enormous bed and grabbed her coat and purse from a nearby chair.

MacLeod had taken the food and service items from the cart, so it would appear he had left her with her dinner. Only the metal plate covers remained to be returned to the kitchen. "Ready?" he asked, reaching for her hand.

"As I'll ever be," she answered, as he helped her into the cart. She curled up in a fetal position on the low shelf, clutching coat and purse to her, and he lowered the linen cloth back down to cover her. She could see nothing but the shadows of his legs through the cloth as he began to push the cart from the room.

They rumbled down the hallway and then stopped, at the service elevator she guessed. *"Garçon,"* she heard a man say in accented French. One of the security guards. She held her breath. "When will you bring our food?"

When MacLeod spoke, it was in his odd, vaguely Pakistani accent, and she bit her lip so as not to laugh. "I do not know, monsieur, but I will go down immediately and ask the chef." The elevator arrived, and he pushed the cart in. *"Bonsoir! Bonsoir!"* he piped cheerfully to the guards as the doors closed.

The elevator moved briefly, then stopped. The doors opened, and she felt the cart rumble out onto another floor, then a stop, a start, then a stop and some rustling sounds. She waited for what seemed like several minutes, afraid to speak, afraid even to breathe too loudly, lest she give them away. Then the linen skirt flipped up and MacLeod was helping her out of the cart.

The cheesy mustache and waiter's uniform were gone, replaced by a tight pair of jeans and a black T-shirt that hugged the contours of his chest. "Where are we?" she whispered.

"Fifth-floor linen closet. I wasn't really going to wheel you down the Boulevard Raspail. Put on your coat," he whispered, donning his leather jacket, and she complied. He stuck his head cautiously out the door, looked around, then motioned for her to follow him out. Once in the hall, he pulled the room-service cart out of the linen closet and left it outside a neighboring guest room. Then he took her hand and they proceeded down the hall as if nothing had happened.

Her heart was beating fast as they descended to the lobby in the guest elevator and he squeezed her hand in encouragement. As the doors opened, they stepped nonchalantly into the lobby and toward the revolving doors.

"Uh-oh." Before she even had a chance to notice what was wrong, MacLeod wrapped an arm around her shoulder and spun her around in the opposite direction. They started walking quickly out of the back of the lobby and into a corridor of meeting rooms. As they passed out of the lobby, Maral turned around and saw a flock of reporters at the door, anxious for a statement about the Palestinian walkout at the day's negotiations, and Farid and his men valiantly holding them at bay.

MacLeod ducked into a room labeled "Degas," empty of people but set for a formal dinner, pulling Maral behind him. They hurried across the chandeliered room and through a small door at the back. They found themselves in a stark, utilitarian hallway surrounded by serving carts and metal shelving.

"I've never been backstage before," Maral whispered. "Where does this go?"

"Your guess is as good as mine." He looked right, then left, then right again."C'mon, this way," he said, starting down the corridor to the left. They'd only gone a couple of feet when a cadre of servers bearing trays of glassware for the Degas Room came toward them in formation, blocking the hallway. "Or not," MacLeod said, quickly changing direction and hurrying back the other way, pulling Maral along in his wake.

Not too far past the Degas Room, they found a metal door labeled *"Sortie."* Maral moved to push on the exit bar, but MacLeod pulled her back. "Wait." He looked around the door, checking for sirens or buzzers that might go off once they pushed the door open, but found none. "Okay, here goes." He tensed himself for an alarm and together they pushed open the door. There was silence.

They ran out into the night, into the alley behind the hotel. The Citroën was parked a couple of blocks away and they strolled leisurely to it, hand in hand, Maral giggling like a schoolgirl at their little taste of adventure. As they drove back past the hotel, surrounded by news vans with satellite transmitters on their roofs, she waved at it in triumph.

When MacLeod heard that Maral had seen virtually nothing of Paris since her arrival, he regretted their grand adventure was taking place at night. There were so many things he would have loved to have shown her, he said—the rose window of Sainte-Chapelle at sunset, the gallery of the Impressionists at the Musée d'Orsay, the Bagatelle gardens in the Bois de Boulogne. Maybe someday. They had to content themselves with a moonlit ride up the elevator at the Eiffel Tower, but the look of delight on her face as she gazed out over the twinkling splendor of the City of Lights when they'd reached the top made up for it all. And the view of Notre-Dame from the deck of MacLeod's barge, lit bright against the night sky, was better than any she could have hoped for. It was a long while before he could even coax her belowdecks. Had it been summer and the breeze off the Seine not so biting, she might have stayed there all night, gazing across the river at the wonders that man could create.

Before he even snapped on the light, she could tell they were in a place uniquely his. It smelled of him, strong and masculine, yet as comforting as her father's favorite sweater. Ali had had a scent like this, warm but powerful, a touch of spice that had slowly leaked away out of their apartment, out of her life in the months after his death. As the lights came on, she thought to herself "Of course"—the room was a natural extension of the man. Both fit and spare, but at the same time comfortable and welcoming. There was beauty in the details, in the objets d'art from many lands adorning the spartan shelves to the simple but extremely tasteful furnishings, and they spoke volumes about their owner.

"Home, sweet home," MacLeod announced, helping her remove her coat. "Be it ever so humble . . ."

"I think it's wonderful," she said. She moved to the porthole overlooking the Seine and watched a boatload of tourists drift past on a moonlight cruise, so close she could almost touch them. "How incredibly free you must feel here." She turned back to him glowing with delight. "How I envy you."

"Well, there are still docking fees and taxes, but there is something about the water." He walked past her and into the tiny galley area. "You hungry?"

Now that she thought about it, "Famished. Is this what adventure does to you?"

"I find that a little adventure stirs up all sorts of appetites." She thought she could detect a delicious twinkle in his eye before his head disappeared into the small refrigerator beneath the counter. "Make yourself at home, and I'll see what I can rustle up."

As he rattled and clanged in the galley, Maral wandered around the barge, picking up hand-carved chess pieces, running a hand along the burnished chrome of an intricate piece of sculpture, trying to get a feel for this man Duncan MacLeod and how he chose to live. At the antique writing desk, she studied the few framed photos he kept there, and the stunning blonde who dominated them all.

She felt his hand on her shoulder. "Château MacLeod, our very best year," he said, handing her a crystal champagne flute of chilled water. "Dinner is served, madame."

"Who is she?" Maral asked, and she thought she might lose her breath at the bittersweet look that passed across his noble face. Whoever she was, God, how he still loved her.

"That's Tessa," he said quietly. "She's gone now."

In those simple words, she could feel it—his grief, his loneliness. All the days he'd screamed at the earth to stop turning because it was empty and meaningless. All the nights he'd begged his heart to stop beating so he could be with her and stop the pain. And finally the acceptance, that he could go on in spite of the pain that would never leave, that somehow he *had* to go on. She could feel it, and in that moment she could feel their souls touch, both wounded, both lonely, both needing.

And then she pulled away. Maybe she wasn't ready after all.

"Maral?"

She moved to the table. "So what's this I hear about dinner?" Then she stopped and stared at the feast he'd laid on. Chilled gazpacho, a full color wheel of patés, smoked goose, a delicate carpacho of Parmesaned greens and cold veal. "Duncan, you can't tell me these were odds and ends you found in the back of the fridge," she accused. "Did you make all this?"

"Of course not, I'm not Superman." He laughed. "White knight on even numbered days, gourmet chef on the odd ones. But I have friends." He pulled her chair out with a flourish. "Shall we?"

As they dined on their cold supper, she told him about the day that had finally led up to her call for help. How the Israeli foreign minister had pulled a key plank from the impending agreement, claiming that he was unaware of it and that his negotiators had had no authority to include it. About how Arafat had staged a walkout to bring what he called deception in front of the international press. How she hated the press, the posturing, the half-truths. It felt so good to have someone to talk to, honestly and without the negotiation games. And he had seemed willing to listen to her talk all night if that's what she needed.

Later, after he'd lowered the lights on the barge a bit and started a cheery fire glowing in the fireplace, they sat on the sofa with pastry and strong dark coffee. Kicking off her shoes, she pulled her bare feet up under her and nestled back into the sofa's soothing folds, luxuriating in the warmth of the fire, at peace for the first time in weeks. During a lull in the conversation, MacLeod reached out and took her left hand in his.

"Tell me about him." He softly rubbed her wedding ring with his thumb.

She wanted to pull away again, then stopped. Something in his eyes, in his voice, in his encouraging smile reassured her. "His name was Ali. He was my student at Bir Zeit. Then the government closed the university, and he . . ."

"Was no longer your student," he finished for her after a moment. She smiled gratefully at his tact.

"We married in '89, during the Intifada. The Israelis called him an 'instigator.' During the first few years we were married, I think he spent more nights in an Israeli prison bed then he did in mine."

"Sometimes the reunions make it all worthwhile," MacLeod said with understanding.

She felt herself blush just a little, remembering, then went on. "When the military closed the schools in Ramallah, I taught children in our home. That was as close to rebellion as I got. That was Ali's calling—war was man's work." She took a swig of her coffee and stared off into the fire. It was still so hard to face.

"And then?" he prompted, gently, already knowing.

"And then he went out one night three years ago and never came back. There was a disturbance. Some kids throwing rocks at some Israeli settlers got out of hand. Ali went to see if he could calm things down. I thought at first he'd been arrested again. And then I prayed to God that he'd been arrested again." She looked down at her wedding band, still safely cradled in MacLeod's hand. "It was a week before they even let me claim his body." It was all so fresh. The waiting and wondering. The charnel house they called a morgue. She didn't want to cry. Not here. Not now.

He reached an arm around her shoulders and tenderly lay his hand against her face, guiding it to rest against his chest. God, he smelled so good. His chest was firm and strong, and she could feel his strength hold her up, bolster her own courage. She leaned against him that way for a long moment, reveling in the feeling of being cared for again. Then she pulled away, grateful, and sat up, peer to peer once more.

MacLeod acknowledged the subtle change in their dynamic with an approving smile. "So then the professor became the 'instigator.' "

"Mediator," she stressed. "Someone has to stop it, Duncan. Someone has to make sure no more wives or mothers go through what I went through. Israeli or Palestinian. The killing has to stop. And if it has to fall to me to do it, I will. No matter what."

She stopped, uncomfortable. He was looking at her in a way she could only describe as wonder. The room had become unexpectedly warm. He reached out both his arms and as his hands drew nearer to her face, she closed her eyes and held her breath, hoping against hope he would touch her in the way she found she was suddenly longing to be touched. She felt his fingers brush her cheeks, then stroke her temples and she opened her eyes again to gaze into his soft brown ones. With slow, deliberate motions, he removed the graceful gazelles from her hair and she gave her head a toss, allowing the full glory of her mane to cascade around her face and beneath her shoulders to her waist. He dug his face and hands into her hair like a parched traveler at an oasis pool.

She hated to break the moment, but she had to laugh out loud. He lifted his head. "What?"

"You've been wanting to do that since the first moment you saw me."

"So?" he said a little sheepishly.

"It's all right, Duncan," she said, "because I've been dying to do this." She reached her arms up behind him and pulled off the fastener that bound back his hair. Then she ran her fingers slowly through his own glorious lion's mane.

The passion of his answering kiss drove her back against the leathery folds of the couch, and she responded with equal fervor. Her mouth hungered to taste all of his flavors. Cinnamon and musk and the smoke of ancient campfires exploded in her mouth and she savored each one. She threw back her head, daring his tongue to take her, needing to feel his kiss deep inside her.

He tried to balance himself on his elbows and knees, sparing her body the brunt of his weight, but she pulled him down on top of her, her agile hands massaging deep into the muscles of his back pulling him closer, closer, wanting to feel him against every pore of her skin. It had been so long, too long since she'd allowed anyone to come near her. Now, even the thin cloth of his T-shirt was more than she could bear between them, and she began to draw it awkwardly off over his head.

With a hand, he stopped her. He stood up from the sofa, moving closer to the warmth of the fireplace, and she joined him there. He pulled the T-shirt over his head in one fluid motion, and suddenly they were like a single creature, all arms and legs, fingers and hands, helping, hindering, until all barriers of clothing were removed.

They both glowed golden in the firelight. She stood in awe

of him. Like Michaelangelo's *David*, Rodin's lovers, every muscle taut and articulated, sculpted from God's own blueprints. God, how she needed him. Her breasts felt heavy and tipped with flame and she longed for him to quench the fire, and, as if privy to the secrets of her mind, he did. She gasped as she felt his mouth upon her, and with her nails she traced the sinews of his thighs to the tight ridges of his belly.

When he released her—her heart wanted to scream No!—he took her hand in his, starting to lead her toward his bed in the bow of the barge.

"No," she said, her voice awash with passion. She had to see him in the dancing light of the fire, watch as the flames played along his magnificent features as they made love. "Here." She knelt to the floor and drew him down on top of her.

Chapter Ten

Paris: The Present

MacLeod came awake before he actually opened his eyes. He could tell from the damp chill against his skin that dawn had not arrived yet, but the noises from outside—the chattering of the birds, the roar of passing trucks, the creaking and rocking of the barge as a towboat went past on the river—told him it was not far away. He opened his eyes to find that, indeed, the rosy fingers of dawn had yet to find their way into the barge. He tried to remember when they'd finally made it to the bed. Not that long ago. He rolled over with a fond smile, replaying in his mind the night just spent, and reached out to kiss Maral awake.

She wasn't there.

MacLeod sat upright in the empty bed, completely awake now. "Maral?" he called out into the predawn gloom filling the barge. He was answered by the sound of the shower coming on.

Relieved, he looked at the clock. Four in the morning. No wonder he felt like he hadn't slept. But there were definitely some things in this life worth losing sleep for. He could still smell her scent on his pillow, on his body. He slipped out of bed, out from beneath the downy warmth of the duvet, and the damp cold of the morning air hit his naked body with a shiver. He padded across the barge to the bathroom.

MacLeod stood in the bathroom doorway for a long minute, watching her through the glass doors of the shower, watching her body dance under the jets of water, before sliding open the door and slipping into the shower behind her. He picked up a bar of soap and slid it down her back. "Can I help?"

She turned toward him with a start. "Duncan. I didn't mean to wake you."

The cascade of water against them was blood hot and he could feel his body come to life in the fiery jets. He kissed her gently on the lips, then began to lather her shoulders, letting his hands roam down her back in large soapy circles. Beneath his firm hands he could feel her muscles relax.

"Hmmm, very nice," she purred. "Do you make house calls?"

He allowed his hands to roam farther, swirling lather down her spine, across and under her tightly rounded rear. He left one hand there, pressing her close against him while he kissed her again as the pulsating jets rinsed the soap from her back. All of a sudden, the barge lurched a bit to one side and Maral pulled away, startled, then the boat righted itself and resumed its gentle rocking motion. "What was that?" she wondered.

"Probably just got caught in something's wake. Happens all the time. Nothing to worry about." He slipped an arm around her waist and turned her around. "Other side." He pulled her close, her slick back against his dripping chest, and she could feel every inch of him press against her, skin to skin, as he soaped her belly and allowed the hot stream of water to sweep the soap away in rivers down her legs.

Slowly, his soapy hands circled upward, lathering her chest, spiraling up her breasts. Feeling a little devilish, he paid special attention to the hollow between her breasts where he'd discovered she was so very ticklish. Laughing, she pulled away from his slippery embrace. "Duncan, if you keep this up, I'll never leave."

"That's the plan," he said, running the soapy bar down her nose.

"No!" she protested, wiping the soap from her nose. "I have to get back to the hotel before six-thirty. Some of us have to work today."

Sadly, he knew she was right. While he could be content to dally in the shower with her all day, much more important matters—at least in the grand scheme of things—awaited Maral. "Okay, Cinderella, you finish up here." He handed her the soap. "I'll start some coffee, and we'll get you back before you turn into a pumpkin. I promise."

He slipped from the shower and grabbed a towel from a nearby bar. He buried his face in the thirsty terry cloth as he walked from the bathroom toward the galley, then tousled it through his damp hair.

"Good morning, Mr. MacLeod."

There, waiting patiently on his sofa in dark suit and Arab headdress, Farid. Assad and two more of Farid's goons were ranged about the barge, their pistols drawn and trained on MacLeod.

MacLeod, preserving his dignity, made no quick moves to hide his nakedness. Instead, he acted as if there was nothing out of the ordinary in receiving groups of armed guests on the barge in his altogether. "You couldn't have knocked?"

"You were otherwise engaged, I think," Farid said with a look that, if he thought Farid actually capable of emotion, MacLeod would have called a smirk. "Where is Dr. Amina?"

MacLeod called into the bathroom. "Cinderella, your ugly stepmother's here." The sound of the shower stopped with an abrupt squeak. "I'd recommend the robe on the back of the door." Chilly, MacLeod wrapped the towel casually around his waist.

"I'd recommend you gather the doctor's things and take them to her, Mr. MacLeod," Farid said calmly. "There is no need for all of us to be shamed."

"I don't suppose you could wait on deck."

"I'm afraid not." Farid and his men watched MacLeod intently as he collected bits of Maral's clothing from around the sofa and delivered it to her in the bathroom. When MacLeod exited the bathroom, he closed the door soundly behind him.

"I was about to put on a pot of coffee. Interested?" Off the Arabs' sullen silence, he gestured down at his towel-clad body, "Look, Farid, it's obvious I'm not armed here. Tell the boys to put the toys away and tell me what's going on."

"What's going on is that we are in the midst of an international security crisis and you're luring this woman away to play your childish sex games." Farid stood and faced MacLeod, nose to nose. "I could have you arrested for kidnapping a diplomat of the Palestinian people, Mr. MacLeod, but I would rather avoid the unpleasant press that would generate. But I will if you force my hand. Do we have an understanding?"

Something in Farid's voice . . . "Whoa, back it up. What international security crisis? This is no longer about Hebron, is it?" Farid seemed unwilling to give him any details, and MacLeod pressed him. "Tell me. If this involves Maral, I need to know." Still nothing. "I make a better ally than enemy, Farid," and the look of warning in MacLeod's eyes gave the Palestinian a taste of what it might be like to go up against him.

Farid conceded and, with a gesture of his hand, told the others to put their weapons away. "A public bus exploded outside Tel Aviv yesterday, killing four Israeli soldiers and a civilian bus driver. Someone worked very hard to make it look like the work of the Jewish fundamentalists, but we have reason to believe it was the work of the terrorist organization Hamas. And that the negotiations are the next target. We thought at first they had kidnapped Dr. Amina."

"Hamas?" Maral stood in the doorway of the bathroom, clothed, her face full of shock. "That can't be. We had their guarantee. They agreed to the truce. They swore—"

"That was before Hebron," Farid pointed out. "Everything's changed."

"No," she breathed, unbelieving, and all the stress and worry she'd managed to leave somewhere between her hotel room and the top of the Eiffel Tower came crashing back onto her shoulders, aging her beyond her years.

"Say your good-byes. We're leaving now," Farid commanded her.

MacLeod looked to Maral, who still seemed stunned by the revelation. He knew he should probably just back away and let Farid do his job. Maral's evening of adventure, their night of mutual pleasure and comfort had ended with the cold cruel dawn of reality. Farid and his men would protect her. It's what they were trained to do. But she just looked so lost. So all alone. And if anything were to happen to her because he'd done nothing . . . Instead of backing away, MacLeod stepped in. "I'm going with her."

"Out of the question," Farid said, taking Maral by the arm to guide her to the door.

"I don't think you heard me," MacLeod said, stepping in front of them, pulling Farid's hand away from her. His voice was pleasant, but carried a hard core of steel. "I said, I'm going with her." Even in just a towel, he could be quite intimidating. "Farid, you need me. If this is a Hamas threat, you're going to need all the help you can get."

"No." Farid's word was final. He started for the door again, gesturing Maral to follow.

"Last time, Farid," MacLeod tried one more tack. "I stay with her, or I go to the press. What do you say?"

Farid glared at him, then inclined his head just a bit, acknowledging his defeat. "You have five minutes."

MacLeod only needed four and half. As he emerged from the bathroom, dressed and ready to leave, he realized he'd walked into the middle of a conflict of wills.

"I will not permit this behavior," Farid was growling at Maral. MacLeod's first instinct was to come to her aid, but then with one look at the stern resolution on her face, he realized that when the war was with words, Maral had the situation well in hand.

"I am not your wife, Farid, and I am not your daughter. You work for the delegation, and, therefore, you work for me. You have no right to treat me any differently than you do the other delegates."

"None of them behave as shamefully as you!"

"Bullshit!" Farid was floored by her use of such a crass Americanism. MacLeod could tell she'd done it just to watch him flinch. "Halabi is a drunkard. Al-Sayyeed has a different whore to his room every night. Don't tell me you don't know," she said over his protests. "Your men are procuring them for him. And I'm sure all their security clearances are just impeccable, aren't they?" It was clear Farid would not allow himself to be bested by a woman, but he was having trouble figuring a way out of this awkward situation. Maral, sensing this, moved in for the kill. "From now on, Farid, you treat me with the same courtesy and respect you do the men, or you and I will be having a chat with the chairman about these breaches in al-Sayyeed's security. Do *we* have an understanding?"

Farid was not a man to shuffle or to hem and haw, even in defeat. He would stand his ground no matter what. His gaze was steady and his voice firm as he said, "As you say, Doctor." He glanced at MacLeod, well aware he'd heard what transpired. "You're ready." It was not a question.

"After you." MacLeod gestured toward the door, grabbing his long dark coat from the back of a chair. He took Maral's arm and wondered, as they followed Farid out of the barge, if the security chief knew just how much she was trembling.

From the air, Paris seemed to go on forever. As Avram watched through the airplane's tiny window, the city grew larger and larger. Descent was one of his favorite parts of flying—second only to the in-flight films. He loved the thrill of barely controlled falling. Nothing between him and a burnt crater in the ground but the skill of a man unseen, unknown, yet entrusted with the lives of hundreds of people. It was as close to life on the edge as he would allow himself.

He'd called Paris home for a couple of decades, six hundred years or so ago. He figured he'd called just about everywhere home at one time or another. Wherever his people had been dispersed, it seemed he'd been there at least once in his travels. A man wandering in search of his identity could cover a lot of territory in two thousand years. In Paris, he'd lived on a piece of swampland known as the Marais. He'd opened a small shop—Avram ben Mordecai, Scribe—and made a pleasant life for himself there in the Jewish Quarter. But only Jerusalem had ever truly been his home, and it wasn't long before the urge to move on had taken him on the road again.

With a few jolts and bumps, the El Al jet touched down at Orly and Avram jockeyed to be among the first off as it taxied to the jetway. He'd checked no baggage, only his government-issue roll-aboard and worn leather rucksack as carry-on, and he moved briskly from the gate toward Immigration and Customs, looking like a young lawyer, or perhaps an accountant, in his conservative suit. The lines at the Immigration kiosks were long, all the morning flights from overseas seemed to arrive at once, but Avram bypassed them all and went instead to a small desk at the side of the throng. He pulled a diplomatic passport from his satchel, clearly marked with the seal of Israel, and flashed it at the Immigration agent, who checked it cursorily to make sure the photo matched the youthful man presenting it and waved him through.

Within minutes, he was out in the bright sunlight of Paris, squinting at the cars in the pickup lanes. He reached into his satchel, pulled out his sunglasses. Better. A dark sedan pulled up at the curb alongside him, and the window slid smoothly down. "Mordecai?" one of the two men inside asked. Avram nodded and hopped in the back.

"Welcome to Paris, Mordecai," the driver said. "Took you long enough to get here."

"Something came up," Avram said, as they pulled away from the curb and out into airport traffic.

"Dr. Amina! Dr. Amina! What do you think are the chances the Hamas threat will disrupt the negotiations?" The lights from the video cameras blinded her as she tried to make her way down the stairs to the driveway.

"Doctor! Do you think there's any hope left for East Jerusalem?" An overzealous hand pushed forward a microphone that nearly hit her in the face before it was deflected by Assad.

"Do you fear for your personal safety, Dr. Amina?" Assad and another security man hardly managed to get Maral through the gauntlet of reporters and sound-bite specialists lying in wait outside the Hôtel Lutétia and safely into one of the waiting cars. The other delegates fared no better.

" 'Do I fear for my personal safely,' " Maral mocked once safely behind tinted glass with MacLeod. "Ycs, I do—from them, the damn vultures. As if this isn't hard enough."

"It's okay," MacLeod consoled her. "It's over for now."

She shook her head. "It's never over—there'll be just as many waiting on the other end."

Normally the trip from the hotel to the anonymous French government building belonging to the Ministry of Education that had been pressed into service for the negotiations would take ten minutes, even in the traffic-logged streets of Paris. For a caravan of six limousines and their police escort, the trip took more like half an hour, creeping through the congested thoroughfares. Every moment, Maral was on edge, and the security men alert for the slightest sound or motion out of the ordinary.

When they finally pulled up to the Ministry building, MacLeod could see that Maral had been right. Another throng of reporters, TV journalists, and the morbidly curious waited outside. But on this end, thanks to an Israeli security detail with no qualms about showing automatic weapons in public, the mobs were neatly contained behind strict lines of demarcation.

Maral explained with a wry smile. "They don't have the same image problem we do. Let a Palestinian wave an Uzi in front of Peter Jennings, and it would be a whole different ball game." As MacLeod escorted Maral into the building, the same sorts of questions were shouted at her, but across the barricade instead of directly in her face they no longer seemed like attacks on her person. She smiled a polite "no comment" and moved inside.

Just inside the doors, a series of airport metal detectors were in place to protect the negotiations. Assad removed his gun from his jacket and placed it on the scanner's conveyor belt, passed through the detection gateway with no alarm, then retrieved his weapon.

Maral placed her purse on the moving belt and walked through the gateway. She was startled when the alarm began to sound.

"Madame?" The attendant motioned her to step back and come through the machine again. Once again the sound of the alarm filled the hallway. "I'm sorry, Madame," the security officer said, motioning her off to the side, "but I must search you."

Maral submitted stoically. It was all too common an occurrence. Searches, metal detectors, road blocks, suspicion. Her privacy violated for little reason. She considered it one of the facts of her life as a Palestinian in an occupied land. MacLeod saw Maral's face blank as the security officer's hands passed over her body.

Chapter Eleven

Warsaw: April 18, 1943

Miriam's face tightened into an emotionless mask as the police officer's hands pawed over her body. He was Polish, supposedly one of her own countrymen, the overstuffed pig, but he carried out the orders of his Nazi overlords with great enthusiasm. "Remove your blouse," he ordered, and when she seemed to hesitate, he struck her hard across the face with the butt of his pistol. Her head jerked back and a ragged gash opened beneath her right eye. "Remove your blouse, *moja lalka*," he mocked her—my little doll.

Biting back tears of humiliation and rage, she complied, slowly unfastening the buttons on her white cotton blouse. At nineteen, any faith Miriam Kavner had once had in her fellow countrymen, or humanity itself, had long ago been crushed beneath the great Wall that was her people's prison. Her father and mother had run an upscale restaurant before the war, which quickly became a soup kitchen for the starving after the Wall had cut the Jews of Warsaw off from their "purer" Aryan neighbors. Then the Expulsions began, and Levi Kavner sold everything they owned to buy himself a place on a German work crew, for the promise of protection that would give his family. But protection was just another Nazi lie—her father sent to a forced labor camp in Germany, her mother and little brother Zvi marched to the railroad cars, taken away to Treblinka. Now only Miriam remained, an unlikely warrior, a courier for the *Zydowska Organizacja Bojowa*, the Jewish Fighting Organization, the ZOB.

In the parlance of the ZOB, Miriam Kavner looked "*gut*"—

with her bleached blond hair and light complexion, she could easily pass for a Polish Christian and walk openly in the Aryan sections of the city, carrying messages, smuggling money and food sent from Jews in America or Eretz Israel, negotiating for the few weapons they'd managed to acquire. She found she was good at what she did, never drawing suspicion as she provided vital information and supplies to her comrades in the Jewish resistance. She thought her family would have been proud of her.

But today, returning from the Aryan side in the midst of a group of munitions factory workers herded back to the Ghetto after their day's forced labor, perhaps Miriam looked too "*gut*." Carrying what could be the most important intelligence of the war, she had somehow attracted the attention of the collaborators who guarded the Gesia Street gate.

Miriam could feel the warmth of her blood as it trickled down her cheek, and she could feel the heat of the eyes of the other Polish police guarding the gate as she pulled the tail of her blouse from the waistband of her skirt, undid the final button, slipped the blouse from her shoulders and dropped it to the ground beside her. Standing in the middle of the street clad in her brassiere, she could not stop herself from shivering despite the warmth of the afternoon sun.

Her uniformed tormentor pulled her roughly toward him, slipped one arm tightly around her waist. "You're very pretty," he said, fingering one of her blond curls, "too pretty for a *Jewess*!" His disdainful laugh echoed in her ear. He was a squat, greasy man, desperately in need of a shave and a bath, and the thought of him touching her sent a wave of nausea through Miriam's core. "Let's give everyone a good look," he said. He reached between Miriam's breasts and forcibly ripped the brassiere from her body. The fabric tore away, leaving her exposed to the rest of the Polish squad, who whooped and hollered their approval.

She shut her eyes and tried to shut down her mind as the officer groped and fondled her breasts, touching places she had never felt touched by a man before, but finally her tears escaped, uncontrollable. She could feel his excitement rising against her as he pulled her closer, and she thought about breaking away and running, knowing full well the machine guns at the gate would cut her down in seconds.

But if she died here, no matter how blessed the relief might be to her, her message would die with her. No one would know the Germans planned to strike at the Ghetto before dawn tonight, no one would be prepared, everyone would die. She needed to stay alive as long as she could, to try to get the word to someone—anyone—who could warn the ZOB. Miriam steeled herself as the Pole rubbed himself against her, his fetid breath hot in her ear, his comrades whistling and applauding. With desperate eyes, she searched the neighboring rooftops for salvation.

Up on the roof of the apartment building at the corner of Gesia and Okopowa streets, across from the massive gates leading out of the Ghetto, Avram Mordecai and Duncan MacLeod were arguing as Avram grabbed an old Mauser rifle and thrust it into MacLeod's hands. "You can do this, *goy*. Five shots, five guards. Pick 'em off from the first-floor window," Avram said, trying to move MacLeod toward the roof door.

"Are you completely insane?" MacLeod stood his ground. "Are you *trying* to get her killed?"

"You see what those pigs are doing to her. I'm *trying* to keep her alive. Now go!"

"Listen to me." As MacLeod tried to move away from Avram, Avram hung on tenaciously. MacLeod may have had almost a foot on him in size, but Avram was bound and determined for MacLeod to go. "*Listen to me*, Avram!" MacLeod said. "A grandstand play in front of two machine-gun emplacements does not make 'alive.' It makes 'dead.' I miss one shot, and they'll be all over us."

"Look, I know you. *You* don't miss."

MacLeod had to concede he was a great shot, but he still knew Avram's plan couldn't work. "Yeah, and what happens when that piece of German crap jams? Miriam and I'll both be Swiss cheese. I'll get up again, but she won't. What does that accomplish?" He gave Avram a firm shake to try and knock some sense into him. "We have to get them away from the machine guns."

Avram stopped and looked at him, hearing his words but frustrated at not being able to act immediately. "Okay, you're right. You're right. We need a Plan B."

Down in the street, two more Polish policemen from the gate joined the officer, forcing Miriam to her knees while their leader bound her wrists tightly behind her neck with strips of fabric torn from her blouse.

Avram's eyes narrowed as he thought. "If he really wants it, they're gonna take her somewhere. Somewhere away from those damn machine guns. Even a pig like that's not idiot enough to pull it out in a public street. It's a crime against the State to screw a Jew, MacLeod. Pollutes their good Aryan blood. Doesn't stop it from happening, but it might keep it from happening in the middle of Gesia Street, where any goosestepper might see it." As if to prove Avram right, in the street below them the police pulled Miriam roughly to her feet and ordered her to walk. She hung back and was rewarded with a rifle butt sharply in the small of her naked back. Stumbling, nearly falling, she obeyed.

MacLeod watched them start to go—Miriam, her head bent low with shame but her eyes defiant, searching for any avenue of escape; the Polish police officer, impatient and flushed with his own power; and his two eager lackeys, their rifles ready and trained on Miriam. "Gesiowska," he said, invoking the name of the hated prison less than half a mile to the east, the direction Miriam was being led.

"I think you're right. Plenty of private little rooms. Very cozy. Damn them." All of a sudden, Avram was a flurry of motion, checking his pistol, grabbing two grenades from a small cache near their lookout position.

"So, what's Plan B?" MacLeod demanded.

"You stay with them. Keep an eye on her—make sure they don't get her inside. Be ready to ride in like John Wayne and get her out of there."

Avram started toward the stairs leading down from the roof. "What's the signal?" MacLeod called after him.

"You'll know it when you see it," MacLeod heard him say as he disappeared down the stairwell.

"Avram!" he called down after him, but there was no response. Damn him and his complicated plans. "Just great,"

MacLeod grumbled under his breath, but one thing he'd learned in three hard months in Warsaw was he could trust Avram's instincts when it came to the Ghetto. He quickly checked over his rifle. Fully loaded, the old German Mauser took five rounds, but he knew there was precious little ammunition left for it. The fact the ZOB had entrusted it, one of less than a dozen they'd managed to procure, to him was proof of how highly they valued his marksmanship. He'd have to make every shot count.

He ran to the far edge of the roof, climbed a short ladder onto the roof of the adjoining apartment building. Racing across the rooftop, he vaulted over the side of the building and landed with a tuck and a roll on another building two floors below. Almost before he landed, he was running again.

In the months since MacLeod had helped Rabbi Mendelsohn escape Warsaw and had seen him on his way to rendezvous with his son, the ZOB had tried as best they could to prepare for the inevitable day the Germans would return to finish clearing out the Ghetto. No one deluded themselves that the brief show of resistance MacLeod had witnessed at the *Umschlagplatz* and in the streets of the Ghetto back in January had caused the Germans to retreat for good. When MacLeod had surprised Avram by keeping his promise and returning to the Ghetto, he found the survivors of the Germans' aborted January *Aktsia* working feverishly, digging a complex series of underground bunkers, called *malinas*, throughout the Ghetto, bunkers in which the noncombatants could hide to ride out the coming fury for as long as they could. For the fighters of the resistance, a web of ladders and bridges and chutes was constructed between the closely packed buildings to give the ZOB a stronghold to fight from cover. They all knew if forced to fight the Germans openly in the streets again, the battle was doomed before it began. Their skirmishes with the Germans during the three-day January uprising had routed the Germans from the Ghetto and stopped the expulsions. But the cost in Jewish lives had been high, and they knew the Germans would not be surprised a second time.

Reaching the end of the next building at a run, MacLeod climbed carefully out onto the narrow wooden bridge across Smocza Street. He kept low so as not to be spotted against the blue sky. He kept moving parallel to Miriam's captors three stories below. Miriam was walking as slowly as she dared, buying herself time, but MacLeod could tell the guards were dangerously close to running out of patience with her.

"No more little Jewish half-men for you," the Polish officer taunted Miriam. "Soon you'll know what a real man feels like." He grabbed her from behind and wrapped his beefy arm across her naked breasts. "I'm going to fill you up until you scream for more, little doll," he whispered in her ear, and pulled her faster down the street.

MacLeod couldn't hear the man's words, but he could read them in the revulsion on Miriam's face. His hand tightening on his rifle, he hurried from the wooden causeway and sprinted across the next two rooftops, clearing the low brick wall separating them like a champion hurdler. After another short ladder and another sprint, he'd pulled ahead of the police by half a block. He hoped to cut them off before they could reach the prison. All the while he was alert for Avram's signal.

MacLeod knew more was at stake than just Miriam's life if he allowed them to take her into Gesiowska. Under interrogation, especially if these pigs turned her over to the Gestapo when they were finished with her, Miriam could compromise the entire operation—not only the ZOB fighters in the Ghetto, but the thousands of Jews in hiding on the Aryan side of Warsaw and the handful of sympathetic Poles, Miriam's contacts, who protected them. Miriam was strong, he knew, but he'd seen firsthand what the Gestapo was capable of. And he didn't want to imagine what they might do to a woman. Almost subconsciously, he checked the sight on his rifle. One way or another, MacLeod knew Miriam would never enter Gesiowska Prison.

With a leap he cleared the narrow open passageway that separated Gesia 122 and Gesia 120, then shouldered open the door to Gesia 118 and started down the stairs, taking them three and four at a time. The building was abandoned and his steps echoed as he pounded down the stairwell. Avram had once described to him the Ghetto before the cattle cars, how the Germans had forced nearly half a million people behind the Wall, crammed ten and fifteen to a room, but the Ghetto MacLeod knew was practically a ghost town.

He kicked open the door of a first-floor apartment whose windows fronted the prison. He passed through the kitchen, where a pot of rotted food stood on the stove. As he moved into the living area, he could see the dust-covered dining table still carefully set for dinner, patiently waiting for the family whose meal was so violently interrupted to return. He opened the front window, looked out cautiously. Miriam and her guards were approaching, less than a hundred yards away. MacLeod readied his rifle. "Any time now would be fine, Avram," he muttered.

Out in the street, as the prison came into view, Miriam realized her time was running out. Rescue was not coming. Any escape she made, whether by foot or by death, she would have to make on her own. Her arms still awkwardly bound behind her neck, she swung back hard, catching the greasy Polish officer in the throat with her elbow, hoping that in his surprise he'd loosen his hold on her. Instead, he threw her to the ground.

"Bitch!" he screamed.

As she lay in the street, he drove the steel toe of his jackbooted foot brutally into her stomach, dragging her across the sharp cobblestones. She cried out in pain and struggled to move away as he drew his foot back and rammed it home again.

Signal or no signal, MacLeod would not stand by and watch Miriam beaten to death. He was out the window and into the street before the third steel-toed blow found its mark.

One of the guards saw him coming at them and shouted out an alarm. "*Uwaga!* Watch out!" He fired off a shot at MacLeod that missed wildly. Before the guard could shoot again, MacLeod fired at him on the run, hitting him in the shoulder. The guard dropped his rifle and fell to the ground in agony, cradling his useless gun arm. At the sound of gunfire, the Polish officer and his second guard turned toward MacLeod, leveling their weapons at him.

"Now would be the time!" MacLeod called out to Avram, not really expecting him to hear.

The two Poles fired simultaneously. MacLeod hit the

ground and rolled, dodging the volley. If nothing else, at least he'd drawn their attention away from Miriam.

Rolling to his feet again, he fired off another shot. It barely missed the officer and whizzed dangerously close to Miriam, who had struggled to her knees and was attempting to stand behind him. *"Vart doh!"* MacLeod called to her, and she obediently dropped back to the ground.

The second guard fired his rifle again and caught MacLeod in the thigh. MacLeod stumbled from the impact, cursing loudly, but managed to keep on charging, closing the ground between them. Mentally, he fought to block out the pain, block out the pain, concentrate on raising the rifle, aiming the rifle, firing the rifle. His bullet hit the second guard squarely in the gut, throwing him back a yard or more before dropping him in the gutter.

Suddenly, MacLeod could sense the presence of another Immortal coming closer. "About bloody time," he mumbled under his breath as he charged, then dodged as the remaining officer fired his pistol. MacLeod could feel the hot rush of the bullet just inches from his head. He spun and fired twice in quick succession, dropping the officer where he stood.

Allowing himself a quick sigh of relief, MacLeod hurried to where Miriam lay in the street, curled in a tight ball to protect her injured belly. *"Alts iz gut,"* he reassured her. Out of the corner of his eye, he could see a German cargo truck barrel around the corner, Avram at the wheel. Better late than never, MacLeod thought. He bent down and began to untie Miriam's hands. "Everything's all right."

Suddenly, blam! and a bullet tore into MacLeod's arm. Through the red-rush of pain, MacLeod looked up to see five guards from Gesiowska, uniformed Germans and Poles, running down the street toward him, guns drawn and firing. MacLeod raised his rifle to fire at the closest German.

Click.

Nothing. Out of ammo. Shit.

"Avram!" he called out. The cargo truck drove directly for the Gesiowska reinforcements. "Avra—" the impact of the German bullet as it ripped into his stomach knocked the air from his lungs. As he fell to his knees, eyes wide with shock, he fought to retain consciousness. He could barely hear Avram scream out from the truck—

"Protect Miriam!"

With what felt like his last ounce of strength, MacLeod managed to throw his body across Miriam, protecting her body with his own. Avram's truck erupted in a tremendous ball of red-gold flame in the midst of the prison guards. MacLeod turned his face away from the intense heat and blinding light. Then something metal seared into his side, and his world faded to black.

"Duncan? Duncan, please . . . please wake up. Duncan?"

As MacLeod began to come back to life, he could hear Miriam's voice, filled with terror. "God in Heaven, help me. Duncan!" Beneath him, as feeling was slowly restored to his body, he could feel her try to move, trying to escape from under what she must have thought was MacLeod's bloody corpse pinning her to the cobblestones. The more her frail, undernourished body fought and failed to free herself, the more panicked she became. "Oh, God, no . . . please, no . . ." she sobbed, struggling. He wanted to comfort her, but speech and motion had not yet returned to his body.

By the time he was finally able to roll to one side, freeing her, she was nearly hysterical. She turned and looked at him in horror. "You were . . . you were . . . dead," she said, barely able to catch her breath

"Miriam, I'm fine, really," he consoled her. He untied the bonds that held her hands. Immediately, without thought, she crossed her arms in front of her to shield her nakedness. MacLeod tried to explain, "I just blacked out. Must've hit my head when I fell." He gave her what he hoped was his most sincere and endearing smile. "C'mon, we've gotta get out of here before more company comes." He scooped her up in his arms as if carrying her over a threshold, and they disappeared into a nearby alley before more soldiers arrived to investigate the explosion.

Avram found them in a stairwell of an empty building several streets away from the prison. Miriam, wrapped in MacLeod's shirt, sat on an upper stair, head against the wall for support, still a little dazed. MacLeod, now shirtless, cleaned the cuts and abrasions on Miriam's face as gingerly as he could with some water he'd found.

"Yeow!" Miriam flinched away as his handkerchief dabbed at the pistol gouge beneath her eye.

"We have to get the gravel out or it won't heal," MacLeod explained. "Just a little more, then I'll stop. I promise ... okay?" His voice was tender, his touch gentle. Miriam sighed, nodding, and closed her eyes, allowing him to continue.

"How's our heroine?"

At the sound of Avram's voice from the bottom of the stairwell, Miriam's eyes flew open. "Tzaddik?" she called out, and then saw him coming up the stairs. "Tzaddik, you're alive!" His shirt lay in shreds on his back, his trousers torn, but he was whole and alive. In his arms he carried two rifles, a pistol and an ammo belt he had liberated from their owners before fleeing the scene of the crime. Miriam jumped up to meet him, eager to touch him, to make sure he was real, but a sharp pain tore through her belly when she moved too fast. Startled, she started to fall and immediately MacLeod's strong arms were there to catch her, and he helped her gently down to the steps again.

"Some cuts, a lot of bruises," MacLeod filled Avram in. "Probably some nightmares she'll never be rid of, but nothing we can do about that right now. I'm concerned about what's going on inside here, though." He touched Miriam's midsection, which she was cradling protectively. "We should find Dr. Cohen." Dr. Israel Cohen, one of the only physicians left in the Ghetto, was a ZOB partisan who during the January uprising had proven himself equally skilled with a grenade as with a scalpel.

"No!" Miriam protested. "There's no time. I have to see Anielewicz. As soon as we can. It's urgent." Using the handrail, Miriam managed to get back to her feet.

If Miriam needed to see the ZOB leader that urgently, MacLeod realized her news had to be grim. "The *Aktsia*?" he asked, resigned to the answer he knew he'd hear.

"Tonight. The Germans strike before first light."

MacLeod and Avram exchanged a look, and Avram handed him the weapons he'd scrounged. Then Avram put an arm around Miriam's waist. "Anielewicz is at the Mila Street base.

Can you walk?" He helped her gingerly down a step, then another, and when the shooting pain did not return, she pulled away from him and started down the stairs under her own power.

"Looks like I'll have to," she said as she reached the bottom landing and turned toward Avram with a little lopsided smile, the best her bruised face could manage. "You seem to have blown up the only working transportation in the Ghetto."

Juggling the rifles, MacLeod attempted to put his jacket back on. "Hell of a signal, Avram. Next time, you might try whistling."

"Hey, stop with the kvetching," Avram protested, "it worked, didn't it? Three of the bastards dead, another five out of commission—admit it, Errol Flynn couldn't have done it better," he said, invoking the name of one of his heroes in the American films he used to like to watch before the war.

"Errol Flynn would have used a stunt man," MacLeod groused as he followed them down the stairs.

Chapter Twelve

MacLeod and Avram escorted Miriam across the Ghetto to the ZOB headquarters in an old building on Mila Street where she could meet with Anielewicz, the ZOB commander, and be tended to by Dr. Cohen. After they dropped her off safely, MacLeod had thought they'd return to their unit to prepare for the coming confrontation. But Avram had other ideas.

He led MacLeod into an apartment building a few blocks away at Mila Street 18. They passed through the lobby to a rear hallway, then down a flight of stairs into an empty basement. Avram knocked twice on a section of the wall that looked no different than the walls around it. MacLeod knew it was the entrance to an underground bunker.

"Tell Shmuel, Tzaddik's here," Avram announced to the empty room. They could hear locks turning, then a section of the wall swung out. They had been granted admission to the bunker beneath Mila 18.

The guard at the door was a big, hulking lug who didn't so much talk as he did grunt as he gestured them down the stairs, and MacLeod couldn't remember seeing him before at any of the ZOB meetings or drills. And a face like that one he knew he would've remembered.

"Who's that?" MacLeod whispered to Avram, as they started down the stairs to the *malina*. Avram shushed him with a wave of his hand.

"Later."

The stairwell was a long one, the bunker far deeper than any MacLeod had seen so far, and there was an odd quality to the light. It was a few moments before MacLeod realized that the light seemed strange because it was coming from light-bulbs in the ceiling. He'd grown so used to candles and oil lamps in the power-deprived Ghetto, he'd nearly forgotten what electric light was like. "Avram, what *is* this place?" he hissed in his comrade's ear.

Avram took a quick look over his shoulder to make sure they were out of earshot of the bruiser manning the entrance. "Welcome to the gangsters' lair, MacLeod."

"Gangsters?"

"You know. Dillinger, Capone, Cagney. 'You'll never take me alive, coppers,' all that stuff—gangsters."

"James Cagney is an actor, Avram, not a gangster," MacLeod corrected.

"Gangster, actor, what's the difference?" Avram said as they continued down the stairs. "Anyway, Shmuel Issachar is the king of the thieves, pickpockets, blackmailers, hired killers—name your vice, he's probably got a piece of it. Chicago hasn't got a lock on corruption, you know."

"And this place is his?" MacLeod looked around in the bright, steady light as they reached the bottom of the stairs. On either side of him, the corridor stretched on for hundreds of yards. He could hear voices through some of the open doorways, and occasionally someone would move from room to room down the hallway.

"When the king needs a place to hole up from the Nazis, he builds the Taj Mahal. Generators, hot and cold running water, game room, library. Rumor has it if the *Aktsia* doesn't start soon, old Izzy's putting in a pool over the summer." Avram pointed out a large, broad-shouldered man moving quickly toward them down the corridor. "Speak of the devil."

"Tzaddik!" Issachar engulfed the smaller man in a bearish hug. "It's been far too long!"

Avram grinned and bore it. "Shmuel, this is—"

"Duncan MacLeod!" Issachar released Avram abruptly and turned to MacLeod. "I've heard so much about you."

"I'm sure you have." MacLeod found something obscene about the gangster's pudgy hands and fatty chins in a city where starvation was the way of life.

Issachar laughed. "A rat can't shit in the Ghetto without me knowing about it. Isn't that right, Tzaddik?" Without waiting for an answer, the man put a beefy arm around MacLeod's shoulders. "So, they tell me you have connections in the French Underground . . ."

"Later, Shmuel," Avram interrupted, pulling MacLeod away from him. "First we need to talk some business."

"Isn't that a coincidence, business is my middle name. Step into my office, gentlemen." Issachar ushered them into a side room full of fine art and antique furnishings, and a desk to rival King Arthur's round table. "Take a seat," he said as he lowered himself into the thronelike chair behind the desk.

MacLeod noticed two more hulking goons, like the one guarding the bunker's entrance, placed strategically in the room. "We'll stand, thanks," he said.

"Suit yourself," the gangster said. "So, boys, what can I get you? Whiskey? Women?"

"Guns," Avram said with finality. He wasn't buying into Issachar's joviality any more than MacLeod.

The false smile left Issachar's face. "Guns," he repeated. "Now, Tzaddik, my dear boy, what makes you think I can arrange for guns any better than you can?"

"Because arranging them wasn't the problem. We'd already done that for you. One dozen brand-new Russian rifles. That conveniently disappeared two days ago between the Aryan side and the Ghetto." Avram sat on the edge of the enormous desk and leaned into the gangster's face. "Face it, Izzy, I know you've got them. Now I want them."

The gangster leaned forward as well, until he was nose to nose with Avram. "Go away, kid. You're scuffing the furniture. I never heard of your damn guns." Issachar raised his hand, and the two goons hauled Avram off the desk.

"You don't get it, do you?" Avram said as he squirmed from the goons' grasp. "You don't give us back the guns, you'll all be dead by morning. And that includes you, big man, and your entire operation. 'Cause I'll tell 'em all about you. Every damn German I can find. I'll sing like a bird. By tomorrow this place'll be crawling with Nazis, you dirty rat." Behind him, MacLeod worked hard to keep a straight face during Avram's Cagneyesque performance. He'd seen way too many movies.

Issachar blanched at the notion of Avram selling him out to the Germans, but he didn't fall for the bluff. "Get them out of here," he told his men.

MacLeod, who'd watched the proceedings with an air of detached interest, spoke up, shaking his head. "Oh, dear. De Gaulle isn't going to like this, Issachar. He'll not like this at all."

"What? What about de Gaulle?"

Seeing he had the mobster's interest, MacLeod milked the part for all it was worth. "Well, I didn't want to tell anyone"— he looked suspiciously at Avram—"but that's the real reason de Gaulle sent me here. To establish a supply line from the French Resistance through Warsaw to the Russians and back. You name it—arms, equipment . . . art . . . *gold* . . ."

"Gold?" Issachar echoed.

"And since you've got similar operations already in place, I thought you and your people would be perfect to recommend for the job. But if you can't even keep track of a dozen guns"—MacLeod laughed at the notion—"then I guess I'll just have to find someone else." He sighed and started from the room.

"Wait, wait," Issachar said. "Guns. Maybe we do have some guns." He motioned to one of his goons. "Go see if we have the boy's guns. Go!"

"And ammunition," MacLeod called after the man, as the goon hurried from the room.

Issachar smiled broadly. "Of course, ammunition. What's the use of guns without ammunition? You'll tell that to de Gaulle, right?"

They left Mila 18 with a dozen rifles more than they had entered with, packed in three wooden boxes. For each rifle, Issachar had come up with twenty rounds of ammunition. Avram laughed as they reached the street.

"What's so funny?" MacLeod asked.

"Izzy didn't steal the ammunition from us. There was no ammo in that shipment. I can't believe you actually got Shmuel Issachar to donate to the cause. You were brilliant!"

MacLeod tried to look humble. "Well, I've done a bit of

acting in my day. Sometimes it comes in handy. And what about you? Was that Cagney you were doing in there?"

"Yeah, what did you think? 'You dirty rat,' " he repeated.

"Frankly, I think you sounded more like Peter Lorre. Maybe gangsters just aren't your style, Avram."

Humph. "Well, at least we got the guns. You take that box, give two of the rifles to Gutman at his base, take the other two back to our unit. I'll deliver these two boxes back to Anielewicz. We'll rendezvous back on the roof."

"Whatever you say, Scarface," MacLeod said, setting off for Gutman's base across the Ghetto.

When Avram and MacLeod met up once again on the roof of the apartment building overlooking the Gesia Street gate, it was well after sundown. Their post was meagerly supplied and sparsely furnished. A battered wooden crate, a stained and tattered blanket. A metal ammunitions box, still stenciled in German, holding a handful of grenades, a few extra rounds of ammo, and a half dozen Molotov cocktails lovingly hand-crafted from old wine bottles during the lull following the January uprising. Over in one corner of the roof, a plunger detonator connected to two thin wires trailing over the side of the building, barely perceptible from the street. The wires disappeared under the sidewalk and eventually connected to a cache of explosives, dynamite mostly, in a carefully constructed cavern dug just inside the Gesia Street gate. It had taken some work, but MacLeod had managed to convince the ZOB leadership to risk most of the explosives they could scrounge on this and a similar mine beneath the Brushmakers' gate. He knew they had to block German access to the Ghetto when the time came, to limit the number of Nazis they'd have to take on at any one time.

"Miriam all right?" MacLeod wondered. He'd dug up a shirt from the closet of someone he knew would not be returning for it. It made him feel like a ghoul, robbing the dead this way, but sometimes it was necessary. He prayed that, somewhere, the original owner might forgive him.

Avram carried a burlap sack with him, which he set down near the crate on which MacLeod sat. "Cohen checked her over. Good news is, no internal injury, no internal bleeding that he can detect. She should be fine. Bad news is, the Germans are still dropping by around four in the morning." He sat down heavily on the blanket with a sigh. "I hate uninvited guests."

"I guess it was inevitable. Doesn't make it any easier, though." As MacLeod spoke, Avram untied the sack and opened it. "I'd had this—I don't know what you'd call it—hope? Dream? That the Germans would keep putting it off until the Russians, or maybe the Americans, could get here."

"You don't honestly believe it would be better with the Russians, do you? You said you'd once ridden with Cossacks. Then you know the Russians feel the same as the Germans."

"I know you're right."

"As for your heroic Allies," Avram went on, "it's obvious by now they just don't care. Shimon Mendelsohn told them. A dozen others, all with the same message. Jan Karski talked to your Roosevelt and your Churchill personally. Zygelbojm went on the BBC from London and told the whole world what was happening here, in Lodz, in Lublin." He began to pull out a few small items from the sack, placing them on the blanket as he spoke. There was no anger in his voice, merely acceptance. He could as easily have been discussing the price of fish at the market. Avram Mordecai rarely wore his anger publicly. "So where are the bombing raids, he asks? Why hasn't anyone blown Auschwitz to hell? Why haven't the great war powers of the West even tried to destroy Treblinka? *I* tried, MacLeod. Me. I'm just one man, but I had to try, even though I failed. Why haven't they? Why? You know why, MacLeod. Because we don't matter. Because to them, the lives of half a million Jews, a million Jews, God only knows maybe *ten* million Jews, just don't matter."

Avram pulled a dusty bottle of wine and three metal cups from his sack. "We have to face it, MacLeod. The cavalry's not riding to the rescue. We're alone in here. All we can do is circle the wagons and try to hang on." He set the cups up carefully on the blanket.

"What are you doing?" MacLeod asked.

Avram pulled out a penknife and set about opening the wine. "This is probably the last bottle of kosher wine left in

Warsaw. I've been saving it for *Pesach* since I found it nearly a year ago."

Although the Jewish calendar had been unfamiliar to MacLeod when he first came to Warsaw, he'd caught on quickly. "Passover starts tomorrow night, not tonight. You're a day early."

"By sundown tomorrow, I don't think anyone's going to be doing any celebrating. If God wants to damn me for starting a day early, then so be it. It would be a shame to waste this—it won't go well with Wiener schnitzel."

The bottle open, Avram set it aside and picked up an old tin can. It was open, and in the bottom was a makeshift wick and a thick layer of wax once melted from burning candles. Actual candles were in short supply, and what few were left were desperately needed to light the *malinas*, the bunkers where the majority of Warsaw's inhabitants would soon be hiding. He offered the can to MacLeod. "Got a light?" As MacLeod pulled out his well-used Zippo and lit the wick, Avram closed his eyes and began to sing in a clear, high tenor.

Boruch Ator Adonoi, Elohainu Melech hor-olum, asher kid'shornu b'mitzvo-sav v'tziornu, l'hadlik nair shel yom tov.

"That was nice," MacLeod said when Avram opened his eyes again.

"A little blessing for the light, such as it is." He took the makeshift candle and set it down so that what little light it threw could not be seen beyond the Wall. Then he began to unwrap the smaller parcels he'd taken from his sack. "I'm afraid it's not much," he said, setting out a few pieces of unleavened bread and two hard-boiled eggs. "I gave most of it to some folks for whom starving to death is more than just unpleasant."

"Eggs? Where on earth did you find eggs?" MacLeod hadn't seen an egg since entering the Ghetto.

"Isn't Rivka amazing? Eggs are a tradition; they represent the triumph of life over death, and she was bound and determined that if there was nothing else, there would be eggs for

Pesach. Oh, that reminds me, Rivka made me solemnly promise to say hello to you. So, hello."

"Rivka did?"

"She's got it bad for you, MacLeod." Avram cracked the egg and began to peel it.

"Rivka?" MacLeod repeated. "She's just a kid."

"So? Tell me you didn't have a crush on someone when you were twelve." Avram thought way back. "Mine was Naomi, the glassblower's daughter. She couldn't have been more than three years older than me, but I thought she was the most beautiful woman in all Jerusalem. I broke more glass that year, just so I could go to their shop . . . I'm surprised my father put up with it."

MacLeod had to smile. Sure, he remembered being in love when he was twelve, too. "I guess it's harmless."

"The poor kid's got nothing left to dream about. She might as well have you." The eggs peeled, Avram picked up the *matzah* and began to sing once again.

Boruch Ator Adonoi, Elohainu Melech hor-olum, ha-motzi lechem min hor-oretz.

The melody was haunting, Avram's voice reaching toward heaven. Then he broke the pieces in half and handed MacLeod his portion. "Blessing for the bread, right?" MacLeod asked.

"You catch on fast, for a *goy*." He picked up the wine bottle and filled one of the three cups, which he placed at the head of the blanket. MacLeod reached for it, and Avram swatted his hand away. "No-no-no," he scolded, "that one's Elijah's." He filled another cup and handed it to MacLeod, who looked at him quizzically. "One cup is set out for the Prophet Elijah," he explained. "It's said that Elijah will come to the seder to bring redemption and rescue his people from oppression and evil."

"Well, if he's coming, I think he picked the right night." MacLeod raised the cup as if to toast, then stopped, setting the cup down. "But first, the blessing for the wine, right?"

"I'm so proud of you," Avram beamed and began to intone the ancient words.

*Boruch Ator Adonoi, Elohainu Melech hor-olum, borai
p'ree ha-gorfen.*

When he'd finished, Avram raised his glass to MacLeod,
then took a drink. Following his cue, MacLeod toasted
Avram. *"L'chayim."*

"Showoff." Avram laughed. "There's one more. You want
to try it with me?"

"Oh, no, no," MacLeod declined with a laugh. "I'll leave
that to you and the angels," and he sat back to listen as Avram
made another joyful noise unto the Lord.

*Boruch Ator Adonoi, Elohainu Melech hor-olum, sh'-hi-
gee-yornu, v'kee-y'mornu, v'higee-ornu, lazman hazeh.*

"So what was that one for?" MacLeod wondered.

Avram translated the Hebrew for him. " 'Blessed art Thou,
O Lord our God, King of the universe, Who has kept us in
life, preserved us, and enabled us to reach this festive season.'
I thought it was appropriate." He picked up a piece of the
matzah and took a bite. "Go ahead, eat. Who knows when
we'll get another chance."

The unleavened bread was much like the soldier's hardtack
MacLeod had known in a dozen campaigns. It was certainly
better than the sea rations he'd known as a ship's pilot.

He'd tried not to think much about food since coming to
the Ghetto. As Avram had pointed out, starvation for him was
a painful annoyance. For the others, it was a daily fight to
stave off death. But as he bit into the egg, he realized it was
possibly the most wonderful thing he had ever tasted. No
sumptuous banquet in a sultan's palace, no culinary delight in
the best restaurants of Paris had ever come close to the grati-
fication MacLeod got from this one simple chicken's egg. It
and the wine were gone much too fast. He looked over at
Avram, wondering if he was having a similar reaction, and
then noticed that Avram was no longer eating. Instead, he sat
cross-legged on the blanket staring into his cup as he moved
it around, watching the light from the nearly full moon reflect
off the ripples in the wine.

"Why is this night different from all other nights?" Avram whispered to himself after a long period of silence.

"Avram?"

Avram looked up at him. "Do you know what Passover is, MacLeod?"

MacLeod laughed. "I may be *goy*, but I'm not stupid." Then he saw the look on Avram's face and realized this was not a time for joking. "It's the night the angel of death slew the firstborn of the Egyptians but passed over the children of Israel. It commemorates God delivering His people out of slavery in the land of Egypt."

"When I was young," Avram reminisced, "my father and I would go to the Great Temple at *Pesach*. We would sacrifice a lamb as the scriptures prescribed, and then we would keep vigil there with the other scholars, discussing Torah until the sun rose. Then the Romans destroyed the Temple. And now *Pesach* is celebrated in the home. In secret, in hiding." He paused for a moment, thinking, remembering, reliving. "In the middle of the fifteenth century, my brother-in-law and I were stoned to death at Passover. The enlightened citizens of Rome said the wine we drank was the blood of young Christian boys." He set the cup down hard and wine sloshed out onto the ground, onto the blanket, putting out the sputtering candle. "Three thousand years later, we're still slaves, MacLeod. If it's not Pharaoh, it's Caesar. Or Tsar Nicholas. Or Hitler. If we're not forced to make bricks in Egypt, we're making bombs in Poland. When does deliverance come? Look at us, still waiting for the angel of death. When does Elijah come to give us back the Promised Land?"

Suddenly, MacLeod hushed him with a raised hand and a look. Noise on the stairs. Avram stood and pulled his pistol as MacLeod moved to the door. "*Vo?*" MacLeod called out.

"*Jan-Warsaw,*" a woman's voice answered.

The correct password. MacLeod opened the door, and Miriam came out onto the roof. "You're looking better," MacLeod noted. After briefing the ZOB leadership, she'd had a chance to wash and change. But it was obvious the shirtdress she wore buttoned firmly from chin to ankle was from some earlier lifetime—the short sleeves only emphasized how reed-thin her arms had grown. She had to belt it tightly at the waist to keep it from gapping open.

She went directly to Avram. "Anielewicz has called a unit commanders' meeting in half an hour, Tzaddik. I'm to take your watch with *Der Alte*."

MacLeod never could get used to that nickname—the Old One. The first time he'd heard the name, at a strategy meeting not long after returning to the Ghetto and throwing his lot in with the ZOB, he'd glared at Avram accusingly, but later, after the meeting, Avram had sworn he wasn't behind it. "Hey, I wanted *schmuck*, but they voted me down." Almost everyone in the organization had a pseudonym, Avram had explained— Antek, Kazik, Green Marysia—it was a safety measure. "You get used to it."

"So what's Tzaddik mean?" MacLeod had asked Avram at the time, his Yiddish getting better but still not quite that good.

"It's a kind of a wandering holy man with..." he had trailed off into a mumble.

"With what? I didn't quite hear you, 'holy man,' " MacLeod had pressed.

Avram had looked a little sheepish. "With, ah, mystical powers." MacLeod raised a critical eyebrow. "I had a few close calls, they think I'm lucky, that's all," Avram had said defensively. He pushed a sleeve back, indicating his smoky-dark arm. "And it's pretty obvious I'm not from around here."

"So how did *I* get to be the Old One? You've got a good fifteen hundred years on me."

"Look at yourself, MacLeod, and then look at them. Most of these kids are barely out of school. They should be studying algebra, not carrying guns. You look old enough to be their father. Hell, you look old enough to be *my* father." MacLeod had speared him with a look that promised violence, and Avram quickly backpedaled. "Adoring older brother?"

Wherever the name had come from, he was Der Alte now in all official ZOB communications, and even people like Miriam, who also knew him as Duncan MacLeod, abided by it. She continued her message. "The commanders are to report to Yossel's base in the Brushmakers' Area."

Avram checked that his pistol was fully loaded and holstered it. "Guess this is it then." He shouldered his rifle. "Keep my seat warm." He headed down the stairs.

MacLeod returned to sit at his lookout position on the wooden crate near the edge of the roof overlooking the gate. The streets of the Ghetto were deserted, but beyond the gate, the city of Warsaw teemed with life. Despite the wartime blackout, he could see automobiles moving in the streets, young couples walking home from the picture show. So close, and yet it might as well be worlds away. Miriam stood anxiously near the door for several minutes before MacLeod noted, "It's hard to stand watch from there. Sure you don't want to come over here? Tzaddik left a little food." She hesitated another moment, then pulled a bundle from the canvas pack she carried. She brought it to MacLeod and presented it to him wordlessly.

It was his bloodied, bullet-ridden shirt.

He took the shirt from her, and she searched his face for answers. She never said a word, yet MacLeod knew instinctively the questions she was asking. Who was he? *What* was he? So many times he'd heard those questions, faced the rejection and revulsion that accompanied them. He reached up and gently touched her bruised face, looking deeply into the dark, serious eyes that studied him so intently. He didn't find the fear he expected to see there, only a burning curiosity and something akin to accusation.

"Don't ask me, Miriam, please," he finally said, with a touch of sadness. "I don't want to have to lie to you."

He continued looking at her, intense, unmoving, until she finally pulled away, not satisfied but knowing somehow she would never know. Moving to the ratty blanket where Avram had been, she sat down. She picked up the full cup of wine there with hands that trembled just a touch and took a drink, looking out at the gate and the darkened city beyond it, avoiding looking at him at all costs. MacLeod could sense she had much more on her mind than the mystery of the bullet holes in his shirt. Her second drink from the cup was a deep one. "I think that was Elijah's," he said softly.

Miriam turned back to him with a mournful smile. "Why would Elijah come all the way to Hell to get a drink?"

"I take it you're not"—he indicated the remains of Avram's impromptu seder—"practicing?"

Miriam shrugged. "I thought I believed. Once. Now?" She reached for the bottle and poured the last of the wine into the cup. "My parents believed. My neighbors believed. You see what good it did them."

It was a spiritual journey MacLeod recognized all too well. How to justify a loving, caring God when all around the world lay bleeding and dying. Where was God's love in agony, in atrocity, in carnage? He'd traveled that road many times, on countless bloodstained battlefields and by the caskets of those he loved, but still he had no answers. He only had his faith.

He swept aside the seder crumbs and sat on the blanket next to her. "Don't blame God." She turned her head and tried to shrug him off, but he grabbed her forearm, determined she would hear him. "*God* didn't kill your parents, Miriam. The Nazis did."

"*He* let it happen."

MacLeod released her, stunned by the depth of her bitterness. After a moment, he leaned back on his elbows, looking up at the bright field of stars stretched above them. "Do you ever just sit and watch the stars, Miriam?" When she didn't answer, he said quietly, "Some people might say God was there to comfort them at their passing."

"And what do *you* say, Duncan?"

"I say . . . I don't know. I say . . . I hope we find out someday." It was the best he could do. It was the truth.

Miriam took another drink from Elijah's cup, then offered it to MacLeod. He shook it off. "I'd better keep a clear head." He pointed skyward. "That one's Polaris. You can navigate a ship all the way to America by that one tiny star."

She put down the cup and sat with her arms hugged around her knees, trying to see what it was MacLeod saw in the heavens. "I never thought much about stars, I guess. When there used to be light in the city, you couldn't see them so well."

"You know what else I like about that star, Miriam? That no matter what happens, she'll still be there. The Nazis will be gone a thousand centuries and Polaris'll still be shining, leading people home."

Miriam said nothing, lost in her own thoughts, lost in the stars. After a while, MacLeod pulled out his watch, checked the time. Still nearly four hours until the Germans were expected. And if there was one thing he had learned, the Germans would be punctual. He closed the watch and slid it back in his pocket.

"I would have been twenty in June," Miriam said so quietly he barely heard her. He couldn't tell if she meant to speak to him or just to the stars.

"Miriam, you can't think that way," he protested.

She continued on as if she hadn't heard him. "I wanted to go to University. Maybe study philosophy. Kant and Buber. Hegel . . ." She paused for a moment, apparently deep in thought, then asked, "Do you think that's silly, Duncan? For a woman to study philosophy?"

"No, of course not." He took her hand in his, rubbing it in encouragement. He knew that listening was the best way he could help her now.

Miriam kept on looking at the sky. "I used to dream that maybe I'd meet someone there, someone sophisticated, an intellectual—maybe even a poet. And he'd love me. We'd travel, we'd go all over the world together, see everything together." MacLeod could hear the tears coming, although she was trying her best to hide them. "Paris is very beautiful, isn't it, Duncan?"

"Yes, it is," he whispered, "very beautiful."

"I wanted to see Paris. I wanted to raise a family. I wanted to grow old with someone who loved me. Was that so much to ask? And now—" Her voice broke and she swallowed a sob.

MacLeod put his arm around her shaking shoulders. "Miriam, you don't know that."

She finally turned from the sky to look at him, her eyes bright with tears. "We die their way or ours, Duncan. That's the choice. You know what we're up against. There are no provisions for winning." She was vehement. "Either we're led like sheep to the ovens or we go down fighting, but there's not an option left for *living*. Not anymore. Not in this lifetime." MacLeod watched her face as she fought to control the anger and frustration, but it was too much. She hung her head in her hands and finally allowed the strength of her sobs to over-whelm her. "Sometimes . . . I just wish . . . I'd never been born . . ."

"Miriam, no . . ." MacLeod reached out to her, gathering her in his arms, and she melted into his chest, her tears anointing his shoulder as she wept. He stroked the back of her hair. "You can't grieve for what hasn't happened yet—what may never happen. You have to celebrate each moment you *have* been given, like it's a gift from God." His arms around her in a comforting embrace, he rocked her back and forth like a child.

"Some gift," he heard her say in a small voice, but gradually the tremor of her sobs quieted until she lay still against his chest.

After a time, while he held her close listening to the sound of her breathing, Miriam stirred. She reached up to him, wrapping her arms around his neck. She placed a kiss on the base of his throat.

"Miriam?"

Slowly, her lips traced the line of finely articulated muscle connecting shoulder and jaw.

"Miriam, what—" He drew in a sharp breath as her teeth brushed the sensitive area where his head joined his body, the vulnerable place that was his sole defense between life and everlasting death. Emboldened by his reaction, Miriam sat up on her knees so she could bathe his face with her kisses. She tangled one hand in his hair and tilted back his head, kissing him hard on the mouth.

MacLeod pulled back—"Miriam, wait"—but her lips urgently sought his again. He grabbed her face with both hands and held her still in front of him. "What are you doing?"

"I want you to make love to me, Duncan." Her voice was breathless, her eyes pleaded with him. "Please . . . I don't want to die without knowing about love." Her eager hands moved to caress his face, fingers tracing the path her lips yearned to follow.

"Sex and love aren't the same, Miriam. You know that." He could feel her pain, her loneliness, her longing welling up inside of her as she stroked the strong, dark ridge of his brow. With the very tips of her fingers, she traced the contours of his lips, the touch of a feather. He could feel his senses begin to awaken.

"Please, Duncan, I want to be touched by someone who cares about me." One fevered hand moved to unfasten his jacket. "I need to be held by someone I care for. Just once." With her other hand she explored the silhouette of his face, the curvature of his ear like someone blind, taking it all in, memorizing the shape, the feel, the sensations. "Please," she said urgently. "Now. Before the Germans come. Show me what it's like to be a woman. Make love to me."

His senses coming sharply into focus, MacLeod looked at Miriam with new eyes. Her bleached hair tied simply back, her face free of the makeup she usually wore to look older to her contacts on the Aryan side, she projected a bittersweet innocence even through the cuts and bruises. She was so very young and fragile. And beautiful. He'd never allowed himself to see how beautiful she was before. But behind the facade of the brave, dispassionate ZOB courier was a young woman barely out of her teens, scared and vulnerable. He was torn. "Miriam, I . . . I can't. We can't."

"Duncan, please, don't say no." Her voice took on an edge of desperation. "I don't want my first time to be like today . . . or some German . . ." The prospect left her speechless and trembling. Her eyes bored into his, filling with tears once again, begging him.

The last thing a wounded psyche like Miriam's needed was sex for sex's sake, loveless, meaningless, mechanical. But he knew that with caring and affection, the act of love could rise above that, become a rite of celebration, an affirmation of life, a ceremony of healing and, as such, not out of place on this night, so different from all other nights. He cared deeply for Miriam, although never until this moment had he thought of her in a consciously sexual way. Perhaps some affection and tenderness could help prepare her spirit for the ordeal he knew would come with the rising sun.

Wordless, he rose to his knees and answered her, moving closer to her face still cradled in his hands, touching her lips with his own, parting those trembling lips and claiming her mouth with his tongue. He felt her shiver ripple through her body and into his own.

He released her for a moment and watched her gasp for air, her body awakening to new possibilities, sensations she was only starting to imagine. Every breath a sigh of longing. He removed his leather jacket and wadded it into a pillow, which he placed at one end of the tattered blanket. As soon as the jacket was off, Miriam began unfastening his shirt with a fierce passion, but her inexperience showed as she fumbled with the buttons. Taking one of her tiny hands in each of his own strong ones, he helped her carefully work each button.

"You're sure you want to do this?" he asked as she pulled the shirttail from his trousers and finished unbuttoning it.

"More than anything in my life," she responded with grave seriousness as she ran her hands under the shirt, up his taut abdomen, and across a chest as firm as steel. She pushed the shirt off each of his shoulders, and he helped her pull it off behind him and throw it aside.

MacLeod leaned forward and kissed her again, pulling her close so their bodies fitted together. He was pleased to feel her tongue dance over his lips, and he opened them, taking her deep inside him. She didn't hesitate, exploring every crevice of his mouth, running her tongue along the slick, hard surface of his teeth. She wrapped her arms tightly around his waist, delighting in the sensation of his naked back rubbing against her palms.

She moved against him as she kneaded the muscles of his back and shoulders, and he could feel the swelling of her breasts grind against his own sensitive chest through the thin, worn cotton of her dress. He took in a deep breath and held it, savoring the sensation. Then he allowed one hand to trail down from where it had rested in her hair, to softly caress her neck, and then her shoulder, before gently cupping a tender breast. She made a sweet little sound in the back of her throat that vibrated deep into his own through their kiss, and he could feel her body respond, straining to reach him through the fabric.

Without breaking the kiss, MacLeod lowered Miriam back onto the blanket, cradling her head on his jacket. Then, with deft hands, he began to unbutton her dress.

Chapter Thirteen

Warsaw: April 18, 1943

"This is the moment we planned for, prepared for, and prayed for. Now is the time to be strong. Not to falter. Not to show fear. And above all, not to lose faith." Mordechai Anielewicz was only twenty-three, but as he paced in front of the gathered unit commanders, gesturing broadly with his hands, outlining strategy, boosting morale, Avram thought he spoke with the wisdom and confidence of a man more than twice that age. "Whether we go to fight in the streets or stand firm in the bunkers, we still resist. Armed Jewish resistance to the Germans is a reality, and, no matter what happens from this moment forward, they can't take that away from us. Or our people. No more will the Jews go peacefully to their deaths. No more!"

They were in close quarters, meeting in the protected basement of an empty butcher shop, and the *"Amen!"* that answered Anielewicz from the throats of the men gathered there resounded from the thick stone walls. He was their elected commander and, since the uprising in January, the de facto leader of the less than fifty thousand Jews surviving of the half a million who once walked Warsaw's streets.

A heavy burden at twenty-three, the fate of a people, but Anielewicz had proven himself equal to the challenge. He had somehow taken Zionists and anti-Zionists, farmers and intellectuals, Communists and Socialists, the devout and the secular, the left and the right, and all the other schisms that had crippled Jewish Warsaw and gotten them to see beyond their ideologies. Avram had once believed that in itself would take a miracle, but now they worked together for a common vision. Some in the ZOB compared him to Eleazar, the heroic commander of Masada. Perhaps, thought Avram, who knew the strengths and weaknesses of both men firsthand, but Avram thought instead of the legends told of Judah Maccabees, who'd led his own small force of poorly equipped Jews against a heartless empire bent on their destruction. But Maccabees had restored the Great Temple to his people; Avram was sorely afraid the most Anielewicz could hope for was to restore his people's honor. Nothing could ever restore the lives of the hundreds of thousands of innocent souls lost in Warsaw alone. Nothing could ever punish their murderers enough.

But if anyone could try, it would be Anielewicz, and Avram followed and supported him like he had no other mortal in nearly two thousand years. From the back of the crowded room, he watched his leader plan for the coming battle. Avram wondered if anyone else was struck by the irony—here on the stone killing floor of the butcher's shop, site of a hundred years of ritual slaughter, the Jews meet to plan the death of their enemies. And very probably, their own.

"Tzaddik?" Anielewicz called to the back, finally getting to Avram. "Your unit?"

"We've set up two stations on opposite corners of Gesia and Smocza. Thanks to the sudden generosity of Shmuel Issachar, each station has a rifle, four or five grenades, and a dozen cocktails. There'll be six fighters in each station, each has their own pistol. Der Alte and I are overlooking the Gesia gate; we're wired for both alarm and the explosive charge in the tunnel under the gate."

It was a run-of-the-mill report. Avram expected Anielewicz to move on to the next unit. Instead, he said in front of all gathered, "I'm still not sure about Der Alte. What's his game? He's not one of us."

"What?" He thought they'd gotten beyond this point months ago. If Avram, who prided himself on his skepticism, had gotten over his doubts about MacLeod's sincerity, he could see no reason why Anielewicz still didn't trust him.

"Take him off the gate, Tzaddik. That mine's too important to risk. Take Glonek up there instead."

"Glonek?" Avram started to push his way to the front of the room. "Glonek is an idiot. He doesn't know anything about explosives. Der Alte's the expert. He's risking his own life to help us, Mordechai." No one present had ever seen Tzaddik angry. The other unit commanders moved back to give him space. "The man *saved* Miriam's life today, for God's sake. What more proof do you want from him?" He stood nose to nose with Anielewicz, two young men who in happier times could be arguing the outcome of a football match, instead arguing over what could mean the life or death of thousands.

"He doesn't belong here," the ZOB leader countered. "What's to keep him from selling us out to the Germans to save his own life?"

Avram wanted to smile a bit in spite of himself. He almost wished he could tell them why that wasn't likely. Instead he said simply, "I trust him with my life."

"Do you trust him with *all* our lives, Tzaddik?"

Avram couldn't blame him. His was an incredible responsibility to bear. As solemnly and sincerely as he could, he impressed upon the young leader, "Yes, Mordechai, I do."

There was complete silence in the room as Anielewicz weighed his faith in Avram against his distrust of MacLeod. Finally, he gave in. "Fine. But God help us all if you're wrong." He moved on to the next unit. "Gutman?"

By the end of the meeting, it was nearly half past one in the morning. The Germans were expected to begin their assault at four. Anielewicz gave the word to the couriers to alert all the fighters to report to their stations and all noncombatants to enter the bunkers they had so carefully prepared over the winter and stay there. Until the end.

One of the youngest commanders, a rabbinical student before God had made other plans for him and placed a rifle in his hands, led them in a brief prayer before they all started back to their units. As the commanders moved to leave, Anielewicz issued his benediction, and his challenge.

"L'shanah habor-or Birushala-yim!"

Next year in Jerusalem.

The final words of the traditional *Haggadah* told every year at the Passover seder. Next year in Jerusalem. They embodied thousands of years of history, of oppression, and most importantly, of hope. They were a beacon uniting the struggle against Pharaoh, against the Romans, against the Tsars, and now the struggle against the Nazis with the day-to-day struggle for life and Jewish identity. With it was the small comfort that the God who rescued his people out of the land of Egypt might somehow deliver them from this evil as well.

As he walked through the dark, deserted streets back to his post on the other side of the Ghetto, vigilant, ready, the words haunted Avram. So many seders celebrated with friends and loved ones in so many lands. Happier times in Spain and Russia, Italy and North Africa, even America—but always the hope that next year they'd celebrate together in the Holy City. But there were so many nights like this one, waiting for the shadow of death to pass over, wondering who among his friends and those he loved would live to see the morning light.

Avram moved silently across the cobblestoned streets. It was a skill he'd learned early on, to not be noticed, to disappear. As a Jew in foreign cities, it had kept him alive more than once. He moved like a ghost through a city of ghosts. Occasionally he could detect weak signs of life—the flutter of an upstairs curtain, shadows dashing furtively between timeworn brick buildings. Mostly he was alone in the dark, alone with the ghosts of Warsaw. Ghosts who had once hoped they, too, would live to celebrate *Pesach* in a Jewish Jerusalem.

Avram himself had returned to Jerusalem only twice since the dark time when the Romans had dispersed his people to the four winds of the earth: once under the Byzantines, once under the Turks. Both times he'd left within a year, unwelcome in the place of his birth. Every street, every hillside was a reminder of what his people once were, once had—and had taken away. The Great Temple, the focal point of his mortal life, gone, destroyed. And in its place, the Dome of the Rock, built upon the blood and ashes of the Jews on the sacred Temple Mount by the followers of Mohammed. He'd vowed he'd never go back until Jerusalem was free once more.

Next year in Jerusalem . . .

He'd crossed out of the occupied Central Ghetto and into block after block of abandoned residences and factories that would never again hear the hum of machinery or the chatter of workers. Once the Ghetto had been bursting with the half million Jews forced behind its Wall. Now, with not even a tenth of its population remaining, most of the Ghetto lay vacant and desolate. This was the territory assigned to Tzaddik's unit, the no-man's-land between the Gesia Street entrance and the Central Ghetto. One last chance to try and stop the Germans before they could reach the last remnant of his people.

Just ahead, he saw a figure dart out of the narrow passageway between two buildings. Immediately, he shrank into the shadows of a nearby doorway. No one should be on this street. Unless they were coming from outside the Wall and had somehow gotten past MacLeod. He drew his pistol and checked it. Footsteps pounded toward him, echoing from the deserted cobbles, running.

Closer. Avram braced himself, cocked the weapon. Then he reached out of the doorway and grabbed the runner.

Rivka screamed.

Avram released her immediately. "Rivka? What are you doing out here?" he scolded, more angry at himself than her for the tragic mistake barely averted. "You should be in a *malina*."

The twelve-year-old, her heart still pounding wildly from her scare, drew herself up proudly, and announced, "I'm not a baby, Tzaddik. I'm a fighter."

Avram always found it impossible to be mad at Rivka's enthusiasm. "Fine, fine, you're a fighter. What are you doing *here*?" he asked with almost fatherly concern.

"Gutman sent me to find Miriam. It's time to report to the unit. Have you seen her?"

"She's at the lookout with MacLeod," Avram answered, and then immediately regretted it as Rivka took off wildly down the street once again. "Rivka, wait!" He started after her.

"I'm sorry, Duncan," Miriam, her open shirtdress drawn loosely around her, nestled back against MacLeod's naked chest and rested her head contentedly on his shoulder. Her throat and chest glistened with the mingled sweat of their bodies under the fullness of the moon. "I'm so sorry."

MacLeod, clad once again in his trousers, sat on the rooftop holding her close. "Sorry for what?" he murmured, nuzzling her ear.

"Hmmmm, that's nice . . ." she purred, her eyes half-closing. She lost herself in the sensation for a moment, then remembered what she wanted to say. "I'm sorry I acted like such a child, you know . . . before . . ."

Smiling into her ear, he idly caressed one gently rounded breast. "I don't see any children here." He stroked its rosy peak with supple fingers. She inhaled sharply and let it out in a slow rolling sigh as he spoke. "I just see a beautiful woman who knows what she wants and isn't afraid to ask. Nothing to be sorry about."

"Really . . . ?" Her voice caught, then trailed off as Miriam felt his other hand trace a silken path up her bare leg. She had felt drained, emptied from more joy than she had ever imagined it possible to feel, and yet at the same time, energy surged through her at his touch.

"Really," he assured her. "Maybe I should be the one to be sorry."

"What for?" He had absolutely nothing to be sorry for in her eyes.

"I don't know," he said, leaning her back into the crook of his arm, cradling her head and shoulders. She was featherlight. He leaned over her and pushed back the folds of the open dress from her belly, exposing the blackish purple contusions, the brand of the Pole on her fragile body. "Maybe for this." Slowly, his lips touched the bruises and he gently covered them with tender kisses, as if he could somehow erase them from her body.

He heard a sob escape her lips and pulled back, afraid he'd hurt her. But one look at her face, transported, told him otherwise. "Or maybe this," he whispered, and gently kissed the gouge beneath her eye.

"You didn't start the war, Duncan," she said after a moment.

"No," he agreed, "but I wish it was within my power to take you away from it."

"You already have." Miriam arched her body in his arms so her mouth could reach his once again, her dress falling back, baring her shoulders, her breasts, her eager body to his touch.

MacLeod's mouth traveled from her lips down her throat. Miriam tilted her head back over his arm, exposing more skin to his caress. Tongue and lips guided by his fingers, he roved over her throat, lingered on the hollow at the join of head and torso, then buried his face between her breasts.

And suddenly felt the telltale presence of another Immortal.

MacLeod closed his eyes and sighed. He'd have to speak to Avram about his timing. But before he could begin to say a word to warn Miriam to dress, the rooftop door flew open and MacLeod found himself looking up into Rivka's widening eyes.

"Duncan?"

At the sound of Rivka's shocked young voice, Miriam sat up with a start and quickly pulled her dress closed, covering her body. Mortified, she turned her back on the twelve-year-old, unable to look her in the eyes.

"Rivka . . . ?" MacLeod was flustered. As he tried to stand up, Avram came pounding up the stairs behind Rivka.

Avram took in the strained tableau and understood the situation immediately. He quickly placed one hand over Rivka's eyes and spun her around with the other so they both faced the opposite side of the roof.

"Hey!" she protested, squirming in his grasp.

"Didn't anyone ever teach you to knock?" Avram scolded her playfully as MacLeod helped gather Miriam's things. "And you, *goy*," he said over his shoulder to MacLeod with a laugh, "no one ever teach you to lock the door?"

MacLeod helped Miriam button her dress in a fraction of the time it had taken him to lingeringly unfasten it. "What is she doing here?" MacLeod wanted to know.

"Miriam's *supposed* to be reporting to her station," Rivka said with more than a trace of petulance. "Gutman sent me to tell her." She squirmed harder. "Let me *go*, Tzaddik."

Avram looked back at MacLeod, who signaled it was safe. Avram released her. She turned around with an icy glare for Miriam and MacLeod. "It's time to go," she announced.

MacLeod moved to her, touched her arm, "Rivka, I'm sorry," but she shrugged him off and ran down the stairs.

Miriam, with a weak smile, turned to follow. "I guess I should go."

Avram gave her a brotherly peck on the cheek. "Be careful, *tsatskeleh*."

She smiled at the term of endearment and moved to the doorway. Then she stopped, one last look at MacLeod.

"God be with you, Miriam," he said.

For a moment she looked tearful, then she smiled again. "And also with you, Duncan MacLeod." She closed the door to the rooftop behind her as she left.

Avram moved across the roof toward MacLeod. He picked up the empty wine bottle and regarded it with a wry smile. "I asked you to keep my seat warm. I didn't say get it hot and sticky."

"You knew, didn't you?"

Avram shrugged. "I suspected." MacLeod was silent, clearly troubled. Avram put a hand on his bare shoulder. "You did the right thing."

"Did I?" MacLeod wasn't so sure. "Miriam's so . . . young."

Avram's eyes were frank, his words brutally honest. "And she's probably not going to get much older. None of them are. And they know it." MacLeod looked away, blinked hard. "Look, I know you don't want to hear it, but that's our reality here. Old morals, old standards, they don't apply anymore. You do what you have to do to survive. That's the only commandment we've got left."

MacLeod's voice was tight. "It's not fair."

"No, it's not," Avram answered, matter-of-factly. "No one should have to die like this. Least of all someone like Miriam."

"Then why can't we stop it?"

Avram could hear the weight of centuries in his friend's cry. It wouldn't help him to know that more centuries didn't bring the answers. They only brought more pain. "Look, Duncan, you made her happy. You gave her light in the middle of darkness. You let her know she was worth something when the whole world tells her she's more worthless than a dog. It's a *mitzvah*, MacLeod, a blessing. Don't rob it of its joy."

MacLeod looked around for his shirt. "What about Rivka?" He found it in a heap behind the munitions crate. He shook it out and slipped it on.

"She'll get over it. Or she won't. She's just a kid. Kids' dreams get shattered all the time, and they survive it. She will, too."

But sometimes dreams are all you have to get you through, MacLeod thought. But he knew Avram was right, they had more urgent things to worry about than the hurt feelings of a twelve-year-old. In less than two hours, the army of the devil would be massing outside the gates.

He and Avram passed the intervening time in relative silence, each preparing for the coming struggle in his own way. Back in the Highlands, the warrior MacLeods would prepare for battle with glad hearts, with boisterous songs and loud war cries, with the clanging of steel to bolster their courage and throw fear into the hearts of their enemies. A glorious sight it would be, the clans arrayed for battle, confident in their bravery, sure in their victory, raising a ruckus that could wake the dead. But here, so far from the green fields of Scotland, victory was far from sure. And it was a very long time since the prospect of war had gladdened MacLeod's heart.

May-Ling Shen, who had helped open the door to the Eastern philosophies to him, had taught him another way to prepare—the *kata*. Visualizing the opponent, practicing defense and attack over and over first in the mind, then again on the practice floor, calmed and readied the spirit for battle. But that required an adversary whose method of attack could be known, whose moves could be predicted, and who would fight honorably. The evil facing them was none of those.

In the end, after physically checking his weapons a dozen times, making sure they were cleaned and armed, ensuring that their makeshift incendiary devices were free of cracks and leaks, and then making sure again, he resorted to a battle-preparedness technique centuries older than himself—vigil. He sat in silence under the stars, unmoving under the nearly full moon that ushered in the Passover, and opened his heart and his mind . . . to God, to the universe, to whatever source whence enlightenment might come. But none came.

After checking and double-checking the detonator and

wires that led to the store of explosives buried beneath the Gesia Street gate, Avram prepared himself in a similar fashion. But where MacLeod had been able to empty his mind, Avram's was full of thoughts and images he couldn't erase. The light fading from his beloved Deborah's eyes as she accepted death at his hands over enslavement to a Roman master on another Passover eve. The defiance in the face of his teacher and friend Rabbi Isaac as he offered his mortal life to the sword of the Crusaders storming the archbishop's palace in Mainz, a place that should have been sanctuary for all. And the children torn from their mothers' arms in the streets of Warsaw, the mothers sent to certain death in the ovens of Treblinka, their squalling children to God only knew where.

His nostrils filled with the smoldering ruin that was once the tiny Russian *shtetl* of Onyetka, and he choked from the memory. He could hear the agonized screams of those consumed by flames as the Great Temple fell around them, their escape blocked by the mighty Roman legion. Slowly, he began to take hold of the memories, to focus. Painstakingly, he folded them together in his mind, building a foundation. And on that foundation of anger and hate and pain, Avram carefully centered himself. When he finished, he was ready to face the enemy. He was more than ready.

MacLeod spotted the shadows at a couple of minutes past four. A truck passing outside near the Wall, stopping every fifty yards or so to discharge a handful of Germans. MacLeod indicated them to Avram with a quick nod of his head as he dropped to all fours on the rooftop. Avram joined him.

"Guess they're here to make sure we don't try to leave the party early," MacLeod said as he made his way over to the detonator.

"I'd never think of being so rude," Avram said. So far there was no action at the gate itself.

Silently they waited, watching over the narrow brick wall that formed the boundary of the rooftop. All around the outside of the Ghetto Wall they could see the German soldiers taking up their positions, readying their weapons. But MacLeod knew that these soldiers were simply laying siege to the Ghetto, ensuring that no one got out. It remained to be seen how many soldiers would be poured into the Ghetto it-self.

Suddenly, off in the distance, the sound of gunfire. Sharp, staccato blasts followed by an explosion. "Ours," Avram identified the sounds and their direction. "Nalewki Street. Couple of rifles and a grenade." Then the sound of automatic fire returned and more grenade explosions. The fiery light from the Molotov cocktails flared and waned in the darkened Ghetto. The battle had been engaged in earnest. Avram could tell that MacLeod was reining himself in, that he wanted to be at the heart of the action so badly he could taste it. "Soon enough," he counseled. "Our time will come soon enough."

It was hard on them both, not knowing what was happening in the Central Ghetto, hearing the guns and the bombs and not knowing who was falling, who was dying. But their duty was to their station—this would not be the only battle, just the first in a long campaign. At one point their spirits were lifted as they heard a loudspeaker outside the Wall warn the men stationed there *"Juden haben Waffen! Juden haben Waffen!"* The Jews have weapons—they'd surprised the Germans after all. But the element of surprise would only work in their favor so long.

Finally there was movement outside the Gesia Street gate. Armored vehicles and a troop transport. Avram's unit had placed several abandoned cars and an old wagon in front of the gate to block it, and it was obvious the Germans were having trouble getting it open. But not for long.

With a tremendous crash, the massive wooden gates were torn asunder. Wood fragments flew in all directions as an armored tank barreled through the gate, pushing the cars out of its way as if they were toys, splintering the wagon beneath its treads. As the tank entered the Ghetto, MacLeod raised the plunger on the detonator. Avram signaled to MacLeod to detonate the mine, but MacLeod shook him off.

"Wait for it . . ." MacLeod hissed. His fingers were itching to blow the bastards to kingdom come but he held back until both the tank and the transport were in range of the mine.

MacLeod pushed down on the plunger with all his strength. The answering explosion knocked him back from the edge of the roof as Gesia Street opened up like a pit from Hell, fire and shrapnel erupting from its bowels. Cobblestones flew and walls crumbled. Windows were shattered for blocks around. The choking cloud of smoke and dust was blinding.

MacLeod crawled back to the edge of the roof and peered through the dust at the street below, where the tank lay on its side, a behemoth beached by its own weight, belching smoke. Behind it, what remained of the troop transport was in flames. He could hear the screams of soldiers as they tried to escape the wreckage. Their luckier comrades retreated on foot back through the gate in terror, abandoning their dead and wounded.

Avram joined him at the edge of the building. His face was eerily highlighted in the glow of the burning transport. "You ain't seen nothing yet," he laughed as they watched the officers scurry back into the darkness beyond the Wall.

Chapter Fourteen

Paris: The Present

MacLeod watched the officers frisk Maral, his hands clenched in fists of impotent anger at the brusque manner in which she was being handled. When the search turned up nothing suspect, another security officer appeared with a portable detection wand. By this time, a handful of spectators had gathered—other security personnel, junior members of the diplomatic entourages, even Omar al-Sayyeed, one of the delegates, stayed to watch.

Maral hadn't moved, hadn't spoken, knowing it would do no good to protest, they would find what they wanted to find. They always did. The hum of the security wand stayed low and quiet as they moved it slowly up her body, then suddenly sang out as it passed her shoulders. She and MacLeod realized what the problem was at the same moment. Making no sudden moves, she raised her hands and pulled the iron gazelles from her hair. Her hair tumbled down below her shoulders but she paid it no mind, handing the combs to a security officer with a steady gaze that said quite firmly she was not embarrassed and by no means ashamed.

MacLeod, on the other hand, was mortified. If not for his gift, so innocent in its intent, this public little drama would never have happened. The small crowd disbursed, al-Sayyeed looking a bit smug, and the security guard gave her back the combs and her purse once a final pass with the wand proved she carried no other "dangerous" objects. "I'm sorry," MacLeod said when he was allowed to rejoin her.

"You, Duncan? It's my fault. I should have known better,"

she said, unsuccessfully attempting to repin her hair as they walked down the corridor. "Everything was so confused this morning, I just wasn't thinking." Passing a ladies' washroom, she turned to Assad. "Do you mind?" Taking it in stride, Assad banged loudly on the door several times, then opened it, calling out to see if anyone was using it. Hearing no response, he went in to secure the room while MacLeod and Maral waited outside. After a few moments, he returned, indicating it was safe. "I'll be right back," she said, and went in.

MacLeod and Assad stood outside the washroom in strained silence. MacLeod's attempts to make conversation— "Is this your first time in Paris?" "How about that World Cup final?" "So, what do you do when you're not a spy?"— seemed to fall on deaf ears. He was relieved when Maral emerged a few minutes later, every hair in its proper place.

"I should go in now," she said. "It's nearly time." Assad led the way down the hall.

The guards stationed at the negotiation room opened the doors as Maral arrived. The centerpiece of the room was a long oaken table, Arabs ranged along one side, Israelis along the other. The Bloods and the Crips, ready to rumble, MacLeod thought. He entered the room with Maral and Assad, but Farid stopped them just inside the door, pointing to MacLeod. "No," the security chief said very firmly. "Out."

This time, MacLeod knew not to argue. While his first thought was Maral's protection, he could sense immediately he was an outsider in this place where two warring peoples were trying to work out their future, and his stranger's presence would not be appreciated here. With a nod of his head to Farid and a wink of encouragement to Maral, he made a quick exit from the room.

He started down a corridor, checking out the building. He noted the video surveillance system and the placement of the security forces posted throughout the area—Israeli, Palestinian, and French personnel working together to ensure the safety of the negotiations—and his confidence in their ability to keep Maral safe rose. After completing a circuit of the Ministry of Education facility and seeing for himself that everything seemed well in hand, MacLeod left the building reassured.

A few members of the press corps perked up as he came out, but for the most part the press were killing time until the delegates would reemerge by playing cards in the back of news vans, gossiping with their colleagues, catching a quick nap. MacLeod skirted around them and started down the street.

As he walked, the smell of coffee called out to him. He realized that in the confusion of the morning, he never did get that cup of coffee he wanted, much less have time for any breakfast. He followed the scent of freshly ground beans as they lured him to a small coffeehouse less than a block from the building that housed the negotiations. The perfect spot for a leisurely newspaper, a pot of coffee, and a bite to eat.

But just as he was about to enter the café, he was alerted to the presence of another Immortal nearby. His eyes scanned the street, but the source was not evident. *So much for that coffee,* MacLeod thought, moving off in the direction of the sensation.

He strode cautiously down the street, his hand itching for his *katana,* but not here, too public. MacLeod contented himself with the knowledge that it was at hand should he need it. He passed several shops and a vacant storefront. Closer, but still no Immortal. Beyond the empty store, an alleyway.

There. MacLeod stopped just short of the alley, collected himself for a moment, then turned the corner, ready for anything.

"Well, if it isn't the *goy!*" *Anything* hadn't really included the sight of Avram Mordecai in a dark suit and a security earpiece, flanked by two more Israeli security men who eyed MacLeod's battle-ready stance suspiciously. Avram, on the other hand, was beaming at him. "Wow, are you out of context."

"Avram? What are you doing here?" MacLeod tried to be circumspect in the presence of Avram's "friends."

"Don't you read the papers, MacLeod? Making sure terrorists don't bring Paris down around our ears before the Jerusalem peace talks are over. Israel calls, and I answer, same as always." Avram turned to his colleagues. "Keep searching along the perimeter. I'll catch up."

As the Israeli security team moved off, MacLeod said, "I

was just going around the corner for a coffee. You got a few minutes?"

"For you, I've got all the time in the world." The two old comrades walked back toward the café. "God, it's great to see you again," Avram said, slapping MacLeod on the arm with almost boyish enthusiasm.

MacLeod had to agree. Although a half a century had passed between them, it seemed like only minutes since they had worked, fought, ate, and died together as one. It felt like they were immediately back in sync, as they'd been in Warsaw. "I tried to find you again after the war. I was afraid you hadn't made it."

"Oh ye of little faith," Avram laughed. "I'm Indestructible Man! Faster than a speeding bullet, more lives than Wile E. Coyote." He paused to open the door to the coffeehouse. "It was chaos after the war. I went through a whole list of new names, new identities, you know how it goes. The British were after me for smuggling refugees into Israel, had to get them off my back."

They took a table by the window, from which they could see the Ministry building, and placed their order. MacLeod explained, "It wasn't until I met Marcus Constantine a few years back that I found out you were still out there raising hell."

"Good old Marcus," Avram said with a fond smile. "I didn't know you two knew each other. Hey, he's invited me for drinks at his place tomorrow night, you should come. Then, when he starts rambling on about the Roman conquest of Galatia, I'll have someone *interesting* to talk to." They shared a laugh.

Their coffees arrived and Avram raised his cup in a toast. "Here's looking at you, kid."

"*L'chayim,*" MacLeod returned.

Avram chuckled. "Showoff." Then his eyes got a far away look and MacLeod realized he was listening to his headset. Avram set his coffee cup down in a daze, concentrating, then his eyes focused and he swung into action, pushing back from the table. "Sorry to stiff you, Duncan. Put it on my tab. Duty calls." Avram raced out the door.

Through the window, MacLeod could see the members of the press scrambling in front of the Ministry of Education building as people hurried out the doors, evacuating into the street. He threw a couple of bills on the table and hurried out after Avram.

Avram pressed through the confused crowd milling in the street outside the building until he reached one of the uniformed French security men trying to maintain order in chaos. "Where's your commanding officer?" Avram shouted over the crowd noise, and the cop indicated his superior, twenty yards away.

Avram ran toward the officer, flashing his ID and yelling, "Get these people out of here! Remember Oklahoma City— the whole block could go!" As he reached the man, he explained more calmly, "Start moving them around the corner, as far away as possible—if that thing blows, this is the last place you want to be." The French officer spoke rapidly into his radio, instructing his men to follow Avram's orders. Before he had even finished, Avram was already racing away into the building.

An Israeli security agent had found a bomb in a second-floor men's room, hidden in the back of a toilet stall. He had immediately called for an evacuation. It was a design all too familiar to Israeli bomb experts. The terrorist organization Hamas had used one exactly like it to destroy an Israeli courthouse in the occupied town of Nabulus only six months before. Avram knew if the bomb detonated, it would take out a good chunk of the Ministry of Education building.

He also knew that this bomb wouldn't actually detonate. It mimicked the Hamas bomb down to the smallest detail, except for a small defect in the wiring. As he was building it, he knew it wouldn't go off because he'd never intended it to go off. Not this time. This bomb, so obviously planted by Hamas, was merely a smoke screen, a ruse to compound the fear, the mistrust, the paranoia that was already rampant between the two negotiating powers. With it Avram hoped to blow open a hole in the negotiations much bigger than any actual explosive device could achieve.

Avram played the part of heroic security agent in the face of danger well, rushing into the threatened building, ensuring that all the delegates had been evacuated, personally shepherding the last few—two Israelis and that Palestinian woman—across the street and around the corner to safety. As they came around the corner, he saw Duncan MacLeod break out of the crowd, through the police line, and run toward him. Avram smiled. Same old MacLeod, always the white knight, rushing to assist him. He started to call to him to let him know everything was under control. "Duncan—"

"Doon-can," the Palestinian woman called out over him, and she hurried to MacLeod. Avram watched him throw his arms protectively around her, and she responded with a hard kiss on MacLeod's lips.

Avram's smile slipped away, and his blood turned to ice. Well, that certainly put a whole new spin on everything. He turned on his heel and started back to the Ministry of Education building to assist in the removal of the Hamas bomb.

Although the wine was sometimes suspect, one could always be assured of a fine brandy in the home of Marcus Constantine. MacLeod leaned back in a leather armchair that smelled faintly of pipe tobacco and old books with a snifter of Constantine's best and listened politely to the curator's tales of the gala opening of his new exhibit the evening before.

"Then, we're standing in the middle of the holographic reenactment of the siege of Alesia and the Minister of Culture says to me"—he cleared his throat dramatically and assumed the officious bluster of the French politician—"'This heroic battle and this magnificent exhibition. I stand in awe of these two great Gallic triumphs!' I didn't have the heart to tell him, A), that the Gauls were crushed at Alesia and, B), that I am not now, nor have I ever been, French." Constantine was amused by the very notion.

"So what *did* you say?" MacLeod was quite curious, as Constantine was often known to speak his mind, damn the consequences.

"Just smiled and nodded, smiled and nodded like any good academic with an eye to future funding."

MacLeod had to laugh. "Really, Marcus, sucking up doesn't seem like your line of work."

"Trust me, after four hundred years of serving Roman emperors, 'sucking up,' as you call it, becomes second nature if you want to survive. Modern academe's not that different than Imperial Rome, truth be told." Constantine raised his glass in mock tribute.

As MacLeod poured himself a bit more from the crystal decanter on the small table between their chairs, Constantine remarked, "So, I saw that Arab woman of yours on the television news last night. Very pretty." MacLeod shot him a look. "What?"

"There's more to her than that, Marcus."

"Oh, please, has the world become so politically correct that a man can't comment on a woman's looks anymore? Or vice versa, for that matter." Constantine threw up his hands with a laugh. "It was a ten-second video clip, Duncan. She may indeed have the intellect of Einstein and the wisdom of Solomon, but in ten seconds I'm afraid all I had time to notice was her lovely face. So sue me. Cigar?" He opened a box of cigars and offered it to MacLeod, who shook his head no. "You really care for her, don't you?"

"We've only known each other a few days," MacLeod said, as if that answered the question.

"Since when did that matter? Or am I more out of touch with the world than I realized?" Constantine asked with a fond smile.

The approach of a fellow Immortal spared MacLeod from answering. "Avram?" he wondered.

Constantine checked the elaborate grandfather clock across the room. "Probably not. Avram phoned to say he'd be a few minutes late. But I've invited another friend to join us. It's rare that a group of us can get together without someone losing their head over it, so I thought I'd take advantage of it. If you'll excuse me . . ." He started for the foyer before the doorbell had even begun to chime.

"I don't believe you two have met," MacLeod heard Constantine say as he returned. "Adam Pierson, this is—"

"Oh, we've met," MacLeod said as he saw Methos lounge in the doorway of the study in his oversize pullover and grungy raincoat. The five-thousand-year-old man was still playing at the perennial graduate student. "But I didn't know you two knew each other."

Methos shrugged out of his raincoat and dropped himself

down on the settee. "It's hard to be a Classicist in Paris and avoid the Big Kahuna of antiquities for very long."

"Glass of wine, Pierson?"

"I don't suppose you have anything that tastes like it was bottled within this century? No, I didn't think so." He propped his Doc Martens up on the coffee table and eyed MacLeod's snifter. "I'll have whatever he's having."

Constantine handed Methos a glass of brandy, then pushed his feet off the furniture. Returning to his seat near MacLeod, he said, "Turns out, we'd met before. I helped him out of a little jam once."

"Marcus . . ." Methos said, a hint of threat in his voice. Constantine gleefully ignored him.

"What was it? Thirty-four? Thirty-five? Our young friend here was Remus, a slave in the household of one Valerius Petronius, Senator, and the horrifying force of nature that was his wife, Druscilla."

"Marcus, I'm warning you . . ."

MacLeod was enjoying the show. He'd never seen Methos squirm quite so much. "*You* were a slave?"

"It was all part of a plan," Methos said a little more petulantly than he probably would have liked. "I was Valerius's *advisor*." He put his feet back up on the coffee table with a loud thud and a glare at Constantine.

"Druscilla the Emasculator, we called her. Wasn't man nor boy on the Palatine Hill safe from her. Voracious she was, absolutely voracious. And Petronius, that poor blind fool, had no idea what was going on. Until the day the Emasculator set her sights on her husband's trusted advisor."

"Look, Marcus, you got your bloody nail. Do you want a pound of flesh now, too?"

MacLeod was intrigued. "So what happened?"

Methos jumped in before Constantine could continue. "Same old ancient saga. I certainly wasn't the first, you can look it up in Genesis 39—I say no, she cries rape, dead slave, game over. *End of story,* okay?"

"Well, not quite the end," Constantine added. "Luckily, Petronius had a certain friend who heard about the incident and rescued young Remus from the cross before he died too many times and helped him out of the country."

"You never touched her?"

It was obvious the idea still horrified Methos. "Touch her? Are you kidding? The woman had six inches and 150 pounds on me—she came near me, I ran like hell. And because of her overactive libido, Caligula became emperor in '37 instead of Petronius. All that work wasted."

"Ah, my friend, but we who remained had to live with Caligula. I think you got your revenge after all," Constantine noted.

Methos slumped back into the corner of the settee. "That's the last time I got involved in politics, let me tell you."

"So that nail in the museum is yours?" MacLeod grinned with smug satisfaction, knowing he had something he could hold over Methos forever.

Methos knew it, too, and was less than pleased. "There, you see, MacLeod, we've all got our crosses to bear. I hope you're happy. Now, can we just move on? No amount of brandy is worth this abuse."

As one, the three men realized there was an Immortal approaching. "Guess that's Avram now. I'll be right back." Constantine excused himself to answer the door, knocking Methos's size twelves from the coffee table as he went by. When he was safely out of the room, MacLeod leaned forward in his chair and whispered to Methos.

"Does Marcus know you're really . . . ?" MacLeod didn't want to say it aloud for fear of being overheard.

"Methos? Not a clue. And I'd prefer to keep it that way, if you don't mind. Otherwise, he'll want to put me under glass and study me for posterity."

Something was still bothering MacLeod. "Why did you come? Small talk with Immortals you've never met has never been your strong suit."

"Just returning a favor I owe Marcus. Besides, I'm perfectly safe. Avram Mordecai hasn't taken a head that wasn't in self-defense in two thousand years. He's too caught up in the affairs of mortals. As long as he doesn't find out about that century I spent as a Samaritan, I'm in no danger from him."

Constantine ushered Avram into the study. "Avram Mordecai, Adam Pierson." Methos reached over the back of the settee to shake his hand, unwilling to relinquish his comfy spot.

"And of course, you know MacLeod. Glass of wine? A little brandy?"

"None for me, thanks," Avram said, seating himself on an ottoman across the room from MacLeod and Methos. Constantine offered him the box of smokes.

"Cigar?"

Avram selected one with a smile. "Whatever your vice, Constantine's your man." Constantine clipped the end of the cigar for him and handed him a lighter. "In the old days, there would have been whores in the back room," Avram said as he lit the thing and took a few preliminary puffs.

"Why do I never get invited to *those* parties?" Methos groused.

"So," Constantine said, settling back into one of the leather armchairs with his own cigar, "I hear you had something of a near miss yesterday."

Avram shrugged it off casually. "When you try to bargain with terrorists, you get what you deserve." He shot a look at MacLeod. "Don't you agree, MacLeod?"

MacLeod wondered where this was leading. "Avram, Hamas planted that bomb, not the Palestinian people. Hamas are your terrorists."

"These days Hamas has more Palestinian support than Arafat and his merry men do, MacLeod. What does that say about your Palestinian people?" Avram challenged.

Constantine intervened. "What is this about, Avram?"

"Haven't you heard, Marcus? Our good friend Duncan MacLeod is shacking up with a terrorist."

MacLeod was angered by the accusation. "Maral Amina is not a terrorist."

"No?" Avram said, standing so he could look MacLeod in the face. "Then what do you call her? That woman is the legal representative of an organization whose stated purpose is the genocide of the Jewish people. You're *shtupping* Hitler, MacLeod!"

MacLeod took a long moment. He knew any immediate response he'd make would only make matters worse, and in his present state might prove violent. Another deep breath. "That was thirty years ago, Avram," he said carefully. "The PLO has changed. The Palestinians have changed."

"People don't change, MacLeod. Their words may change, their propaganda may change, but what's in their hearts doesn't change." Avram spoke with his body, spoke with his hands, the cigar dancing through the air. "They wanted us all dead then, they want us all dead now. And I will not roll over and let that happen. Never again. And if you ally yourself with them, you ally yourself against the Jews. Against me."

MacLeod would not give in to his anger, because he knew too well that was not the way to deal with Avram. "I am not allying myself with anyone, Avram. This is not about politics. It's about an individual woman I happen to be seeing. And who I choose to see is none of your damn business."

"Not like you to pick the wrong side, MacLeod," Avram said, arms crossed in front of him, egging him on.

"There is no right and wrong, Avram, not this time."

"Wrong again." Avram shook his head sadly. "Didn't you learn anything in Warsaw?"

"Yes, I did. I learned that no one group of people has the right to oppress and destroy another people because of their ancestry or how they choose to worship." He kept his voice low and nonthreatening. "Or did I get that wrong, too?"

That stopped Avram for a moment, but just a moment. "Is that what you think this is about? Since when are you so naive? You're buying into her propaganda, lock, stock, and barrel."

"Am I?"

Avram stepped toward him, scrutinizing him intently. As the two men sized each other up, MacLeod couldn't help but be reminded of their first meeting—the same hostility, the same inability to trust. Everything had changed since then, but apparently nothing had. They regarded each other in angry silence, resolute will battling resolute will, the only sound in the room the quiet tap, tap, tap of Methos's foot against the carpet.

Methos could stand it no longer. "Okay, look, a priest, a rabbi, and a chihuahua went into a bar one night—"

"Pierson!" Constantine scolded.

"What?" Methos said, feigning innocence. "You all seem to be confusing what sounds to me like a pleasant roll in the hay with the start of World War III. Chill out a little, would you?

She's just here to negotiate for a few run-down blocks of real estate."

Avram jumped on it. "A piece of the City of God! She has no right. It was taken from us, and now that we have it back, it is *ours.*"

"Well, I'll make sure to tell the Jebusites," Methos said casually, strolling over to the decanter to freshen his drink.

"Pierson, what the devil are you talking about?" Constantine was confused by the non sequitur.

MacLeod didn't appreciate Methos's interjecting into his debate. *"Adam,"* he growled warningly.

"The Jebusites, the people that shepherd boy—what was his name?—David took Jerusalem from in the first place. Under your tautology, looks like they can have their city back. Come to think of it, the Manhattan Indians may want to have a look at this, too."

MacLeod shot him another angry look. "You stay out of this." But Methos held his ground.

"Okay, maybe I am being facetious, but the point is, people have been fighting, and dying, over that same piece of arid hillside for nearly five thousand years. This is not an exclusive Arab/Jew thing. It runs much deeper than that."

Avram countered, "This isn't about land. This is about the preservation of a people. About the protection of a way of life that dates back thousands of years. I have dedicated my entire life to this."

"And what about the Palestinian way of life? Does that mean nothing to you?" MacLeod said, and he was stunned by the intensity of the hate in Avram's dark eyes.

"What's happened to you, MacLeod? Once you were willing to give your life to save a handful of Jews you didn't even know. Once you fought with us, bled with us, mourned with us." He thrust his smoking cigar into MacLeod's face for emphasis. "The Duncan MacLeod I remember wouldn't allow himself to get dragged around by his dick!"

MacLeod grabbed the cigar from Avram's hand and ground it out with such force it crumbled into leaves. Smoke swirled around them.

Chapter Fifteen

Smoke swirled around him, so dense he could feel it against his skin. MacLeod fought for air. For each breath of oxygen he managed to draw in, he couldn't stop the smoke from invading his lungs, tightening his throat. Sweat dripped down his forehead, into his eyes, the heat intense and growing hotter. Guided by the light of an electric lantern reflected eerily from the translucent smoke, he groped around the floor until he found a makeshift pallet. He ripped off the sheet, bit down hard on one edge of the cloth, and pulled with all his strength. The fabric tore. He pulled off a wide strip and tied it quickly over his nose and mouth. It couldn't increase the amount of oxygen in the room, but it might limit the soot and ash filling his lungs.

He tore off more pieces. "Avram, here!" MacLeod called out. "Take these." Avram appeared out of the smoke rapidly filling the *malina* where the remnants of his unit had sought an hour's rest and refuge. He took the cloths from MacLeod and began to pass them out to the others holed up in the bunker.

There were eleven of them in all in the tiny room that had been dug beneath a dry goods shop on Ostrowska Street. MacLeod and Avram; Landau, from Avram's unit, whose arm had been broken not an hour before by a wall that collapsed from a German shell; Rubenstein, another ZOB fighter from the unit; Miriam, who had been forced to seek refuge with their unit after a German squadron had blocked off access to her own while she was couriering messages from Gutman;

and six noncombatants—Singer the shop owner, his wife and son, a nephew, a neighbor woman, and a small, silent boy the nephew had found wandering in the streets.

Miriam had known of the *malina* beneath Singer's shop, and, when Avram realized they would need a safe place nearby to try to set Landau's arm and to rest for an hour or two until nightfall, she'd led them there. Singer and his family had welcomed the fighters happily, offered them part of the little food they had remaining. In return, they begged for news from the outside. How went the battle?

The Germans' most powerful weapon in the war for the Ghetto had not been their tanks or their automatic rifles or the almost constant shelling by the cannons they'd placed just outside the Wall. The most fearsome weapon in the German arsenal had turned out to be the flamethrower. Nearly two-thirds of the Ghetto was in flames or had already collapsed into smoldering ruin. Thousands had been flushed from hiding and captured or shot by the Germans as they tried to surrender. Thousands more had perished in their hidden underground bunkers, overcome by smoke and heat as the buildings above them were systematically burned to their foundations.

Somehow, Singer's block had been spared thus far. It wasn't until Avram had set Landau's arm with an improvised splint, the other fighters had gratefully accepted a little water and some stale bread from Mrs. Singer, and MacLeod had signaled they'd best be moving on that they heard the rushing, the roaring of the beast above them. Thick smoke began pouring through the ventilator shafts. The shop was ablaze.

Rubenstein stumbled in from the narrow tunnel that led topside, choking on the dense air. Avram quickly tied a cloth around the man's nose and mouth. Rubenstein shouted to be heard above the roar of the conflagration above. "Tunnel's clear so far. No fire," but he shook his head at Avram's look of relief. "There's a squad at the end of the street. Six or seven. They'll pick us off as soon as we show our heads." Avram looked at MacLeod, anguished, out of ideas.

MacLeod looked at the Singers, who looked to him with the last bit of hope they had in their hearts. The eyes of the poor little boy too traumatized to tell anyone his name, yet who'd somehow managed to hang on this long, seemed to bore right through him. MacLeod faced a decision he'd hoped he'd never have to make. Would it be more merciful for these innocent souls to die a quick death at the end of a Nazi rifle or a slower one here in the shelter they'd dug for their protection?

Suddenly, Miriam pushed forward. "I have an idea," she shouted. She pulled the cloth mask from her face and dipped it in a cup with a little water still at the bottom. As quickly as she could, she used it to wash the soot and grime from her face, then pulled the scarf from her hair, shaking her hair out so it was full and loose. Then she handed her pistol to Mr. Singer.

MacLeod protested, "Miriam, what do you think you're doing?"

"Cover me," she told MacLeod, hurrying toward the access tunnel. "And be ready to get the hell out of here!" MacLeod followed her up the tunnel. Behind him, he could hear Avram directing the others to do the same.

As she reached the door to the outside, Miriam unbuttoned the top buttons of her shirtdress until the tops of her breasts were visible. She licked her lips and ran a hand through her hair. Then she threw open the door and ran out into the smoky street.

"*Hilfe!* Don't shoot!" she cried out in fairly good German, good enough at least to catch the German squad's attention. "Help me, *bitte! Der Juden,* those horrible Jews, they kept me prisoner. Please, save me!" To add impact to her performance, Miriam dropped to the ground in a swoon.

The squad started down the street toward her at a trot. As they drew near, Miriam reached into the pocket of her dress and wrapped her fingers around the prize secreted there—her last grenade. She and the other ZOB fighters had spent days working on this drill, she could do it in her sleep. She pulled the grenade from her pocket in one fluid motion, pulled the pin, and pitched it expertly into the center of the squad. Leaping to her feet, she took off running in the opposite direction.

A second later she could hear the explosive erupt behind her. Almost instantly, the shock wave caught up with her, knocking her to the ground.

MacLeod watched the explosion from the mouth of the bunker. Soldiers in the air, arms, legs flying apart from bodies. The air was filled with blood and the screams of maimed and dying men. Not a German was left standing. Immediately, he began to pull Landau and the others from the tunnel, pushing them toward the street in the opposite direction. "Run, run, hurry, move!" Rubenstein followed after the Singer family, carrying the little boy out of the bunker. "Go! Hurry!" Avram brought up the rear, herding them all toward a nearby alleyway.

Only when everyone was out could MacLeod turn his attention back to Miriam, who was rising to her feet with a huge smile. *Thank God,* MacLeod thought, as she gave him a thumbs-up to let him know she was fine.

"How was that?" Miriam called out, nearly laughing from relief. She began to run to catch up with him.

"You were magnificent. Now let's get out of here."

She'd nearly reached his outstretched arms when, blam, a single shot rang out. MacLeod watched helplessly as Miriam's body jerked unnaturally in the air, then hit the cobblestones at his feet with a sickening impact.

"MIRIAM!" he screamed, dropping to his knees, reaching out for her, heedless of any danger to himself as two Germans rounded the corner at a run, their rifles firing. Her eyes stared lifelessly into his own and he could see the light was gone. The bullet had shattered her spine, ricocheted into her brain. Death had been instantaneous. "Oh, God, no," he whispered, and closed her sightless eyes with hands dripping with her blood.

A shot whizzed close to MacLeod's head. Before he could even respond, another rifle fired, this one from behind MacLeod, and the closest German fell, one side of his face blasted away.

"C'mon, MacLeod, she's gone. We have to go!" he heard Avram shout behind him as he fired again. "Let her go." He knew Avram was right. He gathered up his rage and grief and managed to fire a shot straight through the heart of the second German before the tears came and blurred his sight. He staggered down the street, toward Avram and the others.

* * *

Midnight. The near-constant shelling from the artillery outside the Wall abated, and the streets of the Ghetto were once again quiet, a quiet broken only by the sporadic burst of gunfire and the shuddering collapse of buildings still aflame.

MacLeod and Avram were still trying to make their way across the Ghetto to rendezvous with the ZOB leadership. It was little more than a mile as the crow flies from Tzaddik's outpost at the edge of no-man's-land and the *malina* on Mila Street where they were to meet, but the route was thick with German patrols, with entire blocks burning out of control and mutilated bodies strewn along the sides of the roads like so much driftwood. The burning streets were bright like day, but on the passable streets, long since burned-out or mercifully untouched, it was black, and the smoke that hung over the Ghetto made it even harder to see. Familiar landmarks were gone, reduced to rubble. The journey seemed endless.

Now MacLeod and Avram faced the added problem of what to do about the family Miriam had given her life to rescue from the Ostrowska *malina*. They needed to find another safe place for the Singers to hide. But they all knew that "safe" was a relative term.

They made their way in complete silence, keeping to the alleyways, staying off the main avenues. They moved a block, a half block, sometimes only the length of a single building at a time. MacLeod and Avram scouting ahead, signaling the others to catch up, they moved their party of ten from shadow to shadow. MacLeod was grateful that Avram's decades in Warsaw gave him an innate sense of the Ghetto. He seemed to know instinctively where they were, where to go, what to avoid in this now alien landscape.

At Lubeckiego Street, Avram signaled everyone to stop. They had no choice but to cross this major thoroughfare. He waited for a few minutes, trying to detect any signs of life, any movement. The street was dark, deserted, silent. Finally, Avram signaled everyone on. They crossed the street single file, each barely able to see the back of the one in front of them in the smoke-filled dark, moving quickly to get to the protection of the buildings on the other side.

"Halt!"

An unseen German barked the command. Suddenly the

street was bathed in a blinding white light. Everyone froze where they were, unable to move, as if transfixed by the light.

The spotlight seared into MacLeod's eyes. He forced himself to try to see beyond it, but his entire world had turned to white. Tears streamed down his face from the effort. Finally, he raised his rifle, closed his eyes, and fired two shots into what he hoped was the center of the brilliance.

The light was extinguished in the shattering of glass.

"Run!" he heard Avram scream as several shots were fired by the Germans into the sudden darkness. MacLeod opened his eyes but could see nothing but the afterimage of the blinding light. He started to run toward Avram's voice, in the direction he thought was safety. He'd gone several paces when Rubenstein grabbed his arm, helped him up the curb, and into the narrow passage between two buildings. As his sight began to clear, he could see the others had made it safely across as well.

"Whoa, nice shooting, Tex," Avram said with a drawl.

"All in a day's work," MacLeod answered. Then, more somber. "Let's move."

Another two blocks brought them to the burned-out hulk that used to house the Bund, the Jewish socialist youth movement. It **was** obvious the building had burned early in the battle, and **the** remains were now cold and dead. MacLeod watched a cloud of anger pass over Avram's face as he surveyed the devastation. "What?" MacLeod asked.

"There once was a library here," Avram said quietly. "Thousands and thousands of volumes they'd managed to save. Generations of Jewish thought, Jewish lives, Jewish dreams. Gone. Just gone. Just like the rest of us. Like they never existed." He waded into the rubble, gesturing MacLeod to help him while Landau and Rubenstein stood guard, pistols at the ready, watching the streets. "The entrance to Mendik's base should be right around here."

MacLeod pulled aside some half-eaten timbers that had fallen, revealing a trapdoor. "Lock's broken," he indicated. "Nazis have been here." He dug into the debris, clearing the door with his bare hands.

"Then why are we still here?" Landau wondered. "The building's burned down, and the Germans would have cleared out any survivors. We can't do any good here—we should move on."

"They can only burn it down once," MacLeod said. It only took Avram a moment to understand his plan. "The *goy's* got a point. If the *malina* is still intact, we may have a place to hide our people." Avram opened the door, releasing a stench of smoke and mildew and rotting flesh. "After you," he gestured. MacLeod grimaced and started down the darkened stairway.

Avram pulled a candle from his pack as they moved down the stairs and lit it. The flame burned brightly.

"Air's breathable, at least," MacLeod noted.

As they reached the main room of the shelter, the flickering light of the candle revealed a tragic tale. Thirty, maybe forty bodies, men and women, their bodies bloated and decomposing, lay dead on the dirt floor arranged as if sleeping. Only the horrifying grimaces etched in their faces bore witness to how slow and agonizing their deaths must have been, suffocated in the smoke that had poured in through their only source of air. Only as the building had cooled had the air through the ventilation shafts become breathable again, too late for those trapped in the bunker by the fire above.

Avram held the candle close to some of the ghoulish faces. Dr. Cohen, who had fought tirelessly throughout the war to save the sick and the dying, and in the end could not save himself. Mendik, the unit commander, and Jana, his wife of less than a year, locked together forever in one last embrace. Nahum, the cantor, whose voice would rise to God no more. Avram turned away as a light flared behind him.

In a jumble of tools and supplies that had been swept off a nearby shelf onto the floor, MacLeod had located more oil for the lantern that had once illuminated the *malina*. As Avram blew out his candle, MacLeod pointed out, "No weapons." The Nazis had indeed been through, stripped the bunker and its victims of weapons and whatever other valuables they took a fancy to, then left the bodies there to rot. "I'll go topside and get the others."

Avram looked at him in horror. "You don't mean to leave them down here with all these bodies? You can't be serious."

MacLeod explained, "The Germans won't look down here

again. They'll be safe here. The dead will protect them. I'll try to prepare them for what they're going to see, then bring them down." He started up the stairs.

When MacLeod was gone, Avram turned back to the bodies of his friends. He knelt beside Mendik and Jana, entwined, and touched Mendik's hand, stroked a lock of hair from Jana's cheek. Softly, he began to sing over them. "*El Male Rachamim,* Thou who dwellest on high. Grant perfect rest beneath the sheltering wings of Thy presence, among the holy and pure who shine as the brightness of the firmament, onto the souls of these who have gone unto eternity." A single tear drifted down Avram's face. So much death he'd seen. So much. "May their repose be in Paradise. May the Master of Mercies enfold them under the cover of His wings forever, and may their souls be bound up in the bond of life eternal." An eternal life denied to him. "May the Lord be their possession, and may their repose be peace."

MacLeod returned, leading the others down the stairs, barely in time to hear the choked sob that broke Avram's "*Amen,*" but by the time they'd made it to the bottom and into the room, Avram was all business once again. He handed his rifle and its remaining ammunition to Rubenstein, ignoring the shock registering on the fighter's face as he took in the gruesome sight of the decomposing bodies. "You and Landau take the watch. We'll be back as soon as we've met with Anielewicz and the others." He quickly turned and started for the stairs. "C'mon, MacLeod. The dead can wait, but we can't."

Chapter Sixteen

Warsaw: May 8, 1943

Their password was a stale one—it had been a couple of days since they'd last seen a courier from the Central Ghetto—but it gained them admission to the smugglers' bunker beneath the apartment house at Mila 18 just before dawn. So far the building seemed miraculously untouched by flame or German shell. They were relieved to be off the streets before the German patrols returned in force.

Issachar met them at the bottom of the stairs as they entered. "Gentlemen!" he greeted them expansively, then put a beefy arm around MacLeod's shoulders. "So, what's the word from the French Underground about our little . . . arrangement?" It was clear the corpulent gangster was in denial of the reality of the tragedy taking place outside his palace.

"You can talk business later, Shmuel," Avram interrupted. "First we need to find Anielewicz."

"In the conference room. East wing, last door on the right." As Avram and MacLeod started down the corridor, Issachar called after them. "Remember, you need anything, you let me know. Everything I have is yours."

MacLeod shook his head in wonder. "Boy, is he singing a different tune. How'd Anielewicz wind up bedfellows with Capone?"

"Izzy is many things, but stupid isn't one of them. He realized a couple weeks ago that he needed us to keep him alive. Safecrackers and cat burglars aren't much help in a firefight. Anielewicz's place farther down Mila got bombed and Shmuel 'generously' opened his doors to the survivors, kind-hearted soul that he is. You know how it goes—I scratch your *tuchas*, you save mine." They'd reached the end of the corridor. Avram knocked on the door on the right. "It's Tzaddik."

The door opened. Inside the room, the remnants of the ZOB command gathered around a table. There were nearly twenty of them, all pale and haggard, hollow-eyed. It was obvious none of them had slept in days, and the nerves that weren't numb were keenly on edge and ready to snap.

"Tzaddik, thank God!" Mordechai Anielewicz said as they entered. "What's the news?"

Avram shook his head sadly. "Nothing you haven't already heard a hundred times, I'm afraid. Miriam's gone. Half my unit went down when the mortar hit the Smocza base. Three more in the shootout."

"Mendik's base was smoked out," MacLeod added. "As far as we could tell, no one made it out."

Across the room, Lilka Minski stood, clutching the table for support. "What about Israel? He was going to Mendik's, Jana was ill. I haven't seen him since." Lilka was the doctor's longtime lover, and it was clear from her face she knew the answer before she even asked the question. "He was there, wasn't he?"

"I'm sorry, Lilka," MacLeod said gently.

"Oh, God." The words caught in Lilka's throat, and her hands went to her mouth. Mira, Anielewicz's companion and aide, hurried to her side and quietly helped her from the room so she could grieve in peace.

Anielewicz gestured for them to join the meeting. "Come, sit." Avram took Lilka's place, MacLeod pulled an empty chair nearby up to the table. "Quite frankly, gentlemen, I am open to suggestions," their young leader said wearily. "If you've been hiding a miracle in your pocket, now would be the time."

There were three hundred people in the bunker—fighters, commanders, thieves, murderers—and an untold number still alive in other bunkers scattered throughout the burning Ghetto. There had to be something they could do to save them. But every idea, every scenario they came up with seemed to work out the same way—death.

"What about the Polish Underground?" MacLeod asked, frustrated. There had to be a way. "Any chance of getting them to attack on another front, draw the Germans' attention long enough to evacuate the Ghetto?"

Zelzer, who had commanded a unit in the Brushmaker's area, shook his head sadly. "Antek and Kazik are both on the Aryan side now trying to talk some sense into the *Armia Krajowa,* but no luck. Apparently the heroic AK is too afraid of stirring up the hornets' nest on its side of the Wall. They claim they're not ready yet."

"They'll be ready enough when the Nazis run out of Jews and start on the Poles. Cowards!" Avram spit.

The door to the conference room burst open. "Mordechai, you have to do something!" The king of the killers and thieves was a quivering mass. "They're here!"

"The Nazis?" Anielewicz asked for confirmation. The other ZOB fighters looked at each other with grave concern.

Issachar nodded, looking back over his shoulder expecting Brownshirts to be following him down the corridor, guns blazing. "They've surrounded the entire block. They're covering all the entrances." He grabbed the young ZOB leader by the arm and shook it frantically. "You've got to do something!"

"Calm down, Shmuel." Anielewicz shook him off. "They won't try to enter the bunker, we know that. They're afraid of the bunkers. *You* need to stay calm and stay put." The underworld prince was twice Anielewicz's age and nearly three times his size, but he backed away.

Suddenly, there was a rumbling, and they could feel the ground move around them. "Grenades," MacLeod said. "They're trying to blow a way in."

Issachar, panicked, opened his mouth to speak, but Anielewicz silenced him with a look. "I told you, Shmuel," he said warningly. "Here's what you have to do. I want you to gather all your noncombatants and get them as far away from the entrances as possible. Now go!" As Issachar scurried away to fulfill his orders, the ZOB leader turned to his people and indicated four of the commanders. "Yossel, Linder, Zaleski, Rabinowitz—gather your fighters, make sure everybody has a rifle. Take every grenade in the place and do whatever you have to to keep the bastards away from the entrances."

As the commanders raced from the room to gather their troops, Avram turned to Anielewicz. "Now what?"

"We wait."

"Wait? They're not going to just go away," Avram said, frustrated at the inactivity.

Anielewicz gave him a look that said he was just as frustrated. "Look, Tzaddik, you got a better idea, we're all listening." Avram was forced to concede that he had no better plan.

Another, more powerful explosion rocked the complex, and the electric lights flickered but held. Close on its heels, a second explosion of equal magnitude. Mortars. MacLeod got up from the table and started for the door. "I'll see what's happening."

He hurried down the corridor. At the base of the steep stairwell leading to the main entrance to the *malina,* fighters were gathering, tense, afraid, pistols and rifles trained on the door to the world above as if waiting for Satan and the forces of Hell itself to come bursting through. MacLeod pushed his way through the young fighters and up the stairs.

The door was locked and barred with metal rods. Yossel, one of the captains, peered intently through the small peephole cut into the door. "Yossel," MacLeod said, tapping him on the shoulder. The captain stepped back so that MacLeod could look out.

"They haven't found the basement yet," Yossel reported, and MacLeod could see that the basement of the building at Mila 18 was empty. He needed to see what was going on outside. MacLeod began unbarring the door.

"What are you doing?" Yossel tried to stop him. "You can't go out there."

"We have to know what's up there," MacLeod said, and another mortar shell exploded above them, causing the walls of the bunker to quake.

Yossel looked at him as if MacLeod was a madman. "You're going to get your crazy head blown off!"

"Then you'll be in for quite a show," MacLeod said as he unbolted the final lock. With a last look through the peephole, he threw the door open and darted into the shadows along the walls of the basement. He could hear the sounds of the door being barred behind him.

He crept along the basement wall, one with the shadows, until he reached the stairs leading to the ground floor. In one quick motion, he stuck his head around the corner, then pulled back to safety. There was nothing on the stairs. Nothing alive, that is. He looked again, more slowly this time. At the top of the stairs, he saw the sprawled body of the gorilla who had guarded Issachar's entrance, riddled with bullets. A white handkerchief was still clutched in his hand. The mobster had tried to surrender to save his own skin. But obviously the Nazis weren't interested in surrender.

MacLeod dropped to the ground and slithered up the stairs on his belly, using the body of the dead mobster to shield his own from sight. As he reached the top, he peered over the corpse into the back hallway of the apartment building where the basement stairs let out. Empty. Another shell impacted against the building with a deafening blast, and MacLeod ducked back beneath the dead man as plaster and wood rained down on his head. When the shaking stopped, he leapt up and over the body and into the hallway. He felt fairly secure that there would be no Germans in the building until the shelling stopped, but still he led with his rifle as he hurried down the hallway.

He reached an apartment that fronted Mila Street. The door had already been forced open and hung crookedly from one hinge. As quietly as possible, he widened the opening enough for him to slip into the empty room. He dropped to the floor again so he couldn't be seen from the street through the shattered windows and made his way across the room to those windows, ignoring the painful broken glass in his path.

At the window he chanced a look out the bottom corner. The street was full of soldiers. He looked again, noting the positions of the sharpshooters scattered among the infantry. He could see only one mortar, its crew in no rush to reload, target, and fire—their quarry wasn't going anywhere. Coming down the road he could see a tank and, in front of it, a German staff car.

The car pulled up near the building, and a German officer jumped out, hurrying to open the back door for his superior. As the man emerged, MacLeod recognized the uniform—that of an SS general. He knew the wearer could be none other than Jürgen Stroop himself, the Nazi butcher charged with the task of completely eradicating the Ghetto.

Stroop's aide handed him a bullhorn. *"Übergeben!"* The general's words commanded the Jews to come out voluntarily, to surrender, but all around him his troops were readying their weapons. Even the mortar crew moved with renewed urgency. There would be no surrender. Only execution.

MacLeod's hand tightened on his rifle and he raised it to just below the level of the window. He knew he would have only one shot. One chance. But if he could take out Stroop, maybe he'd buy the Ghetto a little more life. It might be only another hour or two. But at this point, every additional second of life was a precious gift.

"Raus, Juden!" the general announced. MacLeod spun to his knees in front of the window, aimed and squeezed off his shot—

—just as the general's aide passed in front of him, taking the bullet in the head. His brains splattered across the general's impeccable uniform and the gleaming staff car behind him, but Stroop himself still lived.

Shit. But MacLeod had no time to dwell on his failure, as the air filled with answering bullets. He scrambled from the room and ran for the back hallway. Behind him, the apartment blew apart as a mortar shell ripped into it. The wall beside him as he ran buckled, and the ceiling started to collapse in pieces all around him.

He dived down the stairs to the basement headfirst, hitting the steps two-thirds of the way down, tucking and rolling to the basement floor. He scrambled to his feet, across the basement, and reached the camouflaged door to the bunker just as Yossel opened it and pulled him in, locking the door behind him.

MacLeod sagged against the door for a second or two, catching his breath. Then with a wry smile he pointed out to Yossel, "Well, at least I've still got my head." He hurried down the stairs and returned to the conference room.

He gave Anielewicz and the commanders a full report. What he'd seen. What he'd done. And what he'd left undone. No one blamed him—at least he'd tried. Still, he blamed himself.

Anielewicz seemed withdrawn, as if his brain was working overtime, trying to out think the German general, trying to figure out what the Nazi plan could be.

"Stroop's here," Anielewicz repeated to himself. He turned to his commanders, grim. "He knows. He knows who's down here. He's come for us."

"But who would have told them?" Mira asked.

MacLeod ventured, "I'd lay odds it's one of Issachar's rats."

Avram pulled his pistol and started toward the door. "Where is that son of a bitch?"

"Tzaddik! Wait!" Anielewicz commanded. "It's no use fighting among ourselves. No use fighting the Germans' battle for them." Avram was about to protest when suddenly there was screaming from the other end of the hallway. Everyone in the room grabbed for their weapons as one. Avram rushed out into the corridor.

A yellow smoke began to seep into the conference room through the air vent. MacLeod was the first to notice it. For an instant, he was back on the battlefields of the Marne.

"Poison gas!" he shouted. "Out of the room!" Then he held his breath, but he could already feel the toxic gas burning his throat, his eyes. He grabbed for Anielewicz, who had begun to choke, and dragged him into the hallway and away from the room. He thrust him at Avram. "Take care of him!"

MacLeod rushed back down the hall and into the conference room to make sure the others had made it out. One fighter nearest the vent lay wide-eyed on the floor, drowned by his own body fluid as it erupted into his lungs. Back in the hallway, water flowing from his burning eyes, MacLeod slammed the door to the conference room behind him and took a tentative breath. So far the air in the corridor seemed safe. He assessed the situation.

Zelzer, who'd also been seated near the air vent, was sprawled unconscious near the doorway. As MacLeod bent down to him, he could already hear the gurgling in his lungs as he struggled to breathe. He'd taken in too much of the gas; he'd be gone soon. There was nothing that anyone could do to save him now.

Mira was trying to help one of the couriers, a woman

named Reginka, sit up against the wall. Reginka was coughing up liquid, never a good sign, but it did indicate her body was still trying to fight the gas. MacLeod had transported hundreds like her from the trenches of the Somme. Even the ones who survived would never breathe properly again. Sometimes it was more of a mercy if the gas just killed them outright.

The others seemed to have come through it, more or less. Coughing, swollen eyes, irritation, but if he could find a way to stop more poison gas from entering the bunker, they'd survive this attack. MacLeod started back down the corridor in search of Avram and Anielewicz, cautiously opening each door he encountered. Of the four rooms he checked, he found gas—and bodies—in the first two and quickly closed the doors again. Using his pocket knife, he slashed a big X in the wood of those doors so no one else would be endangered. The rooms weren't airtight, but without a strong breeze behind it, it would take some time for enough gas to seep out through the doors to be dangerous.

In the fifth room, he found Avram and the young commander in the middle of a group of fighters. The room was large, Issachar's game room, and the table tennis and billiards tables were given over to the stricken. Avram saw him enter and moved to him.

"How is it?" MacLeod asked.

"Bad. Real bad. Old Izzy had air vents installed in probably a third of the rooms, plus the entrance. A real stickler for fresh air. Couple of canisters of whatever the hell that was back there was all it took. We've got bodies stacked up in the entrance tunnels and the stairs, they couldn't get out of the way fast enough. No numbers yet."

"How's Anielewicz?" MacLeod could see the young man was pale and coughing, but still seemed to have the reins of command firmly in hand as he directed the head count.

"Completely amazed you would rescue him. I'm sure he half suspected you were the one who sold us out. Who knows, *goy*, you may win him over yet before the war ends." Avram shrugged his shoulders with a sigh. "We should all live so long, right?"

There was a commotion at the door to the game room. Issachar and a couple of his armed goons were trying to force their way into the room over the protests of some ZOB fighters. "Anielewicz!" Issachar bellowed from the doorway. With a resigned look, Anielewicz signaled the fighters to let them in.

Avram pulled out his pistol. "Best watch your manners, Shmuel," he said as he passed by.

Issachar ignored him and went straight for Anielewicz, backing him up against a table, getting right in his face. "I got thirty of my people dead. Dead, Mordechai, do you hear me? Dead! I got another forty so sick they're puking up their guts. What the hell was that? And what do you intend to do about it?"

The young ZOB leader looked at the raging mobster calmly and said, "There's nothing we can do about it, Shmuel. They got into your ventilation system. There's no way to stop it."

"So you're just going to sit here and do nothing and let them come and kill us all?" Issachar said, poking a meaty finger into Anielewicz's chest. The young ZOB leader ignored it.

"It wouldn't be my first choice," he said quietly, but there was an edge of steel running through his words. "But we'll do what we have to do. Are you in or out?"

"You're crazy." Issachar backed away from the young man. "You're all crazy if you think I'm going to stay down here. I'd rather take my chances with the Germans."

Anielewicz shook his head sadly. "They'll kill you, Shmuel. As soon as you step out that door. They don't care how much money you have, they don't care how many people you can intimidate. To them, you're just a Jew. And soon you'll be a dead Jew."

A river of sweat trickled down the pudgy man's face, betraying his fear, but his voice was full of bravado. "We'll take our chances."

Anielewicz signaled to his people, "Get him out of here." Several fighters made a move toward Issachar, who held up his hands and walked out the door on his own, followed closely by his henchmen. As soon as the door closed behind them, Anielewicz sagged back against the table like a puppet whose strings had been cut.

"Mordechai? You all right?" Avram moved toward him, concerned.

Anielewicz waved him off. "Sure, fine. Never better," he

said in a bitter voice. "Let's get together everyone who can still move under their own power. Get them in here for a council in five minutes." Several fighters hurried out to do his bidding.

"What are you going to tell them?" MacLeod asked, as gently as he could.

"God only knows." He looked up at them with anguish in his eyes. "Who knows, maybe Issachar's right. Maybe we should go out and take our chances in the street. One big shootout. I don't *know* anymore." Anielewicz's voice was strained, his nerves to the breaking point. "God help me, I don't *know*!" He struck at the table angrily, then sat down, turning his chair away from the others, unable to face their eyes. He clenched his fists and looked up to the ceiling waiting for answers that would never come. He sat unmoving while the others filed silently into the room, watching him, waiting for his wisdom.

Finally, the commander whom MacLeod knew as Jurek stood up slowly with the help of a cane. His hair was blond and his eyes were blue and once he had looked like a Hollywood film star. Once, before one of his arms-dealing contacts on the Aryan side denounced him to the Gestapo and the sign of his covenant with God, his circumcision, denounced him as a Jew. The ZOB had managed to rescue him from a work camp outside of Warsaw just prior to the beginning of the Uprising, but not before the burns and scars of the Gestapo's interrogation had been branded into his body forever. But he had never broken, never betrayed them, and to an organization full of heroes, he was more than a hero. They all waited intently for him to speak.

"Mordechai," Jurek said, "none of us will come out of this alive—we've known that since the beginning. Maybe it's time to stop struggling for an extra day or an extra week or even an extra hour and accept it." Slowly, painfully, he moved a few steps closer. "I think the question is not how do we try to save our lives, but how do we choose to end them."

Anielewicz turned around slowly, looking at Jurek with new eyes. "Arye, what are you saying?"

"Winning or losing isn't measured in whether we live or whether we die. We know we can't save our lives—but we can save the honor of our people, the honor of mankind. We can show the world that the bastards didn't break us, and they didn't beat us. We can take winning out of their hands."

"Oh God, no," MacLeod heard Avram whisper beside him as he echoed the words in his own heart. Didn't they understand? While there was life, there was still hope. They needed to hang on, to fight for every precious second. They couldn't just throw that away. But MacLeod also knew this wasn't his decision to make. It wasn't his battle, his life, his people at stake, and so he remained silent.

Beside him, Avram was pale. His eyes were shadowed, and he could see all the way to the heights of Masada with those bottomless eyes. He looked almost lost, distracted by the voices of a thousand ghosts in his head. Then he stepped forward as if to challenge Jurek. "No! You don't know what you're saying. That's not the answer. That's never the answer."

"Tzaddik, don't you understand?" Jurek said. "What we do here will be remembered forever—our deeds will be immortal, and no matter what the Germans do, they can't take that away."

Avram turned to Anielewicz, pleading with him. "Mordechai, please, there *has* to be another way."

His young leader was as torn up inside as Avram, but he understood the wisdom of Jurek's words. "What other answer is there, Tzaddik?" he said softly. "The ovens? The Gestapo? The gas? Don't you see, this way we are the masters of our own destiny, not the slaves of the Germans. Surely you can understand that."

"Only too well." Avram knew it was the answer. He knew their backs were to the wall, that there was no hope remaining for an outcome that didn't end in the death of everyone. But knowing it was logical couldn't make it any easier to face. Especially not again. There was so much Avram wanted to say, couldn't say, but he saw the look of determination in Anielewicz's eyes and knew their destiny was sealed. "If this is what you want."

"But no one should be forced to do this against their will," Anielewicz continued. "Anyone who wants to take their chances with the Germans is free to go. Tzaddik?"

Avram shook his head. "I live and die with you, Mordechai. You know that."

Jurek spoke again. "But who pulls the trigger?" There was silence in the room.

"I say we draw lots among the commanders." Avram couldn't believe the words were coming out of his mouth, but it had worked all those centuries ago. It would work now. He cast about the game room, looking for anything that could be used, and spied a deck of cards on a poker table. "Aces high," he said, shuffling the deck. "Low card does the deed."

One by one, the unit commanders came forward to draw their card. Jurek drew the five of diamonds, Arieh Linder the seven. Anielewicz himself drew the queen of hearts. Then the others. Finally, only Avram remained. He took a deep breath and drew.

The two of spades. He looked stricken, as if the foundation of the world had been kicked from under him.

Mira touched his arm, "God will be with you, Tzaddik, I know He will." She kissed him softly on the cheek, then took her place at Anielewicz's side.

Jurek moved painfully to Avram and embraced him. "This is a holy thing you do, Tzaddik, remember that. And in days to come, the world will know: we rose up for a helpless people and saved as much honor as we could. What more can we ask for?"

Avram stood unmoving, eyes closed, gathering his thoughts and his courage. Then, coming to peace with himself, pulled his pistol from his belt. "I'm ready."

"Who will be the first?" Anielewicz asked the assembled. "Who will be the first to say damn the Nazis, we're taking back our lives? We're taking back the honor of the People of God?" There was a deadly stillness in the room, everyone afraid of the inevitable, no one rushing to be the first.

After a long silence, MacLeod stepped forward. "I will." If this was truly their wish, he would try to make it easier for them.

Anielewicz looked at him with gratitude and a new respect. "Tzaddik was right. You are a hero, MacLeod. My apologies."

MacLeod wished he was truly making a sacrifice. He knew the guilt of this moment, of not being able to give his life for these people, would stay with him forever. "You're the real hero, Mordechai. Me, I was just along for the ride."

"Go with God," Anielewicz pronounced his benediction.

MacLeod moved to Avram. He embraced Avram to him and whispered in his ear with great concern. "You cheated. I saw you palm that card. Why?"

"No one should have to die with this on his head, MacLeod. No one." Avram's voice was tight.

"Be strong," MacLeod whispered, and stepped back. He closed his eyes and nodded for Avram to proceed. He heard the gun fire . . .

Chapter Seventeen

Warsaw: May 8, 1943

Slowly, awareness came back to MacLeod. He knew nothing at first but the burning in his chest, the throbbing pain that was the center of his existence. He could not see or hear or even feel, but he knew the pain. As it began to subside, he became aware of the rest of his body—head, arms, legs—and he became aware of himself. He knew he was Duncan MacLeod of the Clan MacLeod.

Suddenly, his body shuddered, and, with a choked gasp, air seared deep into his lungs. He was alive again. His eyes opened and hearing returned, and he instinctively started to move. Then he remembered the Ghetto, the Nazis, the suicide pact, it all flooded back. He feigned death once more, looking around the room as best he could through eyes mostly closed.

There were Nazis no more than ten feet away from him. Gas masks hung at their belts, but the air was clear of their noxious gas. All around MacLeod, the floor was awash in a tide of blood that pooled around the contorted bodies of his fallen comrades. He stilled his breathing as best he could, realizing how lucky he was the Germans hadn't noticed his first gasp for life. There were three of them in the room, walking through the blood to search the bodies of the Jews for weapons and valuables, kicking them to ensure they were dead. Out in the hallway and in the rooms beyond, he could hear others, laughing and joking in German.

"Feige Juden," one soldier remarked to the other two in the room as he cut off a finger from the cold hand of Arieh Lin-

der and pried his wedding ring free. "Cowardly Jews, not even a proper fight," the Nazi groused.

As he lay on the floor amid the other bodies, using the discipline and skills he'd once learned in the East to try to keep his breathing to a minimum, MacLeod realized he couldn't sense Avram. Either he was gone from the room or had not yet come back to life. From his position, he couldn't make out the identities of most of the victims in the room. Avram could be any one of them.

Then he felt it. Very weak, but getting stronger. Coming from across the room. Coming from just beyond where the Nazis were looting the bodies of his friends. MacLeod knew that at any moment Avram would breathe the gasp of life, that there was no way to stop it, no way to control it. And the Germans would be right on top of him when he did.

A distraction. He needed a distraction. Cautiously, he lifted his head, looked around. The Germans had their backs to MacLeod as they busied themselves collecting their petty spoils of war. MacLeod quickly searched his pockets. The bastards had taken his knife and his watch, but he'd been lying on his lighter. He pulled it out and, checking to make sure the Germans were still otherwise engaged, rolled to his side and threw it as hard as he could into the hallway, where it bounced off the far wall and clattered to the floor.

MacLeod dropped back to the ground and watched the startled Germans hurry toward the door. Almost simultaneously, he thought he could hear the soft intake of breath that signaled that Avram was back among the living. Now if they could just play dead until the Germans left, they might still get out of this place.

But it was hours before the Germans finally left the *malina* at Mila 18. Hours of lying among the ranks of the dead, wondering what went wrong, what he could have done differently, replaying in his head how he'd failed his people once again—Avram was merciless on himself.

When they were finally truly alone, MacLeod got up and moved to Avram. Avram's eyes were tightly closed. MacLeod touched him lightly on the shoulder. "Avram?"

At his touch, Avram opened his eyes and MacLeod could see the tears he'd trapped inside. "Why does this keep happening?" Avram sat up. "Everyone dies, and I keep living on. Just me and the memories. Why, MacLeod? Why am I cursed?"

MacLeod knelt beside him. "Maybe it's because books and libraries don't last forever?" He put an arm around Avram's shoulders. "A very wise old *Rebbe* once told me that unless the truth is known, everything your people are, everything they were, will vanish into nothing, like the smoke from the camps. And then the Germans will have won. Maybe some-one has to be left to remember them, to make sure it never happens again."

Avram laid his head against MacLeod's shoulder and fi-nally allowed the tears to flow. "I tried . . . Oh, God, I tried so hard. And it still happened . . ." MacLeod could hear the an-guish of a thousand years in his voice. "I couldn't stop it."

"It's not your fault. You have to believe that."

"It's like trying to save the beach from the sea, MacLeod. For every one I think I've helped, I lose ten thousand more."

"You're not God, Avram," MacLeod said gently. "You can't save everyone. But if you've helped one person live one day, one minute longer, you've won. Look at how you saved Miriam."

"Yeah, and she's still dead," Avram said bitterly.

"But you gave her three weeks of life that she wouldn't have had. Remember what you told me? It's not a curse, Avram. It's a *mitzvah.*"

Avram smiled a bit. "Oh, Lord, what have I done? You're starting to sound like a Jew, MacLeod." Avram got to his feet, wiped his face with his arm. He took one last look around the room, at the friends and comrades who'd been his only fam-ily, who'd chosen the dignity of death by their own hands. "But you're right. I'll make sure no one ever forgets what happened here. As long as I live, another year or another two thousand, their sacrifice won't be forgotten. And it will *never* have to happen again."

There were still German patrols stationed at the Mila Street entrances to the *malina,* but the enterprising smug-glers who'd designed the bunker had allowed for a back door as well, which was, for the moment, unguarded.

MacLeod and Avram emerged onto Zamenhofa, cautious, weaponless. It was still dark, which would provide them some protection as they made their way back to Mendik's base. Still, to avoid the patrols, they kept to the alleyways and building courtyards.

In a courtyard less than a block away from the carnage at Mila 18, another abomination waited. As they entered, MacLeod counted nearly fifty bodies, neatly arranged in patterns of five and six, then gunned down by firing squad. Fresh blood pooled between the paving stones like the water's edge at ebb tide, and the stone floor was rust with a stain that would never come clean. Many of the groups were naked, ordered to strip before their execution, the clothes on their backs worth more to the Germans than their lives. Two piles of the dead closest to the entrance were still clothed and in disarray, their executioners grown tired or bored with their game or simply running out of time.

"God in Heaven," Avram whispered. He hadn't thought he still had the capacity to be horrified but the cold, calculated nature of the massacre and the obvious pride the murderers had taken in their work sickened him. MacLeod waved one hand to shush him.

"Listen!" From within one of the piles of corpses near the entrance, MacLeod could just make out a sound. The mewing of a cat? The crying of a child? MacLeod hurried over, Avram following. Together, they began to roll bullet-ridden bodies from the pile. Death was recent—not all of the blood had dried, and it smeared MacLeod's hands and leather jacket as the two men worked in respectful silence.

Suddenly, a scream! And from out of the pile, a bloody hand buried a knife through the leather and deep into MacLeod's forearm. Surprised, he pulled back, freeing the blade from his flesh, and the knife came after him again. This time, he was able to grab the arm wielding the blade and haul the wielder out from beneath the corpses.

Screaming, crying, covered in blood, Rivka fought like a wildcat to free herself. "Let me go, you bastard!" She flailed with the knife, kicking and clawing.

"Rivka, stop! It's me, Duncan." He pried the knife from her hand and gathered her to him in a tight embrace, restraining her until she would hear him. "*Alts iz gut.* It's okay, you're safe now. It's Duncan and Tzaddik."

Rivka looked up at him and the veil of terror left her eyes. "Duncan?" She stopped struggling, but he could feel her heart beating out of control against him. "Duncan?" she said again, not believing what she saw.

He touched her face. "It's me, *Rivkaleh.*"

The twelve-year-old melted against him, her relief so great she could barely stand. "Duncan . . ."

"Hey, look what I found," MacLeod heard Avram say behind him. He turned to see Avram pull a little girl, no more than five, from the midst of the charnel. She'd had a quiet little cry, as if she no longer had the strength, but it had been strong enough to lead MacLeod to her. Avram settled her on one hip and she wrapped her arms gratefully around his neck.

"That's Zara," Rivka explained, still in a daze. "I tried to get her to stop crying, I tried really hard, but she wouldn't. I thought for sure the Germans had found us."

"Rivka, tell me what happened," MacLeod said.

Rivka looked around the courtyard wide-eyed, the horror still too fresh. She tried to speak, but couldn't. MacLeod smiled at her encouragingly and held her hand, and suddenly the words came flooding out. "They . . . they found our bunker. They took people out, a few at a time, and they never came back. They took Zara's mother. And then they said if we'd tell where the other *malinas* were, they wouldn't kill us. But nobody told the pigs anything. I told Zara that as soon as she heard a gun, to fall down and pretend she was dead. And the guns fired and we fell down. Then there were people on top of me and they were too heavy and I couldn't get them off. And there was blood, there was so much blood . . ." Rivka began to shake as she looked down at herself, covered head to toe in other people's gore. "Oh, God, Duncan . . ."

MacLeod held her close to him once again. "Shhhh, *Rivkaleh* . . . it's all right," he consoled her. "You're with me now." He looked up at Avram. He could see little Zara was holding on to Avram like a vice, as if she'd never let him go. She was quiet now, her head resting against his shoulder, eyes tightly closed. "What do we do?" MacLeod asked.

"We've got to get them out of here."

"Right." MacLeod started walking out of the courtyard, leading Rivka by the hand. "We'll get them back to Mendik's base, then—"

"No, MacLeod, I mean out of the Ghetto." Avram and Zara caught up with him. "Out of Warsaw. Out of that monster's reach." Avram wasn't sure there was even such a place anymore, a world safe from Hitler, but he knew now they had to try to find it. "Rivka, Zara, Moshe Singer and his family back at Mendik's base, anyone else we can find still alive. We'll get them out of here."

"Avram, there's no way out." Mila 18 had finally convinced MacLeod how hopeless their situation was. He stopped walking, grabbed Avram by the arm. MacLeod's face was dark, his jaw firmly set against the frustration that threatened to overtake him. "They've got the Wall surrounded, they've got tanks at the gates. They're patrolling the streets in and out of the Ghetto. We're trapped." The ache in his voice begged Avram to prove him wrong. "How, Avram? You tell me *how*?"

"I don't know. Dammit, I don't know! But we have to try." Avram pulled away and started down the street. Zara could sense the tension that hung between them and began to cry softly again. Without a thought, Avram reached up with his free hand to pat her head, whispering calming words, and Zara settled down again.

MacLeod wished it was that easy. He, too, wished he could comfort Rivka and the others, free them from this prison, but how could he give hope to others when he himself saw no hope left? No way out. He'd begun to see that Miriam, Anielewicz, all of them, had been right after all. Theirs was not a choice between life or death. The choice for them was between death or death. Death on their own terms or at the whim of the Nazis.

"The sewers?"

"What?" MacLeod almost didn't hear what Rivka had said.

"The sewers," she repeated. "I got under the Wall through the sewers once. It's really disgusting and deep in parts, but I've done it."

MacLeod looked to Avram with renewed hope, only to see him shake his head. "We've tried. Even if you managed to find the tunnels under the Wall, you come out of one of those manholes on the Aryan side, they've got you. There're informants on every corner, just waiting for some Jew to stick his head up. We've probably lost a hundred couriers in the sewers. Not an option."

A thought came to MacLeod. "Who says we'd have to come up on the Aryan side? How far beyond the city do the sewers go?"

"No one knows. We've never been able to map them. You don't know what it's like down there, MacLeod. It's a labyrinth. You could wander for days and come up to find you're back in the Ghetto again. Or in front of Gestapo headquarters. If you don't drown in shit higher than your head, first. I said no."

MacLeod disagreed. "I like those odds better than what we've got up here. Look, I saw a compass back at Mendik's. If we could keep to one heading, say north, we might eventually have to reach the end of the tunnel, right?"

Avram was unconvinced. "Maybe. If they don't all starve to death first."

"If we don't do something, they're going to starve anyway. So, when we reach the end of the tunnel, if we're not out of Warsaw, we're at least beyond the active patrols."

Avram finally saw. "Right . . ." He began to piece it together. "And from there, you could get to the forest. You can hide ten people in the forest for a couple of days, no problem. We've done it before. They're so intent on the Ghetto right now, they probably won't even be looking out there."

"And a couple of days is probably all I'd need to arrange some transport out of the Reich. I've still got some connections."

Avram looked happier than he had since the Germans had entered the Ghetto three weeks earlier. "MacLeod, you are a genius!"

MacLeod shook his head, humble. "Don't start passing out the Nobel prizes yet. We've got a long way to go." He quickened the pace. "Let's get back to the others."

Rivka looked up at MacLeod with undisguised awe as they hurried down the alley. "I always knew you'd save us, Duncan."

MacLeod looked helplessly at Avram, who shrugged and laughed in relief. "No pressure, MacLeod. No pressure at all."

They stopped at Mendik's *malina* only long enough to collect Rubenstein, Landau, and the Singer family, and to gather what they would need to attempt to escape the Ghetto. The compass, the lantern and oil, a dimming flashlight, all the food and water they could find, which sadly only amounted to a day's worth of crumbs when split among a dozen people. They hurried to make ready before dawn, when the Nazi patrols would return in force.

In the predawn silence they slipped from the bunker beneath the ruins of the Bundist library in two groups. MacLeod led Landau, Moshe Singer, and his wife and son through the alleyways. Singer's son, Jacob, no longer a child but not quite yet a man, shouldered the responsibility of caring for Zara, while his father and Landau covered MacLeod with their pistols as he took the point on their trek to Muranowska Square. At the last minute, Rivka, who had been assigned to Tzaddik's party, declared she couldn't leave Zara's side, and traveled with MacLeod instead.

They passed through the streets like ghosts, unseen, unheard, and finally rendezvoused with Tzaddik's party at the edge of the square, in the shadowed doorway of a long-closed bank. Muranowska Square marked the northernmost boundary of the Ghetto. Rubenstein and Singer's nephew, Tosia Gross, were in the square, Rubenstein already down the manhole into the sewers to make sure it was unguarded. Tosia stood at the mouth of the hole, exposed, unprotected, waiting for Rubenstein's signal. He looked around nervously, not comforted by the fact Tzaddik's rifle covered him from the shadowed doorway.

Suddenly, Tosia dropped to his knees by the manhole, listening intently. Then he waved frantically to Avram and MacLeod.

"This is it," Avram said. "You first, *mamelah*," he directed Mrs. Singer. She looked at him fearfully and then at her husband.

"Moshe?"

Avram reassured her. "He'll be right behind you. Now, go, the sun is nearly rising." He gave the woman a gentle push and she ran across the square to her nephew, who helped her into the hole and guided her down the ladder to where Rubenstein waited. "Now you, Moshe," he directed her husband, who hurried toward the hole, head looking rapidly in all directions, waving his pistol wildly.

MacLeod leaned closer to Avram. "If we're not all shot by Moshe Singer first, this might just work," he whispered.

"Just don't let him get behind you."

The Singers' upstairs neighbor was the next down the manhole, helping the little boy who had no family, no name. The sky was starting to lighten in the east. Jacob dashed out of the shadows with Zara clinging tightly to him. At the hole, Tosia managed to loosen Zara's hold on his cousin and take her from Jacob, who scrambled down the hole. Then he handed Zara down.

"You're next, Rivka," MacLeod prompted.

"Can't I wait for you?" she asked.

MacLeod laughed. "I'll be right behind you, I promise. Now, go!" She turned to go.

"Rivka, wait!" Avram told her. She turned to him, eyes wide and questioning. He bent down and kissed her gently on the forehead, tousling her pigtails with one hand. "Be brave, *Rivkaleh*," he whispered. Then he swatted her on the backside, saying "Go!" and she took off across the square.

"Avram?" MacLeod could sense something was troubling his comrade.

Avram ignored him, turning to Landau instead. "Send Tosia down, then you follow. Hurry, it's almost dawn." Landau stepped from the shadows and made his way to the manhole.

"You're not going." It wasn't even a question. MacLeod could read the certainty on Avram's face.

"Take this," he said, handing MacLeod the rifle. "You'll need it. I can find another one."

"Why, Avram?" MacLeod pressed. "Tell me why."

"My place is here, MacLeod. With my people. As long as there's one Jew left alive in Warsaw, I have to be here. I have to help."

"Then I'll stay with you."

Avram shook his head, touched deeply by MacLeod's gesture, but adamant. "No. You're their only hope. You get them out of here. You get them safe." Then he grabbed MacLeod firmly by both shoulders and stared intensely into his eyes, as if imparting his commandment upon him: "And then you find a way to stop that bastard, you hear me?"

Both men's eyes began to tear, and MacLeod could feel his lower lip begin to quiver. "I swear," he answered in a voice deep with sorrow, then he embraced Avram to his heart.

After a moment, Avram pulled away. "Daylight's coming," he said, trying to put on a brighter face. "Time to roll." He started across the square toward the manhole, MacLeod following, holding the rifle.

MacLeod started down the ladder into the sewer. "Hey, Tzaddik," he called up out of the hole. Avram looked down at him from the street. "God be with you."

"You, too *goy*." Avram slid the manhole cover into place, leaving MacLeod in darkness.

Chapter Eighteen

Paris: The Present

"You're a *goy*, you've always been a *goy*." To Avram, there was no longer anyone in the room but MacLeod. Constantine, Methos, both had faded into the background of his awareness, leaving him alone with the man he felt was his betrayer. "I never expected you to understand what it's like. To never have a place you can call your home. To be hunted down like a dog in the street because of what you are. But I never thought you'd be the one to side with the murderers."

MacLeod understood all too well. He knew what it was like to be run to ground like an animal by a pack of English butchers and their hounds, his only offense wearing a kilt in defiance of English law. He knew what it was like to be exiled and outlawed from his homeland on pain of death. But he knew as well that all explanations would be lost on Avram in his current state.

"She's *not* a murderer." MacLeod tried again to get him to hear, knowing as he did he might as well be shouting into the wind. "She's trying to create peace between both your peoples."

"Peace?" Avram's laugh was without humor. "You think this is peace? They'll spend weeks of negotiations building up this fragile house of cards that no one likes, only to tear it down before the ink is dry on the page. They only want one kind of 'peace,' MacLeod. The kind that comes at the point of a sword. The kind that comes when the enemy is totally annihilated. The kind of peace the Germans brought." The two men stood toe-to-toe once again. Avram's head might only come to MacLeod's chin, but filled with rage he seemed larger. "I wonder what Miriam Kavner would think of her 'hero' now?"

Behind him, Constantine and Methos exchanged a look. Constantine was horrified at the row taking place between two good friends in his normally staid and quiet home. Methos was wishing he had popcorn to go along with the evening's entertainment.

"Miriam believed there were things in life more important than politics," MacLeod said carefully, stepping away from their battle stance.

"You said it yourself—this isn't 'politics.' " Avram spit out the word. "This is about murder. This is about Treblinka. This is about Warsaw. This is about making sure they never happen again. Never again!"

MacLeod knew there was nothing more he could say to Avram to sway his mind. Maybe later, some other time, they could talk as they once had. Friend to friend. Man to man. "I'm sorry you feel this way, Avram."

"You're sorry, all right. One sorry piece of shit." He grabbed MacLeod tightly by the forearm, forced him to look him in the eyes. MacLeod didn't pull away. "You remember what we did with collaborators in the Ghetto, MacLeod?"

MacLeod answered, "I remember," but gave no ground.

"You'd better." Avram shoved him away and stormed out of the study. They could hear the slam of the front door echo through the house.

MacLeod stood where he was, staring at the study door until long after his sense of Avram's presence had faded into the night, replaying in his mind what had just happened. Was there any way he could salvage Avram's friendship? And yet still not compromise his own values? If there was an answer, he couldn't see it.

"Well, that went about as well as could be expected." Methos's cheery voice split the silence once again. Unfolding himself from the settee, he reached for his raincoat. "I think I've had about all the entertainment I can stand for one evening," he said with a self-satisfied grin.

Constantine looked at Methos askance. "You don't have to look like the cat that swallowed the canary, Pierson. Don't tell me you actually wanted that to happen."

"Of course I did," Methos said with no trace of remorse.

MacLeod was more than a little annoyed. "And I suppose for your next trick, you'll rub salt in old wounds?"

Methos heaved a dramatic sigh, as if he couldn't believe he actually had to explain himself. "Look, the first step toward peace is always getting the grievances out on the table. Drag them out into the light of day, and suddenly they're no longer the monsters under the bed. They're something rational human beings can discuss and, with luck, come to terms with. But the first step is to get them out in the open."

Both MacLeod and Constantine seemed unconvinced. "If that was your clever scheme, it failed," MacLeod said, sagging into the leather chair and retrieving his drink.

"I'm afraid Avram is far from rational at the moment," Constantine added.

"Hey, Rome wasn't built in a day, you know. Patience. You have to wage peace like you wage war. This was only the first skirmish, not the whole battle." Methos slipped his coat on as he headed for the door of the study. "*Ciao*, guys," he said, then stopped, turning to Constantine. "We still on for Saturday?"

"Of course we are. I feel lucky," Constantine said with a greedy smile. Methos's wicked "ha ha ha!" could be heard down the hallway as he left. Constantine saw MacLeod's raised eyebrows and explained, "Departmental poker game. Pierson's been on a winning streak lately. I intend to crush him like a bug."

"He never struck me as the gambling type."

"Ah, one hell of a poker face, though. And if he thinks he's got a winning hand, he's unstoppable." Constantine could tell from his face MacLeod's mind was not on poker. "Look, Duncan, two thousand years ago Avram watched the Romans drive the Jews out of Palestine, and there wasn't a day in those two thousand years—certainly not even an hour, when he was with me—he didn't think about returning. And now, finally, the Jews have it back. Giving it up again . . . it must be impossible for him even to contemplate."

"But does that give him the right to do what the Romans did? To drive people out of their homeland? To rob them of their culture? Their identity?"

Constantine poured himself another drink. "Aye, there's the rub, isn't it? That's the problem with the politics of Palestine. Everyone is in the right. Everyone is in the wrong. Everyone believes that God is on their side. Meanwhile, people are dying on both sides. More?" He offered the decanter to MacLeod, who shook his head. "And God, in his wisdom, seems to have decided to stay well out of it. Which is what I would advise you to do, if you weren't already in the middle of it up to your ears."

"So what do I do?" MacLeod hoped that Constantine's millennia of experience would yield an answer he had yet to think of.

"Not much you can do, I'm afraid. Stop seeing the girl because one of your friends doesn't approve? Seems rather adolescent to me. Besides, if you did, and then something should happen to her"—MacLeod's stricken face at Constantine's words told him all he needed to know—"you'd never forgive yourself. Speak to Avram? Certainly not tonight. Maybe in a couple of days, but you may have more luck talking to a doorpost. When he digs in, it's nearly impossible to move him."

"That's for sure," MacLeod agreed, remembering their time in the Ghetto.

"Or let him hate you, if that's what he wants to do. It's not the end of the world. You can't make everyone happy all the time, but, no matter what Avram says, you've got the right to do what makes you happy." Constantine looked at his worried friend honestly. "Sometimes I think you forget that."

When MacLeod returned to the Lutétia that night, he felt no better than he had leaving Constantine's. If anything, the security checks, the bureaucratic red tape, the pervading sense of fear and paranoia that surrounded the sumptuous palace only reminded him he was caught in the middle of a war. A war without battlefields. A war of words, of emotions pulled so tight the slightest incident could cause them to break. A war of rocks and bottles and hidden bombs that went off unexpectedly, in a bus or a school or in the mind of a fanatic.

Assad waited patiently outside the door to Maral's hotel room. Didn't the guy ever sleep? He nodded a perfunctory greeting at MacLeod and stepped aside to allow him to knock.

MacLeod rapped on the door lightly. "Maral?" He could hear her hurry to open it.

"Duncan." The door opened partway and she pulled him in, closing it firmly behind him. Her hair was down, a hairbrush still clutched in her hand, and she wore a simple pair of satin pajamas which he found more attractive than any sexy peignoir or the most revealing teddy. She had the ability to make anything look good.

Maral gave him a quick kiss on the cheek, asking, "How was your meeting with your Israeli friend?" and resumed her nightly ritual of hair brushing. He didn't know where to start. What to say? But his anger and disappointment showed in the way his body moved as he walked into the room. She set down her brush. "Not good, was it? Was it because of me?"

He shrugged and went to sit on a tapestried couch across the room from her. There wasn't really anything he could tell her.

"Would you like a drink? Something to eat?"

"No, thanks."

She moved to the couch and sat beside him, concerned about the shadows behind his eyes, the world-weary set of his shoulders. "Do you want to talk about it?"

"No, not really," he said. She didn't believe him, but she wasn't going to push.

She put an arm cautiously around his shoulders. They were tense, the muscles wound in knots. When he didn't seem to mind her touch, she snuggled a little closer to him. Still no response. Her other hand she laid across his chest and began to unbutton his shirt. She kissed him softly on the side of the neck, moving up toward his ear. The sinew connecting throat and jaw felt twisted and taut beneath her lips.

He reached out and gently pushed her away. "Not now, Maral, please."

She looked at him a moment, a little stung, wishing she could figure out what was going on in that lovely head of his. "Okay," she said, "help me understand this. You don't want to eat. You don't want to drink. You don't want to talk, and you don't want to play. May I ask why you *are* here, Duncan? You could just as easily be not doing all these things on your barge. Why come to me?"

Why? That was a good question. Because . . . "I just wanted to be near you. Not to make love or fool around, but . . . just to have you close." He smiled a wan little smile. "Sorry I'm not better company tonight."

Her heart melted at this peek beneath the white knight's armor, a glimpse of the vulnerability locked inside. Suddenly, she wanted nothing more than to hold him, to banish his demons and comfort him. Settling back into the couch and pulling her legs up beneath her, she put her arm around him once again and gently guided his head against her shoulder. "Close enough?"

She smelled of sandalwood and fresh rainwater, and he nestled against her. "This is nice." The satin of her pajama top was cool where it brushed his skin, and her thick jet hair cushioned his head like no downy pillow ever had. Gradually he could feel the tension and anger start to seep from his body.

"Why don't I tell you my good news?" she said, allowing her other hand to softly stroke his temple. "I think we finally have an agreement."

"That's fantastic." He tried to sit up, but she wouldn't let him.

"You can listen just fine where you are," she scolded playfully, starting to massage his temples in soothing circular motions. "It is only a preliminary step, all about timetables and troop redeployment, but still, it's a start. We meet again tomorrow morning before the sabbath recess to make sure all the i's are dotted and the t's crossed and all the *alefs* and *sifirs* are in the right places. If all goes well, Arafat and the Israeli Prime Minister arrive on Monday to sign the agreement."

"And what will the people think?" He closed his eyes, listening to the low timbre of her voice, feeling her healing touch.

"Those who want the killing and the fear to stop will embrace it as a necessary step toward peace. The self-righteous, the extremists, the ultraconservative on all sides will despise it, because we all must make some painful concessions. This agreement won't bring peace. In the short term, it will probably make things worse, until people have a chance to get used to it. But it lays the foundation for a lasting peace." She moved her hands to his shoulders, her fingers digging deep into the muscles, releasing the tension, smoothing it away. "My grandfather says that a lasting peace is like a good marriage. Sacrifice and compromise are constantly required of both the bride and the groom, and the minute you take the relationship for granted, it's gone."

"Wise man, your grandfather."

"Sometimes I think he was blessed with a very old soul." If he'd thought he could, he would have turned around to see what exactly she meant by that, but his spine was quickly turning to jelly under her care. "He lost his land, he lost his wife, he lost one son to alcohol and the other to an Israeli bullet, yet he never became bitter. He kept his faith in Allah, but he didn't use that faith to condone vengeance against those who wronged him as so many have. I have a lot of respect for him."

"You're a lot like him, I think."

"I just wish I had his faith."

MacLeod reached up and touched her hand with his own. "You have faith in your fellowman, which is sometimes more difficult to keep."

She laughed. "I'm naive, you mean?" She worked on his shoulders for a few minutes more, the only sound in the room the sound of their breathing. She remembered nights when Ali would come home like this, tired in body, wounded in spirit, when only her touch could bring him peace.

"Your Israeli friend will probably not like this agreement," she said after a while.

"He thinks I've picked the wrong side," MacLeod said, unable to suppress a huge yawn. While he found the conversation interesting, Maral's touch, just her very presence, were lulling him into a state of complete relaxation. Even his anger at Avram had washed away, replaced by compassion and a sense of pity.

"There are so many like that," she said sadly, "Arabs and Jews. Men whose idea of peace is not marriage, but bondage. The other side must be conquered completely, unable to cry out, unable to voice their dissent. Only then can there be peace. I feel very sorry for them." She thought for a moment. "I don't think the side of true peace is ever the wrong side, do you, Duncan?" There was no response. "Duncan?"

Almost against his will, he'd fallen asleep against her shoulder. The tense lines of worry around his eyes and across the planes of his face had softened, and now he looked like an overgrown child, or perhaps an angel, as he slept. Maral didn't have the heart to wake him. She slipped out from under him carefully and lowered him so his head rested on a pillow at the end of the couch.

Maral wrestled the enormous bedspread from the bed and carried it back to the couch, tucking it in around MacLeod's sleeping form. He looked so beautiful as he slept, she couldn't help but kiss him sweetly on the forehead before she turned out the lights.

Climbing into the spacious bed and sliding under the covers, Maral realized that for once she wasn't struck by the same gut-wrenching loneliness the bed usually inspired. Just hearing the easy even sound of his breathing from across the room was like a lullaby, and she felt safe and protected. She smiled a little smile in the darkness and closed her eyes.

It was the middle of the night when she was gently awakened by the jostling of the bed. She rolled over and felt his warmth as he slipped under the blankets next to her. She reached out to him, and they held each other close until morning.

"Are you sure you're ready for this?" MacLeod asked Maral the next morning. The Palestinian delegation was gathered in the lobby of the hotel preparing to leave for the negotiations, but first the gauntlet of media arrayed outside the doors had to be faced. The press had been promised a statement regarding the impending agreement, and it had been decided that Maral, as the most telegenic and Western-friendly of the delegates, would be the one to issue it.

"Why can't we just get this over with?" she complained, pacing nervously like a prizefighter before the first round. "It's the waiting that's killing me."

Farid came out of the glass revolving doors back into the lobby. "CNN has arrived," he announced. "Now we can proceed." He gestured the others to follow him out.

A small podium had been placed at the top of the stairs just outside the door, and representatives of the best and brightest of the world's media services were jockeying for position around it. Farid cleared a path, and MacLeod escorted Maral to it, Assad sticking close to her to deflect the microphones and cameras pushing and shoving their way toward her. "Dr. Amina!" "Professor!" even "Maral!" the insistent voices called, but she ignored them until they reached the podium. The other delegates ranged themselves around her in a show of solidarity.

Maral stepped up to the podium. Assad stayed just behind her, MacLeod off to one side with the delegates, both men vigilant. At the microphone, she cleared her throat politely, and the clamoring news crews settled down to hear the prepared statement.

"Ladies and gentlemen of the international press"—she could barely see through the sea of camera flashes and television lighting—"on behalf of President Arafat and the Palestinian Authority, I thank you for coming." It was probably the last thing she really wanted to say to the press, but she had to be the "nice" one. "Late Thursday evening, a tentative preliminary agreement was reached between negotiators for the nation of Israel and the Palestinian people regarding the military redeployment and political autonomy of—"

Suddenly, MacLeod felt it. An Immortal. Close. And getting closer. He scanned the sea of press . . .

"—East Jerusalem. The details of the agreement will be finalized today. The Israeli and Palestinian cabinets—"

. . . and there he saw, wedged between some reporters, the light of a flashbulb reflect off the barrel of a gun.

"—will vote on the agreement on Sunday. The signing—"

"Bundoo'aya!" MacLeod screamed out. "Gun! Take cover!" Almost before the words were past MacLeod's lips, the automatic was firing. MacLeod dived for Maral, but Assad was there first, knocking her away from the podium, driving her to the pavement, covering her with his body.

As MacLeod went for the ground, he pulled the legs out from under the delegate standing beside him. The man fell heavily just as a bullet passed through the empty air where his heart had been a moment before. The bullet shattered the window surrounding the revolving door to the hotel and several of the Palestinians crawled frantically through the broken glass into the safety of the lobby.

He saw Omar al-Sayyeed take a bullet in the thigh and blood geyser out of a severed artery, spraying the other delegates. As al-Sayyeed dropped, MacLeod grabbed him and started to drag him behind the podium. Suddenly, fire seared into his own shoulder and he lost his grip on the delegate.

MacLeod steeled himself—*block out the pain, no pain, no pain*—and succeeded in getting the screaming al-Sayyeed to relative safety behind the podium. The other delegate whose life MacLeod had saved was crouched behind it. MacLeod grabbed his hand and pressed it hard into al-Sayyeed's bleeding wound. "You let go, he dies," he warned the man, then peered around the podium to find the gunman.

All around, there was chaos. Reporters screaming, some dropping to the ground where they stood, others running for cover. There, in the midst of them, MacLeod spotted the shooter.

Avram. In a baseball cap and ultrabaggy jeans, looking like a teenaged gangbanger.

MacLeod didn't allow himself time to be surprised. He started after Avram who, knowing he'd been spotted, ceased firing and took off running, through the traffic at a standstill in front of the hotel on the Boulevard Raspail, bolting across the Square Boucicaut, past the nesting pigeons, past the dead French king. MacLeod followed, breathing fire.

At the edge of the square, just as MacLeod thought he was gaining on the smaller man, Avram mounted a motorbike he'd secreted behind a bush and roared out into traffic, weaving in and out of the stopped cars as he disappeared down the street.

MacLeod knew he'd lost him. He vowed it wouldn't be for long.

He turned around and started running back to the hotel. Off in the distance he could hear sirens, police and ambulance on their way to help the wounded. The wounded. *Oh God, Maral.* He hadn't thought he could run any faster, but the very thought spurred him on with a herculean burst of speed.

Assad was dead. He knew the instant he pushed through the bystanders ringed around the spot where he and Maral had gone down. A shot through the head and one in the back.

And Maral. She lay so still, covered in blood and gore. He couldn't tell if she was breathing. Farid crouched by her head along with another somber man MacLeod prayed was a doctor. He forced his way over to Farid. "Tell me," he commanded grimly.

"She's alive," Farid said, and relief washed over MacLeod, "but unconscious. We believe she may have suffered a head injury when she fell. Most of the blood you see belonged to Assad, peace be unto him."

"He saved her life," MacLeod realized.

"That was his job, Mr. MacLeod. He was very good at his job." The first of the ambulances pulled in front of the hotel, and the man with Farid hurried to meet it. Farid was quiet for a moment, as if he didn't know how to phrase what he wanted to say. "And you saved delegates al-Sayyeed and Mokhtari. Assad had told me he thought you were very good, as well, and I did not believe him. I believe him now." The two men's eyes met, each holding a new respect for the other. Then Maral, moaning, began to stir. "Come, now we must help Dr. Amina."

Chapter Nineteen

Paris: The Present

"Amy!" Constantine called out as he entered the office of the assistant curator of the Musée National des Antiquités without knocking, as was his usual custom. "Amy?" He was surprised to find it empty. The young archaeologist was generally quite diligent about her work.

He saw a figure walk past the office door, and he hurried out into the hallway. It was his secretary. "Naomi, where's Dr. Zoll?" Naomi always knew everything. Some days Constantine wondered how he'd ever functioned for twenty-five hundred years without her. She directed him to the lunchroom and he set off in search.

The lunchroom wasn't much. A few half-empty vending machines, a microwave, a coffeepot half-full of tepid mud, and an ancient television. All the money in the museum's modest budget was spent on the public areas and the exhibits. As Constantine entered the lunchroom, it appeared that more than half his staff were gathered around the TV.

"What the devil's going on here?" Constantine fumed. The staff snapped to attention at his approach, their guilt plain on their faces. "We open in ten minutes and there are already busloads of twelve-year-olds stacking up outside." He spotted the assistant curator still staring at the screen, wide-eyed. "And you, Doctor, were supposed to have those attendance projections on my desk this morning."

"Look, Marcus, I know *you're* not interested in years that have four digits in them, but could you possibly show a little compassion here?" The young archaeologist was always the only member of the museum staff with the guts to stand up to Constantine. The old general often thought what a fine Centurion she would have made. She was also a hell of a poker player, almost as good as his friend who was calling himself Pierson. "There's history happening, Marcus," she chided him.

"What do you mean?" Constantine asked, but his colleague shushed him.

On the TV, the news anchor spoke in clipped, somber tones. "Once again, two are confirmed dead in this morning's shocking attack: Nigel Coles, a veteran cameraman for the BBC, and Ibrahim Nasir Assad, a member of the Palestinian delegation's security team . . ."

Constantine was appalled. "When did this happen?"

". . . Among the wounded, which some sources have placed as high as thirty, are three of the Palestinian delegates:" The talking head was replaced by silent video of Maral giving the Palestinian statement to the press. "Former PLO terrorist turned negotiator Salim Ghassan, who's been taken to Hospital in serious condition; Omar al-Sayyeed, the deputy minister of labor, who is listed in good condition; and the spokesperson, Bir Zeit University professor Maral Amina, who is reportedly undergoing tests at this hour . . ."

"Poor Duncan," Constantine murmured. "And that poor woman."

The video panned away from Maral and the other delegates and swept across the mass of media personnel and equipment covering the Palestinian statement. "Several of the other delegates were treated at the scene for minor injuries and released." And then for a second Constantine saw him. Avram. Clear as day in the sea of reporters. As the muted video panned back to the podium, the delegates began to shudder and fall as the assassin's bullets hit their marks. Then the camera spiraled to the ground and the video ended. The image of the news anchor filled the screen once more. "Within minutes of the attack, a Jewish fundamentalist organization called *Oneg Shabbat* had claimed responsibility in a call to Paris police. *Oneg Shabbat* is also implicated in the massacre of forty-three Muslim Palestinians outside a Hebron mosque exactly one week ago."

"Marcus, are you okay?" the assistant curator asked, concerned by the uncharacteristic look of horror on her boss's face.

Constantine was already out the door. "I have to use the phone."

MacLeod's barge was not at all what Avram expected. When he learned that MacLeod lived on the Seine a stone's throw from Notre-Dame, he'd pictured a luxurious yacht, a few servants, perhaps some scantily clad beauties lounging on deck—a real 007 pad. This, on the other hand, was simple, without ostentation. He could respect that. It was also ridiculously easy to break into. He couldn't respect that.

Know your opposition. The first rule of chess, of business, of war. Only by knowing him could you anticipate him, stay in front of him . . . know his weaknesses. A standard background check on MacLeod was meaningless, full of forgeries and lies just like his own. No, to get into the head of Duncan MacLeod, he needed to see firsthand how he lived, what he threw away and what he felt was important to keep, how he treated the things that were precious to him. A man's home was his castle, but it was also a blueprint to his soul.

Avram's time gathering intelligence with the Shai, before Israel's War of Independence, and later with the Mossad, had taught him many things, not least of which was how to violate a person's privacy and yet leave no trace. He studied the photos on MacLeod's writing desk. The blonde would be "Noel, Tessa; DOB: 24 August 1958; killed in a random mugging incident" or so MacLeod had reported it to the police at the time.

Carefully sorted in the drawers, MacLeod's personal correspondence and bookkeeping. In an age of instantaneous communication, MacLeod obviously still enjoyed keeping in touch with a well-crafted letter. But he was also not averse to picking up a cellular phone, as his monthly statement indicated. A lot of calls to the States, primarily two numbers. Avram recognized one immediately as MacLeod's business in Seacouver. He would run a trace on the other, but he suspected it might correspond to an establishment called "Joe's," a neighborhood bar that seemed to be MacLeod's only other interest back in the U.S.

Avram continued around the room, scanning the titles of the CDs on the shelves, pulling down random books to see how well thumbed they appeared. MacLeod seemed to actually read the weighty tomes he collected. He was stymied by a piece of statuary on prominent display—burnished chrome, very modern, very dramatic, very stark. Very out of place amid the pottery and other world folk art in the rest of MacLeod's collection. It didn't fit in with the profile he was creating of the man and that bothered him . . . until he remembered reading that the dead girlfriend had been a sculptor.

On a table by the couch, the phone and answering machine, blinking, blinking an open invitation to press the play button. So he did. "MacLeod?" Avram recognized his teacher's voice before he identified himself on the tape. "It's Marcus . . . Hello? Are you there? Damn, you're probably still at the hospital. Look, MacLeod, I saw the news footage. It was Avram. Do you hear me? *Avram.* We have to do something. The museum closes at three today. Meet me here. It's important." The tape clicked off.

Avram's time with the Mossad had indeed taught him many things. Another lesson hard learned had been that you never know who your enemies are until they stab you in the back, so trust no one. Now all the pieces fit. Constantine was against him, too.

Constantine had just shooed the last straggler out of the exhibit in preparation for closing when he sensed that MacLeod had arrived. He threaded his way back through the gallery, turning off displays as he went. The doomed holographic hillfort at Alesia disappeared into smoke. The crowds filling the stands at the Coliseum urging the lions on were silenced. The names of the societies driven to extinction by the empire of the Romans ceased their ceiling-to-floor spiral. Constantine had expected to meet up with MacLeod somewhere midway through the exhibit and was surprised when he made it all the way back to the replica of the Arch of Titus that formed the entrance without seeing him. Then he realized it wasn't MacLeod he'd sensed at all.

"Avram," Constantine acknowledged, friendly but wary.

He was standing just outside the arch, studying the tableau that was carved into the face of the gateway. "What kind of sick joke is this, Marcus?"

"What do you mean? It's no joke." Constantine passed through the arch to the side where Avram stood, concerned that someone had graffitied or vandalized the reconstruction, but the faux marble was just the way he had commissioned it.

Avram's face hardened. "Then you deliberately meant to exclude the Jews?"

"What are you talking about?"

"It's the rape of the Temple, Marcus!" He gestured angrily at the frieze carved into the arch, where members of Titus's victorious legion were systematically stripping the Great Temple of its holy treasures to carry away in triumph to Rome. "For two thousand years, no Jew in Rome has willingly walked under this obscenity, and now you've left us no choice!"

Constantine was horrified. "Avram, I had no idea."

"No, you just didn't *care*," Avram shouted over him. Constantine was even more horrified at the violent reaction his unintentional insult had provoked in his student. Avram had never been one to wear his anger openly, not when mocked and attacked back in the streets of Rome, not even under the reign of the Inquisition. This man was no longer the Avram Mordecai that he'd once known.

"Which one were you?" Avram pointed bitterly to the image of a Roman officer supervising a gang of Jewish slaves carrying off the *menorah* from the sacred altar. "Is that you looting the Temple, Marcus? Or is that you defiling the holy vestments?" He turned on his teacher with hate in his eyes and venom in his voice. "Or were you too busy defiling the Jewish virgins with the rest of your legion?"

"You know I wasn't like that, Avram," Constantine said carefully, trying not to inflame him further, but he could tell it was far too late.

"You were like that, you were *all* like that! The Romans, the Crusaders, the Turks, the Nazis. You were all alike. Butchers, rapists, destroyers—every one of you determined to wipe us from the face of the earth. But we're still here. *I'm* still here."

"And now it's the Palestinians?" Constantine beseeched his student. "Avram, why are you doing this? Why did you try to kill all those people today? All they want is peace."

"Peace?" Avram couldn't believe he'd heard the word. "This isn't peace—it's surrender. This is rolling over and closing our eyes and hoping that if we give the murderers half of what we have, they won't come and kill us for the other half in the dead of night. Well, 'make nice and hope they go away' doesn't work, Marcus. You and your kind keep coming." His anger and his voice were escalating to a fevered pitch. "You take the other half, and you take our families, and our homes, and our people, and our God, and all you leave are *ashes*!" He screamed out the word, and it ricocheted like a gunshot from the marble walls of the vast exhibition hall.

Before the echo died away, Avram continued. "There will be no surrender. No compromise. I have been fighting for Israel for two thousand years. I've watched a hundred generations bleed and die for her—and I'll be damned if I'll see her handed over to them, no matter what."

"Even if that means becoming a butcher yourself?" Constantine wondered, full of sadness for him.

"I finally know my purpose. Now I know why I'm still here—I am her champion. Don't you understand? I do whatever I have to do. And there's nothing, nothing you or MacLeod can do to stop me!"

"What's happened to you? You were never a murderer."

"*You* made me a murderer. You and Silva and your damned legion. What I'm not any longer is a *victim.*"

Constantine understood him all too well. "The best defense is a good offense?" He touched Avram on the arm, friend to friend, teacher to student. "Avram, listen to me. That's not a way to live your life. It will eat you up inside and destroy you."

Avram slapped his hand away. "Are you going to be the one to try and stop me, Marcus?"

Constantine, resigned, "I will if you make me."

Avram drew his sword, one he'd once liberated from a Cossack sacking his village before driving it into the Cossack's heart. "So be it."

Constantine kept his hands in plain sight, still trying to placate him. "It doesn't have to come to this, Avram. I'm your friend. We can talk this out."

Avram snorted derisively. "The talking's long done, Roman. This is a fight we should have had two thousand years ago, before I let you enslave me and drag me to Rome." With that, he slashed wildly at his teacher's head. The blade was neatly deflected by the blur of a Roman *gladius* as Constantine swiftly withdrew it from hiding.

It had been a long time since he had taken the sword out in battle, but for a thousand years on a thousand campaigns he had slept with it, eaten with it, killed with it, died with it. It was a natural extension of his arm, and the patterns long ago ingrained in his mind and his muscles returned to him at its touch. The curator might be a bit rusty, but the general was far from overmatched.

"You were never my slave, Avram." Constantine stayed on the defensive, turning back attacks, blocking thrusts and jabs that would have killed a lesser fighter, but he was reluctant to attack, unwilling to try for his friend's head. "You were my student. You came with me willingly."

"Because you'd left me nothing. My city was gone, my people were gone." Avram swung at Constantine, and their two swords locked, hilt to hilt. "What else could I do," Avram snarled. The two men faced off momentarily in a test of strength and will, then Avram slipped under Constantine's guard and hit him hard in the stomach with his shoulder, driving him back against a leg of the arch. His sword freed, Avram swung for the head, but Constantine, with barely enough room to maneuver, managed to dodge at the last second.

Avram's sword bit deep into the faux stone and Constantine took advantage of the precious seconds it took to free it, spinning out of Avram's reach and slipping through the arch to the other side. He turned to look at Avram and saw his resolve waver—Avram almost followed him through, but he couldn't bring himself to enter the hated archway. Constantine hurried deeper into the labyrinthine exhibit.

Behind him, he could hear a popping and a tearing sound. The dividers between the displays were simple drywall. Avram was ripping himself a path directly into the gallery with his sword, bypassing the despised monument.

Constantine's sword led around every corner. He had the advantage of geography, he knew every nook and jog of his creation. Still, he trod warily, expecting Avram around each bend, behind each case.

Avram knew better than to attempt to surprise the general on his home field. When Constantine found him, he was standing openly in the middle of the corridor, sword ready.

"You can still stop this, Avram," Constantine offered, conciliatory. "It doesn't have to end this way."

"It's the only way it can end."

Constantine nodded, resigned. "As you wish." He unleashed a flurry of blows that Avram, surprised by Constantine's sudden aggression, was hard-pressed to beat back. Then the battle was joined in earnest.

The Roman scored first blood, slicing a bloody line down Avram's upper arm, but the Jew held the sword firm, seemingly oblivious to the pain.

They fought through the corridor, in and around the displays, hacking, slashing, thrusting. Each man tallying minor hits on the other, neither man gaining the upper hand. Each determined not to be the one to yield.

At last, despite the fatigue that was creeping into his own arms, Avram could see the Roman was also tiring, and he pressed his advantage with a series of slashing blows to the head that Constantine managed to parry, but that forced him back, little by little.

To avoid being maneuvered against a wall, Constantine ducked into the room of the Great Temple. Avram continued to hammer away—at his unprotected left side, at his legs, at his throat—but each time Constantine was ready with a block or a parry and an attack of his own.

Frustrated, Avram brought his sword down in a massive two-handed slash. Constantine spun out of the way, dodging the blow, the impact of which landed on the display case holding the model of the Temple, shattering the glass.

The shock of seeing the contents of the case was enough to slow Avram momentarily. That's all he needed—Constantine saw his opening and Avram suddenly found himself impaled through the gut on the general's sword. He sank to his knees and howled in pain. The sword did not yield.

"I don't want to kill you, Avram," Constantine said between labored breaths, exhausted from the fight. "Swear to me you'll stop this senseless holy war, and I'll let you live."

Avram, each breath a lesson in pain, glared at the Roman with hate in his eyes, but did not speak.

"Dammit, Avram, swear it!" He turned the sword in Avram's wound, just a bit. An old trick, but an effective one. He saw the wave of agony shoot through Avram's body.

"I swear," Avram finally managed through clenched jaws.

"On your honor," Constantine pressed.

"On my honor."

Constantine removed his sword from Avram's belly and Avram slumped to the floor like a broken toy. "It's over, Avram. This is over."

Constantine had barely finished speaking when a searing pain blossomed in his chest. He staggered back against the shattered Temple display, unable to breathe. His hands clutched desperately at the boot knife suddenly protruding from his body.

"*Now* it's over." Avram struggled to his feet, a look of grim satisfaction on his face. He moved toward Constantine, his sword at the ready.

"On . . . your . . . honor . . ." Constantine managed to croak out as his heart began to die.

Avram shook his head. "Honor is meaningless. *Life* is all that matters." And with a mighty swing, he cleaved his teacher's head from his shoulders.

Constantine's body hung there for a moment, taunting him, then the momentum of the blow carried it backwards, crashing onto the Temple, demolishing it.

Then, as if out of the ruins of the Temple itself, the tendrils of the Quickening rose like a mist on the moors, coalesced, dancing in the air, and sought its new home in the vessel that was Avram.

Its first touch flowed through him like lava and he howled,

a wild, feral sound, as his identity was consumed by the great chaos that claimed him by force.

Lightning arced from Constantine's body and slammed into his own, igniting the circuitry of his nervous system, uncontrolled power surging through him. The intensity of the bolts drove him across the room, pinning him against the wall, his arms outstretched, forcing him to take in all that was Marcus Constantine.

As Constantine's essence overwhelmed him, he screamed even louder and the lights hung overhead exploded in a rain of glass and shooting stars. Avram was oblivious to the jets of flame that shot through the gallery, kindling the displays, for he was no longer Avram the Jew, but Constantine the Roman—the warrior, the leader, the lover, the scholar. Suddenly, he knew Constantine, understood him far better than he did himself, for he *was* Constantine. Constantine was in him and with him and around him.

Alarms rang and a shower of water cascaded from the ceiling to douse the fires, but still the lightning coursed through the crucified form of the body called Avram as two Immortal essences fought for control. He was Constantine. He was Avram. He was Constantine. With a thundering cry ripped from his soul, the lightning stopped—

And he was Avram. Avram, son of Mordecai. And he was alive.

He slid down the wall and sprawled on the floor, spent, exhausted, deaf to the alarms sounding around him. The water from the ceiling sprinklers anointed his head like a soothing rain and slowly brought him back to the world. He struggled to his knees and forced himself to look at the body of the man he had defeated, lying in the ruins of the shattered Temple. He felt no joy, no elation at the sight, only a deep, abiding sorrow. He'd been forced to kill his father once again.

Suddenly, his weakened body was assailed by the presence of another Immortal. MacLeod. He couldn't face him, not now, not like this. They would have their time later. Avram staggered to his feet, retrieved his sword, and stumbled toward the exit.

Chapter Twenty

As MacLeod pulled up beside the Musée National des Antiquités, he had a vague premonition that something was wrong. He had remained at the hospital until he was sure Maral was out of immediate danger. He'd left her sleeping peacefully in her hospital room, ably protected by Farid, and returned to the barge. It was already three o'clock when he retrieved Constantine's message from his answering machine. He left the Citroën in a loading dock and ran into the museum, the tails of his black overcoat fluttering wildly in his wake.

The lobby was empty, the last of the patrons gone for the day. As MacLeod hurried through it and into the glassed-in cloister walk through the sculpture garden that connected Constantine's exhibit to the rest of the museum, he noted that it seemed the employees had gone home for the day as well. He was midway down the walk when he heard an explosion. Simultaneously he could feel a vibration in his soul—there was a Quickening.

MacLeod broke into a full run just as another explosion rocked the cloister. The fire alarm began to sound its urgent wail. He slammed through the massive wood doors leading to the marble gallery, not waiting for them to swing open at their own automated pace. "Marcus!" he screamed out over the alarms and the lightning and the water cascading from the ceiling.

He found the giant rend in the temporary wall of the entranceway near the Arch of Titus. Drawing his *katana*, feeling the weight of it in his hand, he pushed through the hole into another corridor. He ran in the direction where he could sense an Immortal. Then, just as suddenly as it had started, the Quickening ended and all that remained were the sound of the alarms and the sprays of water dousing the fires.

"Marcus!" he called out again, but the sensation grew farther and farther away, until it was gone entirely. MacLeod's heart went black. Had Constantine been the victor, he wouldn't have run from his own museum.

Dear God. Marcus. MacLeod stood in the doorway of the Temple room for a long minute, unable to will himself to enter, but unwilling to abandon his friend, even to go after his killer. And MacLeod had no doubt about the killer's identity.

He finally moved into the room, close to the body sprawled across the fragments of the broken Temple. In the back of his mind, he could hear Constantine's voice. "And never, ever get involved in the politics of Palestine. It will only bring you grief."

"You were more right than you'll ever know, Marcus," he said, his voice husky with sorrow. He reached out and touched his friend's body, trying to convince himself that it was real, that this awful thing had happened to a man who meant no harm to anyone. He saw the boot knife embedded in Constantine's chest and pulled it out angrily.

Then, in the debris near the body, he spotted the gray figurine Constantine had identified as his own. He was right, it wasn't a very good likeness. With a fierce shake of his head to fend off any tears, MacLeod thrust the figurine and the knife into the pockets of his overcoat and stormed from the room.

There was no trace of Avram in or around the museum. MacLeod knew there wouldn't be, but he had to look anyway. He had to keep moving, had to keep busy, or the full impact of Constantine's loss would cripple him.

The Hôtel Renaissance was next, the safe haven of the Israeli delegation. An enormous crowd of reporters was gathered in front of the stately building, barely held in check by a ring of security operatives. Their weapons weren't drawn, but the men in the suits made it obvious they meant business.

MacLeod double-parked the Citroën against a news van

and forced his way through the mob, not caring who or how many he jostled and elbowed on his way to the front. Avram wasn't among the security team. No surprise.

A dark man on an angry mission, he pushed past a security guard and made it as far as the first step before being stopped by two more guards, their weapons drawn.

"Avram Mordecai," MacLeod growled at them.

"Who?" The security man was purposely blank.

"Avram Mordecai," he repeated, enunciating each syllable carefully. "He's one of your security guys. I want to see him," he said in that tone that clearly meant that "no" would be the wrong answer, "now."

"Never heard of him." The Israeli was unintimidated. "Now get lost before we take you out of here in a bag." MacLeod opened his mouth to protest, then thought better of it when he realized the eyes of the entire security team as well as the international press were upon him.

MacLeod backed off, started back to his car. He'd find some other way in. Avram wouldn't elude him for long. The crowd parted for him to pass through. He had nearly cleared the mob when a French photographer recognized him. "He was with the Palestinians this morning!"

MacLeod took off at a run. He dodged around two journalists trying to block him and slipped the grasp of a television soundman in the back of the crowd. In the clear, he raced for the Citroën and jumped in before the reporters dogging his heels caught up with him. He barely pulled away before the pack of newshounds smelling "lead story" could surround his car.

MacLeod returned to the barge feeling tired and defeated as the sun was setting over the Seine. In the three hours since he'd discovered what Avram had done to Constantine, he felt like he'd accomplished nothing. As he got out of his car at the Quai de la Tournelle, how he wished for Maral's healing hands to soothe away his pain. He could almost feel her soft touch on the back of his neck, but then the feeling was blasted away by his sudden awareness of another Immortal.

Pulling his *katana*, he looked warily around, his eyes taking in the embankment, the road, the barge. There, cross-legged at the bow, a figure silhouetted in the sunset sat motionless, staring out at the water. MacLeod, striding rapidly toward the barge, mentally readied himself for combat and issued his challenge.

"Avram!"

The figure turned to him. "Afraid not," Methos said, uncoiling his body and standing.

MacLeod sheathed his sword again and started grimly up the gangplank. "Constantine's dead," he said, and there was a mixture of sadness and anger in his voice.

"I know. Amy, his assistant curator, phoned me. She was his Watcher." Methos looked thoughtful for a moment. "You wouldn't happen to play poker, would you?"

"Methos . . ." MacLeod growled, not in the mood. He started belowdecks.

"It was just a thought." Methos followed him into the barge. "How is Dr. Amina?" Helping himself to an apple from a bowl of fruit on the coffee table, he plopped himself down recumbent on the sofa, his head propped up on one arm.

MacLeod removed his black overcoat and tossed it on the back of the sofa near him. "Better than Avram would like, I'm sure. She's got a nasty concussion. They were running a CAT scan and some other tests when I left the hospital, to see if there's any permanent damage. Either way, she'll be in for observation for at least a few more days." He opened the fridge, took out a bottle of mineral water for himself. On second thought, he reached in and grabbed another bottle. "There's some short-term memory loss. She can't remember what happened," he said, lobbing the second bottle at Methos, who, surprised, dropped the apple to catch it.

"That's probably a blessing." Methos twisted off the cap, but didn't drink. "So what are you going to do?"

MacLeod rooted around some more in the fridge. Nothing looked appealing. He knew he wasn't really hungry, just empty. "What do you mean, what am I going to do? I'm going to find him, that's what I'm going to do." He closed the fridge door with finality.

"And then?" Methos raised a quizzical eyebrow.

"And then . . ." MacLeod felt himself start to flounder,

"and then . . . I don't know what then." Restless, he wandered over to the cold fireplace and began raking out the dead ash.

"It never gets any easier, does it?" Methos took a long, contemplative drink from the bottle as he watched MacLeod work. "Okay, let's say he wasn't your friend. Let's say you'd never met him, and then he comes along and kills Marcus Constantine. What would you do?"

MacLeod reached into a bin by the fireplace for fresh wood, glad to have a simple, mindless task like starting the fire to keep him occupied. "What, you're my ethics professor now?" He pointed sternly with a piece of kindling. "*You* are the last person in the world to lecture me about ethics."

"Humor me. What do you do?"

"I'd go after him." MacLeod's face was dark as he shoved the wood into the fireplace. "I'd make him pay with his own head."

Methos was intrigued. "Really? Would you? Revenge, just for playing the Game?"

MacLeod stopped his work and turned on Methos. "Avram doesn't play the Game," he growled. "This was personal."

Methos kept his tone light. "Ah, ah, but we're not talking about Avram, remember. One Immortal takes another Immortal's head. That's the Game. Reasons don't matter. Motives don't matter. 'There Can Be Only One'—and it's not going to be Marcus Constantine."

The words ripped into MacLeod's already painful wound. "You're one heartless bastard, Methos."

"Just realistic. So, do you go after his killer?" he pressed.

"Maybe."

"Fair enough. Now, say you have a friend, a mortal like that chef friend of yours, Maurice." As Methos spoke, MacLeod returned to his fire, carefully arranging the kindling, setting it alight. "One day, Maurice picks up a gun and aces six people who complained about his bouillabaisse, and only you know it was him. What do you do? Turn him in to face mortal justice, or go after him yourself?" Methos looked at his watch and began making tick-tock tick-tock noises with his tongue. "Your answer, Contestant Number One?"

MacLeod laid down the bellows he'd been using to flame up the fire. "I can't just turn Avram in to the police. Don't you see, that's just the kind of publicity he wants. My God, the Palestinians find out that the man who massacred dozens of their people works with the Israeli delegation . . . I don't want to imagine the consequences." MacLeod sat down heavily on the coffee table, the weight of the world pressing down on him.

"Point to you," Methos said. "Now, for the bonus round: Say you do track down and kill Avram Mordecai. Do you honestly believe it will make a bit of difference in the grand scheme of things? Please remember to phrase your answer in the form of a question."

MacLeod looked at him sourly. "Okay, how's this: What the hell are you going on about?"

Methos finally sat up, feet on the floor, down to business. "There are three kinds of peace in the world, MacLeod. There's the peace achieved by one side defeating and dominating the other—what Marcus would have called the *Pax Romana*. There's peace negotiated by two sides each seeing the error of its ways and truly dedicated to what's best for both sides—call it the Platonic ideal of peace, if you will—and if you give me a week, I might be able to find an example where that's actually worked. Then there's the brokered peace like your friend is working on, each side forced to give up something they can't live without. You can see how well that solved that little problem in Korea half a century back. Face it, that's not peace, it's just the absence of war."

"So you're saying you don't think these agreements are going to change anything."

"No piece of paper is going to change what's in people's hearts. Their fears, their prejudices, their thousands of years of history. So, yes, I do think a year, or a decade, or a century from now, we'll all be back here again."

"But that doesn't mean Avram doesn't have to pay for murdering all those people."

"True, but I don't want you to go out there thinking that whacking one overzealous Hebrew is miraculously going to solve the crisis in the Middle East." Methos looked at the floor by his feet, bent low to look under the coffee table, then ran a quick hand under the sofa pillows. "Don't suppose you saw where that apple went?"

MacLeod tossed him another. "Whose side are you on, Methos?"

"None but my own." He bit lustily into the fruit and chewed with obvious relish before trying to finish his thought with his mouth full. "I find if you stay out of other people's wars, you live longer."

Moving back to the fire, MacLeod put some more fuel on. The fire was already blazing, but he just couldn't seem to shake the deep chill that had settled into his bones. He poked idly at the burning wood, accomplishing nothing. "I just . . ." he started, then tried again. "I really feel for him. All the horror he's seen, the pain that he bears for his people."

"And the guilt," Methos added, thoughtfully.

"What do you mean, guilt?"

"You've felt it, MacLeod. We all have to some extent. The guilt of living on while everyone around you dies." Methos's eyes grew dark and far away. "The guilt of knowing that some cruel and capricious fate has selected you to be the one to witness the suffering of everyone you've ever cared for, knowing that you're powerless to stop it. Or to share it." Methos spoke from deep within his own heart. "Or to forget it."

"To carry the memories of a hundred generations," MacLeod said softly, "to protect their history and traditions. To ensure their survival. What an impossible burden."

"On the other hand"—the brief window into Methos's soul closed abruptly and was quickly replaced by his usual smug facade—"he did just try to waste your girlfriend."

MacLeod sighed. "And he killed Marcus."

"You know," Methos shrugged, "Marcus was a great believer in cosmic justice. What goes around, comes around. Somehow I think he always knew that when his card came up, it would be at the hands of someone he had wronged in the past. Maybe now, somehow, honor has been satisfied for him."

"But not for Assad," MacLeod said. "Not for those men praying at that mosque. You were right—reasons and motives don't matter. I understand why Avram feels he has to do what he's doing. But he's got to be stopped before he causes another war. Before more people die."

"And?" Methos prompted.

"And," MacLeod was resigned, "I'm the only one who can

stop him." He grabbed his coat from the sofa and started for the barge door. "I have to find him."

Methos called out to him as he opened the door, "Where are you going?"

"It's a Friday night. Where would you go if you were a devout Jew who'd just killed his teacher?" As MacLeod left, Methos settled back on the sofa to finish his apple and enjoy the heat of MacLeod's fire.

The cantor had just intoned the final *"Amen"* when Avram knew with great certainty there was another Immortal in the synagogue. He stayed in his seat, head bowed beneath his prayer cap, his *yarmulke,* while the rest of the congregation filed out, trusting that MacLeod—for he knew it could be no other—would have sense enough to wait until they were alone to confront him.

He hadn't enjoyed killing Constantine. For all Avram's complaints to the contrary, for all his bitterness, Marcus had been like another father to him during a very dark time in his life, a time in which his soul was so black he might have considered suicide had he thought it even possible for one as cursed as he. Marcus had shown him life. Marcus had made him see that his Immortality didn't mean he was damned by God; instead, that he was being called by God for a different purpose. Even so, it was centuries before he truly realized what God wanted—a champion for his chosen people.

And then Marcus betrayed him, plotted against him and, by so doing, betrayed the People of God. He had to be stopped. Avram had no choice.

MacLeod was close by him now, he could tell, so he didn't flinch when something metallic dropped onto the bench beside him. "I think this is yours," MacLeod's voice said, and Avram turned to see the bloody boot knife he'd used to silence Constantine. He looked up to see MacLeod glowering above him—dark eyes, dark coat, dark countenance.

"Is this what you do on Friday nights, MacLeod? Cruise the synagogues? You need a life," Avram sneered, standing.

"*Oneg Shabbat* isn't a terrorist organization; *Oneg Shabbat* is you," MacLeod accused.

Avram gave him a little smile, posturing before MacLeod's

anger. "I've always done some of my best work on the Muslim Sabbath. And you must admit, it was quite a surprise."

If they weren't standing on Holy Ground, Avram knew he'd probably be dead now. But instead, MacLeod was forced to swallow his rage and fight only with words. "You take the work that your friends in the Ghetto gave their lives for and you pervert it into this . . . this abomination! The Lutétia, Hebron, how many people have you killed in their name?"

Avram decided to change the subject. He pushed past MacLeod, out into the aisle, and started to walk toward the front of the synagogue. "Boring conversation. Let's talk about Gamal Ali Mustapha, instead. Name ring any bells?" Noting MacLeod's blank look, he continued. "It should. You're screwing his wife."

"Maral's husband is dead."

Avram nodded. "Sad, but true. At the time of his death, he was wanted for questioning in two car bombings and a fire at an Israeli preschool. Ali Mustapha got off way too easy."

MacLeod followed Avram. "And that makes him different than you exactly how?"

Avram turned on MacLeod angrily. How could this man he once trusted be so blind? "He was a murdering bastard, MacLeod. I'm just—"

"A murdering bastard." MacLeod looked at Avram, searching. "Avram, when did 'What is hateful to you do not do to anyone else' become 'Get them before they get you'? That's not one of the commandments you used to follow."

"You do what you have to do to survive. That's the only commandment we've got left, remember?" There was a time Avram would have given his life for this man. Now he could hardly stand the sight of him. "You remember Rivka, MacLeod? Cute little thing, always a fighter?"

"Of course I do. I helped her get to Israel after the war. Then I . . . I had to move on." Part of the penalty of Immortality, never being able to stay in someone's life for very long. Never being able to stay and watch a young girl blossom into a woman. "We lost touch."

"I saw her not too long ago. Did you know she helped Antek and Zuvia start a Ghetto Fighters' Kibbutz? She served three terms in the Knesset. An amazing woman. Now she's raising hell in a retirement community outside Haifa. She thinks ol' Tzaddik has a heck of a grandson. And you . . ." Avram shook his head in amazement. "She still venerates you like some kind of prophet, MacLeod. Thank God she doesn't know what you really are. It would break her heart."

"Your point?"

"Her eldest son served in the Yom Kippur War, was killed in the Sinai. Ten years ago, her daughter lost a leg and her unborn baby in a terrorist bombing. *My point is,* what had that little pigtailed girl ever done to anyone to deserve a life like that? To lose one family to the Nazis and another to the Arabs?"

"Nothing," MacLeod answered.

"Wrong! She'd been born a Jew. Born a Jew in a world where it's open season on Jews. Well, no more, MacLeod. No more little girls will ever have to grow up like Rivka, I swear it!"

"What about the little Palestinian girls whose fathers were at that mosque?" MacLeod didn't want to believe what he was hearing, but he wasn't going to let Avram get away with it. "You believe that it's all right for *you* to murder? That it's fine for you to butcher innocent men and women, why? Because you've suffered, Avram? Because you've been persecuted? And you think God *approves* of this?" MacLeod was livid.

Avram shouted over MacLeod. "Protecting His chosen people is a righteous act in the eyes of God!"

" 'Thou shalt not kill.' *That* is what's 'righteous' in the eyes of God." MacLeod had had enough. "Okay, Avram. You and me, outside. Right now. It's time to settle this." He was more than ready.

Avram smiled, shook his head. "No work during the Jewish Sabbath, MacLeod." He looked beyond MacLeod, saw someone entering the sanctuary behind them. "Rabbi!" he called out. "A word if you have the time." Then he turned back to MacLeod. "But soon. Soon enough."

"Not soon enough," MacLeod muttered under his breath as Avram hurried away to meet the rabbi, then he stalked down the aisle and out of the synagogue.

Chapter Twenty-one

"Duncan, I'm all right. Stop fussing over me, you're worse than my grandfather." While ordinarily Maral didn't mind being fussed over a little bit—it had been a while since anyone had—after three days in the hospital as the constant center of attention of nurses, doctors, technicians, and a host of security personnel, she'd reached her saturation point. "I *can* walk, you know."

"'Hospital policy, Madame,'" MacLeod mimicked Maral's doctor as he pushed her wheelchair down the corridor. "Just sit back and enjoy the ride." He had become her stalwart protector, standing in for poor Assad, who had made the ultimate sacrifice so that she might live. More than once she had awakened in the middle of the night breathless and shaking as the dead had come to claim her in her dreams, to find MacLeod in the chair beside her, awake and ready to comfort her. Sometimes, when he thought she was sleeping, she would watch him through slitted eyes. He would be far away in his thoughts. Dark thoughts, she could tell. Thoughts that seemed to haunt him, to make him angry yet sad. She wished he would share his thoughts with her, but as soon as he knew she was awake, he was all smiles and pleasant conversation again, banishing the dark thoughts and refusing to speak of them.

Farid led their way to a service elevator. The bulk of his men were downstairs, controlling the members of the press gathered at the main entrance to the hospital, awaiting Maral's release. An elite team guarded the hospital kitchen, where the service elevator let out, and MacLeod's car, parked around the back of the hospital next to the kitchen door. Together, MacLeod and Farid managed to spirit Maral out of the building and away from the prying attention of the media.

"Where are we going?" Maral asked once they were safely free of the hospital. "I'll need to freshen up and change before the signing this evening." The Israelis and the remaining Palestinian delegates, spurred on by their anger at the act of terrorism at the Lutétia, had worked diligently to nail down an agreement that both their cabinets would approve.

"You're sure you want to go? You know you don't have to."

"I *have* to," Maral protested. "I can't let them think they can scare me away. I have to be there—for Assad."

MacLeod nodded. He had known that would be her answer before he even asked. "Your things are at the Jordanian Ambassador's residence. Your delegation has moved there. More secure."

Maral was looking tired already. "I don't think anything can ever be secure enough."

A convoy of police and security vehicles ferried the Palestinians from the secure compound of the Jordanian Embassy to the even more heavily armed and gated Israeli Embassy, where the leaders of the opposing sides would meet to sign the East Jerusalem agreement. In the back of one of the cars, Maral was uncharacteristically quiet. The somber suit that she wore only enhanced the pallor of her usually vibrant complexion. The strain of the event was already beginning to tell on her, and it hadn't even begun. She opened up her handbag and checked her hair in a small mirror for the third time.

"Maral, you look fine," MacLeod, sitting next to her, reassured her.

She put the mirror away self-consciously. "I just need something to do with my hands," she explained. He reached out and took her hand in his.

"How's this?" he asked, and she smiled gratefully at him, sitting there so calmly, strong and handsome in his own dark suit. She ran her free hand up his forearm. "These are beautiful," she said, admiring the golden studs securing the cuffs of his hand-tailored shirt. "Are you going to tell me they were made by some quaint East African tribe?"

"Would you believe West African?" MacLeod said with a grin, content to make small talk with her all night, if it would help relax her. "Aborigine?"

The car slowed at the gate to the Israeli Embassy, and the driver showed their credentials to the gate guard. As they were stopped. MacLeod noticed Maral shiver from a sudden chill. "Are you cold?" He put an arm around her shoulders to warm her.

"No," she said. "I just don't have a good feeling about this."

"It will be fine," he assured her with more certainty than he actually felt. He was certain that Avram would try something at the signing. But it would do no good for her to worry, too. "I'll be close by all night. You'll be fine. I promise."

It made her laugh to think he could chase away the bogeyman with only his word. "Well, if you *promise*," she smiled wistfully. If only he could . . .

The signing ceremony took place in the ballroom of the embassy, a functional but not ornate reception area in the eastern wing of the building surrounded by the offices of embassy officials. Maral took her place with the other representatives of both peoples on a raised dais that stretched nearly the length of the room. Just in front of the dais was a podium with a cloth-covered table on which lay a copy of the historic agreement, waiting for the signatures of the two men upon whom the fate of two nations rested. The walls of the room had been tastefully decorated with the flags of the two peoples, and the theme was repeated on the table in a gold-embossed mahogany pen stand, which featured miniatures of the two flags and the actual pens used by Menachem Begin and Anwar Sadat to sign the Camp David Accords two decades before.

The rest of the room was filled with the world's media, arranged in their standard pecking order–CNN, the BBC, and the big three American networks jockeying for space up front, while the lowly print journalists from the smaller Asian or South American papers had to settle for room at the back.

Once he was sure Maral was settled in, MacLeod roamed the ballroom and the surrounding hallways looking for trouble—looking for Avram. He knew there were both Palestinian and Israeli agents throughout the crowd and on every entrance, but he was also well aware that only he knew what they were looking for. Periodically he would make sure to return to the front of the room, where he hoped Maral would see him and take some comfort from his presence.

The French Foreign Minister served as moderator for the event, quite proud of France's contribution to this historic moment, as he pointed out many times in his endless opening remarks at the podium. As he finally wound down, he introduced each of the Israeli delegates who worked on the agreement, then the Palestinians as MacLeod paced through the assembled media, poised, alert.

Every security operative in the room seemed to tense when the Foreign Minister introduced the Israeli Prime Minister, Benjamin Netanyahu, and the President of the Palestinian Authority, Yasser Arafat. The two men entered from opposite sides of the room, crossed the dais, and shook hands at its center. The press stood to applaud and the ballroom was aflame with the flashes of a thousand cameras. Although he couldn't see him through the crowd and lights, MacLeod suddenly sensed another Immortal.

As the two leaders took their seats near the podium, MacLeod found him. Avram had entered through the side door with the Israeli Prime Minister's retinue, but remained off to one side of the dais with some other security men. As the French Minister droned on, MacLeod carefully made his way across the room. Then, to another round of applause, Arafat took the podium for his remarks and Avram ducked out the side door.

MacLeod was right behind him. He followed him down a corridor lined with offices and out the east entrance into a manicured garden. Two security men stood vigil at the entrance, one Israeli and one Palestinian. As he stalked Avram across the garden, MacLeod knew he'd have to wait until they were out of sight of the two guards and the security cameras on the grounds before he could reach for his *katana*.

At the edge of the garden stood a garage of maintenance

vehicles. Avram passed behind it and MacLeod followed him cautiously, expecting an ambush, but when he cleared the corner, he saw Avram standing in a patch of light behind the building, waiting for him.

"I've heard that the cameras in this sector are out of order. It's a shame no one will be able to fix it until tomorrow." Avram drew his sword. "Now we settle this. We'll let God decide."

"Is that what you told Marcus before you killed him?" The *katana* was in his hand. MacLeod was ready.

Warily, the two Immortals began to circle. "I didn't want to kill him. He gave me no choice."

"And those men in Hebron," MacLeod said, looking for an opening. "I'll bet they were a threat to you, too. Weaponless, on their knees, praying to God. Some threat." He was trying to get Avram angry, get him off-balance.

Avram wasn't biting. "They served their purpose," he said calmly. "Some mistrust here, a little fear there, sprinkle on a good dose of hate, and little by little the peace train goes off the tracks. And when it finally derails, they won't even know which side did the final deed." He feinted with a quick jab to the right which MacLeod's *katana* easily batted away. "I'm just sorry you had to get in the way, MacLeod. Losing your head over a piece of Arab tail—I hope she was worth it."

MacLeod knew when he was being baited, too, and didn't allow his anger to impair his judgment. He lunged to his left, then, when Avram had committed himself, corrected, and slashed to the right. Avram, overbalanced, couldn't recover in time to block, and the *katana* left a neat slice down Avram's face in its wake. First blood. "Now *I'm* giving you no choice. Fight me."

Avram didn't command the power that MacLeod could put behind his blade, but he was quick and he was cunning. His fighting style combined the precise tactics of his Roman teacher with years of desperation, centuries of fighting with his back against the wall. It made him unpredictable, and that, along with the difference in their heights, allowed him to get under MacLeod's guard more than once, scoring a jab to ribs, a slash across the abdomen.

But despite the difference in their ages, MacLeod was the more experienced and better-trained swordsman, and in time experience won out. A combination attack, right and then left and then hard to the left again, and Avram was off-balance again. A slash to the head, and he was on his knees, the *katana* to his throat. MacLeod kicked the sword out of Avram's hand.

Avram glared up at MacLeod with defiance. "Go ahead and kill me. Everyone in that room's dead anyway."

MacLeod stopped dead in his tracks, his sword poised at Avram's neck. "You put a bomb in your own embassy?"

"Kill me or don't kill me, I still win, MacLeod. Go on, take my head." Avram deliberately bared his throat against the gleaming blade of the *katana*. "Take my head! And by the time you're finished with the Quickening, there'll be nothing left of that agreement but a pile of rubble."

MacLeod shook his head. "You're bluffing. You'd never kill your own Prime Minister." He could feel his hands sweat on the ivory hilt of his sword. It was a hard call—the Avram he knew had been a lousy poker player.

"C'mon, coward, do it," Avram goaded. "Remember Marcus. Think about how I made him beg me before I killed him." He rubbed against MacLeod's blade so a thin line of crimson appeared at his throat. "And that Arab you're screwing. I bet I could make her beg me, too—if she wasn't already dead." He looked up at MacLeod, his eyes filled with victory. "Or do you think you still have time to save her?"

"God damn you, Avram," MacLeod growled through clenched teeth. He pulled back the *katana* for the killing blow, swung hard—

—and sliced him viciously across the midsection. Avram's eyes grew wide, and he gurgled out a single sound. Then he fell to the ground, dead.

For now.

MacLeod ran back toward the embassy building with all his strength. When he was barely within earshot of the guards at the east entrance, he was yelling to the Palestinian. *"Tawari'*! It's an emergency! Give me your communicator. I have to talk to Farid!" At the door the startled guard handed him the earpiece and started pulling the transmitter from his pocket. MacLeod was already running into the building with it. "Farid, can you hear me? It's MacLeod. There's a bomb! Clear the dais! Now!"

He raced down the corridor of offices toward the ballroom. As he neared the side door he and Avram had exited, the hallway began to fill with frenzied people. Farid's signal to evacuate the dignitaries had started a panic among the press.

"Out of my way!" MacLeod screamed, pushing upstream, flailing against the current to get back to the ballroom. No time for niceties, he pulled and hit and fought his way through the door and into the room.

The Israeli and Palestinian leaders were gone, taken out immediately. The last of the delegates were fighting for the door behind the dais. He didn't see Maral. In the hall itself, the media were climbing over their equipment and each other in their hurry to escape, except for two cowboy journalists in the midst of the chaos determined to report live from the scene.

Farid and his men were combing the room for the device side by side with the Israeli security, overturning chairs, scouring the dais, examining equipment cases, but still nothing. MacLeod looked wildly around the room. If he were Avram, where would he put it? Where would he plant a bomb?

If he were Avram . . . ". . . *they won't even know which side did the final deed.*" Suddenly, spotting the crossed Israeli and Palestinian flags, he knew.

"Farid!" MacLeod screamed into the communicator. "The pen stand! It's in the pen stand!" Across the room, he saw Farid dive for the podium. When Farid grabbed the pen stand, MacLeod could tell from his face he'd guessed correctly—the weight was all wrong.

Farid clawed desperately at the device, trying to open it, but no success. "Farid!" MacLeod shouted into the security chief's earpiece. Across the room, the two men's eyes locked. "Throw it." MacLeod gestured with his arms. "I'll get it out of here." Farid looked around, looking for some other option, finding none. "THROW IT!" MacLeod screamed into Farid's headset.

MacLeod waved everyone away from him as Farid drew back his arm to throw the device, and the press didn't need to be told twice to scatter. As the small wooden box spiraled through the air, Farid muttered a quick prayer to Allah and braced for detonation on impact.

MacLeod fielded the box into his midsection to cushion the hit, but even he was surprised it didn't go off as he caught it. He headed for the ballroom door.

MacLeod charged into the hallway yelling "It's a bomb, out of my way!" To his dismay, the corridor was filled in either direction with the panicking press. They started to scream and run at his approach. He didn't have time to think, to plan which way to go. He just had to get out. He ran straight across the hall to one of the offices. With a powerful kick, he broke open the door.

A window. Thank God.

Leading with his shoulder, MacLeod crashed and rolled through the plate-glass window as if it were paper. Somewhere far behind him he thought he could hear Maral scream.

"DUNCAN!!"

Once outside, he threw the bomb away from him into the night for all he was worth. Instantly, his world exploded.

He was pain. A ball of pain. A throbbing mass of pain. Pain was his only reality. Pain was his awareness. He had no senses—no sight, no sound, no sensation—but he knew the pain. It moved in him and through him like a thing alive.

Hearing returned first. Off in the distance, almost as if in another world, he could hear shouting and screaming, the insistent wail of a siren. Somewhere a woman cried . . . a woman . . . and then he remembered. He remembered Maral, the bomb, Avram, he remembered Immortality, he remembered the Highlands of Scotland so many, many years ago. He was no longer pain. He was once again Duncan MacLeod. He gasped for air, and it seared down his throat like molten lava.

But MacLeod was still in pain. He struggled to force his eyes open and the night sky he faced was full of smoke and debris. He tried to turn his head—muscles and bones alike protested as he moved—and he could see figures move in the smoke. He knew he had to get up, to move away from the site of the explosion before anyone found him, before he was forced to explain, but his spine and his legs could not yet bear his weight. He pulled himself along the ground, half crawl, half drag, every inch new agony, until he reached a stand of bushes. He managed to roll beneath them, out of sight, and he lay there without moving, eyes closed, waiting for the healing, feeling the pain slowly start to recede.

Scant minutes after the blast, the driveway in front of the embassy was pandemonium. Emergency vehicles clogged the roadway, spilling over onto the manicured lawns, leaving little room for the limousines and government cars attempting to spirit away the officials from the signing ceremony. Stunned delegates wandered in the midst of the equally shocked press corps, their faces ashen in the flashing lights of the fire trucks as they transmitted their reports across the world, and Farid's security men were desperate to herd together their charges and evacuate them to safety.

Farid had Maral tightly by the wrist, and she fought him hard, trying to escape. "No! Let me go!" she screamed out.

The security chief didn't want to hurt her, but his duty was clear. "You have to go. There are assassins everywhere. You're not safe." He escorted her firmly away from the embassy building, leading her, dragging her.

Still she struggled to get away from him. "No! Duncan's out there. I have to find him." Even Farid's veneer of cold professionalism could not help but be touched by her impassioned plea, but he knew there might be little left to find. Even so, he offered her what comfort he could.

"We'll find him, Doctor. I promise you, we'll find him." He opened the door to a waiting security car. "Now get in the car," he said firmly, forcing her in.

"Farid, you don't understand. I *have* to see him. I have to *know*!" she begged him through tears. His only response was to shut the car door and signal the driver to drive on. He turned back to the chaos.

The car moved forward several yards, then was forced to stop and wait as another company of fire equipment arrived at the scene, a hook and ladder blocking the gated entrance. Maral saw her chance and threw the door open, scrambling out of the car, taking off at a run back to the embassy. The driver sounded his horn frantically to get Farid's attention, but in the midst of the sirens and the crowd, it was just another blare of noise.

Maral ran around the back of the emergency vehicles, careful to stay away from the building, out of Farid's radar. She stayed in the shadows of the perimeter fence as it ran parallel with the front of the building, then cut across a crowded parking area, ducking beneath the tops of the cars, until she reached the garden that ran alongside the eastern side of the embassy, where the bomb had detonated.

She slowed her pace, horrified at the damage she could see. A twenty-foot hole had been clawed into the side of the embassy, sections of two floors lay open to the night air. Inside, she could see the first firefighters on the scene crawling carefully through the smoldering debris that used to be someone's office. Outside the hole, a massive crater had been gouged in the carefully tended lawn. She was stunned. If that had gone off during the crowded signing . . . Duncan MacLeod had saved hundreds of lives.

Duncan . . .

She ran on, weaving through the rescue equipment, smoke and tears threatening to blind her as she scanned the garden, the firefighters, the debris for any sign of MacLeod. She found the window he'd crashed through a few short yards from the gaping wound in the embassy.

"Duncan!" she screamed, trying to be heard above the din of the emergency vehicles and the rescuers, trying to be heard in Heaven if that's where he was now. "Duncan!" She dropped to her knees, heedless of the broken glass all around, searching for any trace.

She'd crawled several feet beyond the window when she found blood pooling on the grass. "God, please, no," Maral whispered. She reached out, almost touching it, then pulled back. Glimmering in the moonlight in a black pool of blood she saw one of MacLeod's golden cuff links.

"DUNCAN!!!!" she wailed as if her heart was bursting. Clutching the bloody cuff link tightly in her fist, she rocked back and forth, back and forth, sobbing his name. She had let him into her soul and let him rip open the scar tissue that had formed around Ali's death, and now she grieved for both of them as if both wounds were still raw and bleeding. "Duncan . . ."

* * *

As if in a dream, he heard his name. Carefully, he opened his eyes, tested his body. Arms. Legs. Head. All seemed to move in the ways they were originally designed to. He rolled to his side beneath the bushes. The effort exhausted him, but he noted the pain was nearly gone. He looked down at himself. Covered in blood, clothing in tatters, but the cuts and rends and punctures that had peppered his body were finally beginning to heal. Then he heard his name again, realized it wasn't a dream.

From his sanctuary, he could see Maral not fifty feet away, moaning her grief to the heavens. His heart was torn—he knew he should wait and disappear into the night, leave Paris, leave this life, let them all think he'd died in the blast. It would be simpler for everyone. But as he watched Maral, saw the despair in every inch of her body, heard the devastation in her voice, something in his heart told him no. He couldn't leave her like that. Once again alone, once again not knowing, waiting for the phone call that in this case would never come.

MacLeod rolled out from under the stand of bushes. "Maral," he called out, first making sure there was no one else in earshot. All the rescue activity seemed focused nearer the front of the building where he could see the tremendous hole. "Maral," he called a little louder.

Somehow, through her anguish, she heard him. She turned, startled, and from the look on her face he could almost see her soul come back to life as she saw him, stumbled to her feet, ran to him. "Duncan!"

Maral dropped to her knees beside him and MacLeod sat up to meet her. She threw her arms around him in great relief, and although he tried not to, he winced a bit at her touch on some still open wounds. Pulling back from him, she took in the blood, his tattered clothing. Cautiously, she reached out to touch a jagged, bloody gash dangerously close to his right eye. "You're hurt. I'll get help." She moved to stand.

"No!" MacLeod barked, grabbing her arm to stop her. Then, more gently, "Maral, no." It was hard for him to know what to say to her, how to tell her, so he settled for, "Wait."

"But—" she began to protest, but the beseeching look in his

eyes made her hesitate. He took her hand and placed it where it had been, near the angry slash by his eye.

"Wait."

And then she realized that the cut was not nearly as bad or as deep as she'd first believed. A trick of the light in her excitement. But even as she thought that, she noticed that the wound had narrowed, the swelling receding. "Duncan . . . ?" she said, fear battling with curiosity in her voice.

MacLeod took her hand from his face and held it between both of his. "Maral, I can explain," he started, meeting her eyes gravely. "There are things I need to tell you."

She pulled her hand away and touched his temple again, gently stroking where the wound had been, feeling for herself the soft perfect skin concealing where his face had been ravaged moments before. "My grandfather would say you're one of the *Djinn*," she said, awestruck. "Or a guardian angel sent from Allah."

MacLeod shook his head. "Assad was your guardian angel, Maral. I'm just a man. But I'm . . ." It was always so hard to open up and confess the truth, to live through that longest moment in the world as she took in his words, worked through the anger, worked through the revulsion, and came either to accept or despise him. For good or ill, their relationship would never be the same. It might have been kinder to both of them if he had just disappeared. He took a deep breath. "Maral, I am—"

She kissed him hard on the lips to silence him. "Don't explain," she said as she released him. "Whatever it is, I don't need to know. I just need to know you're safe."

"Maral, are you sure?" He had made up his mind he would tell her if she wanted to know.

She nodded, her eyes filled with unshed tears of relief. "You're here. That's all that matters."

He kissed her again. She would never cease to amaze him. "Thank you," he said from the heart.

Maral helped him to stand. "Now let's see if we can get you out of here before anyone else finds out you should have been blown to Hell."

Chapter Twenty-two

In the end, it had taken Farid's assistance to get them out of the Israeli compound unseen. Farid, who, if MacLeod had thought him actually capable of emotion, looked distinctly happy to see MacLeod in one piece—or at least relieved MacLeod hadn't died on his watch. Farid, who understood implicitly the meaning of "no questions asked."

Once Maral was safely behind the gates of the Jordanian Embassy again, MacLeod returned to his barge. He showered the blood from his body and changed his clothes—black jeans, black sweater, black coat. It was the deepest part of the night, and a bone-chilling cold had settled over the Seine. A light fog had begun to condense along the water. He went up on deck and climbed to the roof of the pilothouse where he sat, sword across his lap, waiting. He could issue no plainer invitation.

Vigil. MacLeod sat in silence under the stars, unmoving, trying to empty his heart and mind of distraction and concentrate solely on the task before him, but he dreaded what he knew he had to do. He'd come close to killing Avram once that night, and he wasn't certain it was only the threat of the bomb that had stayed his hand from the final strike.

MacLeod was raised to protect his people, and it was a lesson that Ian MacLeod had instilled deep within his son's soul, so deep that, four hundred years later, Duncan MacLeod of the Clan MacLeod was still bearing that onus on his shoulders. He had killed for his clan and died for his clan, and he of all men could understand what it meant to put your responsibility to your people ahead of everything—ahead of love, ahead of happiness, ahead of life.

And he, too, had witnessed horror. Not on a scale that could ever rival what Avram had been forced to face, but horror that had eaten away at his soul and his mind all the same. He had seen his people slaughtered by a heartless nation bent on their annihilation, men, women, children made to suffer and to die on the bloody fields of Culloden and in their homes and in their churches and wherever else the English bastards could track them down.

And he had vowed they would pay. *He* would make them pay. And he, like Avram, had vowed "never again"—not as long as there was breath in Duncan MacLeod of the Clan MacLeod. He'd butchered men as their wives screamed to him for mercy. He'd killed them in front of the eyes of their crying children. He'd murdered men whose only crime was to be born in the land he despised more than Hell itself. Perhaps the only difference between himself and Avram was that Ceirdwyn had found a way to reach him, to stop the killing, without resorting to the sword. And MacLeod had failed to do that for Avram.

Who was he to say the Palestinians weren't as much a threat to Avram and his way of life as the Nazis were? He was an outsider. He'd lived in Avram's world only a brief time—and back then he was more than willing to kill as many Germans as he could to try and save Avram's people—they were his people, too, they were his clan for the time he was there. Certainly in Avram's mind, this threat seemed as real. To Avram, losing Hebron, losing East Jerusalem, could only remind him of the Jews losing their shops and their homes prior to the deportations, the expulsions, the ovens.

Who was Duncan MacLeod to proclaim that the Nazis were evil . . . Cumberland's English were evil . . . but the Palestinians, they're not evil? And then expect Avram Mordecai, a Jew from Biblical Palestine, a man fifteen hundred years older than he, with different experiences, different values, different morals, to bend to his judgement? Who was he to decree what constituted evil for anyone but himself?

Maybe only God could do that.

Maybe only God could judge Avram. But MacLeod knew, right or wrong, he had to stop Avram before more mortals died. Israeli mortals. Palestinian mortals. Their race, their religion, their politics didn't matter.

And maybe someday God would judge MacLeod for that act, as well. But until that day of reckoning came, he could live with the knowledge that no more innocents would die at Avram's hand.

MacLeod didn't have to wait long for his invitation to be answered. Still more than an hour before sunrise, he felt Avram approach, saw him along the foggy Quai.

"You failed," MacLeod pointed out, as Avram came within earshot.

"You win some, you lose some." Avram's demeanor was calm, resigned. "Arafat and the Prime Minister signed the agreement in the back of the security van after they evacuated the embassy. Guess I pushed them into each other's arms." He approached the gangplank. "It's only one battle. You have to fight a lot of battles to win a war. There'll be others." Despite his words, he seemed less than enthusiastic at the prospect.

MacLeod shook his head, standing. "Not for you, Avram." He climbed down from the top of the pilothouse.

"Guess we have to finish this," Avram said. MacLeod nodded his head, sad but resolved. Avram tried one more time to get his old friend to understand. "Duncan, you know why I had to do it." He started up the gangplank.

"And you know why I have to stop you." The *katana* was heavy in his hands.

"'Cause you'll always be the white knight, *goy*, champion to damsels in distress everywhere." Avram pulled his sword and leapt from the gangplank onto the deck of the barge. "C'mon, hero," he challenged, darting to the flat open deck of the bow, "let's go. Time for the O.K. Corral."

In two long strides, MacLeod was there, and, with no formality, he laid into Avram, three quick slashes to Avram's head. Avram's sword was ready to deflect, deflect, then he twisted out of MacLeod's reach.

Avram circled to MacLeod's left, tried to thrust in behind his blade, but the *katana* that had saved MacLeod's life more times than he could remember was already there, waiting to block the blow. MacLeod spun to face him and pressed a flurry of attacks—hip, head, head, thrust—that drove Avram back, then back again as he struggled to defend against the powerhouse blows.

He realized MacLeod was maneuvering the fight into the narrow prow of the barge. The boat's hull and the collection of pipes and winches and equipment would negate what little advantage his natural agility gave Avram against MacLeod's superior sword skills.

Avram feinted at MacLeod's legs, drawing the *katana* down, then an overhead slice at the head, to lure the *katana* into a defensive position perpendicular to MacLeod's body. Quickly, he slipped inside MacLeod's guard, catching the *katana*'s blade at the hilt and, putting all his weight and strength behind it, he powered his sword down and away, dragging the tip of the *katana* into the deck of the barge.

Avram jumped back quickly and swung before MacLeod could raise the sword back into proper position to defend. He caught MacLeod across the right arm, a wicked slash that severed the tendons. First blood, and a much-needed advantage. He slipped out of the narrow confines of the barge's prow.

MacLeod spun away, howling, but he held firm to the sword with his left hand. While the *katana* wielded two-handed was a powerful killing weapon, one-handed it was still formidable. Holding his damaged arm close to his body, MacLeod spun the sword expertly in his hand to show Avram he had gained no advantage, then attacked aggressively.

They battled across the deck of the barge, MacLeod on the attack. Again and again, Avram found himself forced to retreat to what he hoped was a better position. With a roar and a mighty slash of his sword, MacLeod locked blades with Avram and pressed him back against the raised roof of the living space belowdecks. To avoid falling, Avram scrambled on top and over it, running nimbly across the narrow passage between the pilothouse and the side of the barge, MacLeod on his heels.

Reaching the stern, Avram stood his ground, sword ready, waiting for MacLeod's attack. He was winded, on the defensive, and the edge of the barge, where the dark Seine beckoned to shield his escape, was tantalizingly close. But he was not going to take the coward's way out—one way or the other, they were going to finish this.

Grimly, MacLeod came at him, to the head, to the gut, to the shoulder. Even Avram's quickness was not enough, and he took a painful slice across the collarbone. He howled with the pain and tried to dart away, but MacLeod was right on him.

As MacLeod swung again, Avram ducked to a crouch and came up under the larger man's guard. He shouldered MacLeod into the side of the pilothouse, and the sword went flying from MacLeod's hand.

Avram pressed in closer, going for the kill. An instant later he found himself on his ass, swordless, the *katana* to his neck. In one seamless move, MacLeod had caught the *katana* midair with his healed right arm and pulled Avram's feet from under him with a sweep of his leg.

"Duncan!" Avram gasped, and the plea in his voice made MacLeod stay his hand. Avram held him with his eyes for a long moment. Then he folded his hands in front of him and closed his eyes in prayer. "Blessed art Thou, O Lord our God, King of the universe, Whose judgments are true." Then, with a sigh, he tilted back his head, exposing his throat.

MacLeod could feel the tears rise up in his throat. "*Shalom,* Avram. Peace." The keen edge of the *katana* sliced cleanly.

Avram's body fell to the deck of the barge, and, a moment later, the *katana* followed, as if its owner could no longer bear to hold the weapon that had slain his former comrade. The gentle breeze along the Seine stirred into a wind that caused currents of fog to dance around the barge.

The shattered vessel that was Avram gave up its Quickening like wisps of smoke which curled into the air, intertwining with the dancing fog. Suddenly, the wind became a gale, the dance a frenzy, as the Quickening writhed in the whirlwind, then sought shelter in Duncan MacLeod.

Its touch was the touch of liquid fire that seeped through his pores and overwhelmed his soul, stripping away all that he was, all that he is, all that he would be, and leaving in its place an acute, never-ending loneliness that filled him up until he could hold no more. He fell to his knees from the ache and a deep moan, torn from the very fiber of his being, escaped from his throat.

Shafts of lightning exploded from Avram's body, shattering the windows of the pilothouse, scarring the deck and the sides of the barge with their intensity before snaring MacLeod in their web. Power shot through him unrestrained, and the moan became a scream as cosmic fire sparked his nerves, his cells, his very atoms.

Through the pain, through the loneliness and the despair that held him prisoner, he reached into the maelstrom within his essence and grasped the memories churning there, desperate for identity. Lightning pierced the physical form once called MacLeod, sending it writhing to the deck of the barge, but he was Avram, son of Mordecai the Pharisee, and he was marrying the most beautiful woman in Judea. He lifted Deborah's veil and looked into her chestnut eyes, and they were the lifeless eyes of Debra Campbell and he was Duncan MacLeod of the Clan MacLeod and his world was coming to an end at the base of a cliff in the Highlands of Scotland. Tongues of fire shot from the bilge pipes quenched with a hiss in the waters of the Seine and he was assailed by the smell of burning wood and burning flesh and he was Avram the schoolteacher fighting on alone in the village that had died around him as the Cossack's horse rode him down and he rode and he rode on the heels of that butcher, Kern, who'd destroyed his family, and he vowed someday MacLeod of the Lakota would have his revenge.

He roared, a wild howl filled with anguish and sorrow, and he reached for heaven as if he could almost touch it, first one hand, then both. Almost, but not quite.

Suddenly, the lightning ceased, the fog blowing past the barge on a gentle breeze as if nothing to disturb the fabric of space and time had just occurred, and he was once again MacLeod, Duncan MacLeod, born in Glenfinnan in the Highlands of Scotland in 1592, and he was the victor.

But there was no joy in this victory. MacLeod collapsed back onto the deck, a puppet with no strings, exhausted. And he wept.

* * *

Minutes, hours, days later, he felt the approach of another Immortal. Barely lifting his head, he reached out for his sword. Then he looked up to see Methos mounting the gangplank. "You," MacLeod said.

"I came to watch the fireworks." Methos picked his way carefully across the shattered glass and blasted decking. "I hear it's Palestinian Independence Day." With the tails of his grungy raincoat, he wiped off a spot on the deck and sat down beside MacLeod.

MacLeod sat up, looking at his *katana* as if it was a stranger to him. "I didn't do it for the Palestinians."

"I know," Methos said with more compassion. "Still, I suppose it had to be done."

Now that the deed was done, MacLeod was firm. "He couldn't keep on killing innocent mortals."

"True," Methos said, examining a shard of glass he'd picked up near his feet. "Much better to let the mortals go on killing each other."

MacLeod looked at him oddly. "What do you mean by that?"

"Me?" Methos shrugged, tossing the glass fragment into the river. "I dunno. Sometimes I just like to hear myself talk."

MacLeod stood, putting away his sword. "I've got to go." Methos nodded sagely. MacLeod walked to the gangplank and off onto the Quai. Methos looked around the wreckage of the barge.

"Guess I'll just tidy up a bit."

It was dawn when he knocked on Maral's door at the Jordanian Embassy and he was surprised when she opened it almost immediately. Her eyes were red and shadowed. She hadn't slept.

"Duncan!" She thought that she'd never see him again, that by coming so close to whatever secret he was forced to conceal, she had lost him forever. She wrapped her arms around him and pulled him into her room.

The door closed, he pressed her back against it and kissed her, a soul-searching kiss, as if he never wanted to let her go. A kiss so full of hunger, so full of need, she could tell something had happened. Something had changed him almost imperceptibly, had left him with this deep aching loneliness.

"Duncan . . . it's all right." She stroked his head, brushed back his hair, trying to comfort him. "Let me help."

"Just hold me," he whispered. "Please . . ." There was nothing he could tell her.

Author's Notes

Working on *Zealot,* I've come to appreciate how very different writing fiction for the printed page is from writing for the TV screen. So many more words are needed! You can't just map out the dialogue and rely on an actor to provide the character's description, expression, and reactions. When writing a book, you don't have the luxury of an Adrian Paul or Peter Wingfield calling the writers to say, "You don't need to put in that line—I can say it in a look," and they do, beautifully. On the other hand, you don't have the producer calling to say "Masada? Have you gone totally insane? Where am I supposed to double Masada in Paris?"

One luxury that you have when putting a book together, unlike a television show, is what you're reading right now—the author's notes. Many's the time the writers of "Highlander" would have loved to put a banner across the bottom of the screen that said something like, "Well, it was *supposed* to be Waterloo, but it snowed the day of filming." So, having been given this precious opportunity, here are a few notes.

On May 16, 1943, SS Major General Jürgen Stroop reported to his superiors that "The Warsaw Ghetto is no more." The 50,000 Jews who had remained in the Ghetto after the mass deportations of nearly 500,000 to the death camps, and the roughly 1,000 young Jewish rebels who had risen up in arms against the Nazi war machine to try and protect them, were gone—captured and sent to Treblinka, shot where they stood, or consumed by the fires the Nazis set to ravage the Ghetto. Of the actual heroes and villains involved in the Warsaw Ghetto Uprising, I've put my words in the mouths of only a few—Ghetto commander Mordechai Anielewicz and his companion Mira, Jurek, Issachar Schmuel the gangster king, General Stroop.

Little is known about the last hours of Masada, except what is reported in Flavius Josephus's *The Jewish Wars*. Josephus, a one-time Jewish rebel turned Roman collaborator, purported he got his facts from two women who survived Masada by hiding in a cistern. Recent archaeological evidence does support much of what Josephus wrote, including the pottery shards inscribed with the commanders' names which were used to draw lots. The shards confirm the presence of Eleazar ben Yair, the legendary commander of Masada, who I've borrowed for this book.

A note about Jewish naming conventions. According to Rabbi Morrison David Bial, the practice of naming children only after deceased relatives was originally an Ashkenazic tradition (Jews from Central Europe), not biblical or talmudic in origin, and so wouldn't have been adhered to at the time of Masada.

Of the many books and references I consulted, three really stand out: *Resistance: The Warsaw Ghetto Uprising* by Israel Gutman; *The Struggle for Peace: Israelis and Palestinians* edited by Elizabeth Warnock Fernea and Mary Evelyn Hocking; and *Masada,* by Yigael Yadin, the archaeologist who uncovered the rock's mysteries in the 1960s.

Thanks to "St. Catherine's fifth grade"—Jennifer, Darla & Dr. Amy—for the beta testing.

Thanks to Sara Schwager, who brought the Hebrew in line with the pronunciation used in the 1940s.

Thanks also to the United States Holocaust Memorial Museum in Washington, D.C., for refusing to let memories die away like the smoke from the camps. And to the writings of Elie Wiesel, who brought Avram Mordecai into sharp focus for me when he wrote of having to remember, even if "condemned to live as long as God himself."

THERE CAN BE ONLY ONE. . . .

But not when it comes to new *Highlander*™ novels! Watch in May 1998 for a new novel by Rebecca Neason, author of *Highlander: The Path*.

The Immortal known as Darius began life as a leader of the Goths. His army swept out of the Urals, sacked Rome, then headed to Paris—where Darius's life was changed forever by his encounter with a holy man whose Quickening he took. As a result, Darius became a priest and forswore the Immortals' game. This is the story of his centuries-long friendship with Duncan MacLeod, in which the two face danger and treachery, in the name of Immortal brotherhood. . . .

By the year 2000, 2 out of 3 Americans could be illiterate.

It's true.

Today, 75 million adults… about one American in three, can't read adequately. And by the year 2000, U.S. News & World Report envisions an America with a literacy rate of only 30%.

Before that America comes to be, you can stop it… by joining the fight against illiteracy today.

Call the Coalition for Literacy at toll-free **1-800-228-8813** and volunteer.

Volunteer Against Illiteracy. The only degree you need is a degree of caring.

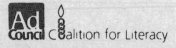

Ad Council Coalition for Literacy

Warner Books is proud to be an active supporter of the Coalition for Literacy.

HIGHLANDER™
THE CARD GAME

FREE UNIQUE CARD OFFER!

Now you can play an Immortal in the fast paced card game that lets you pit your sword against others in the quest for The Prize.

In celebration of the new series of original novels from Warner Aspect, Thunder Castle Games is making available, for a limited time only, one Highlander™ Card not for sale in any edition.

Send a stamped self-addressed envelope and proof of purchase (cash register receipt attached to this coupon) to Thunder Castle Games, Dept. 120, P.O. Box 11529, Kansas City, MO 64138. Please allow 4-6 weeks for delivery.

Name: _____

Address: _____

City: _____ State: _____ Zip: _____

Age: _____ Phone: _____